D0629227

THE
MISSING PIECE
OF CHARLIE
O'REILLY

REBECCA K. S. ANSARI

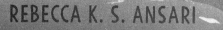

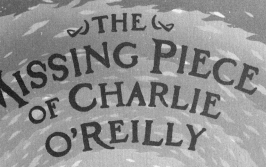

THE
MISSING PIECE
OF CHARLIE
O'REILLY

WALDEN POND PRESS
An Imprint of HarperCollins*Publishers*

Walden Pond Press is an imprint of HarperCollins Publishers.
Walden Pond Press and the skipping stone logo are trademarks and
registered trademarks of Walden Media, LLC.

ISBN 978-0-06-267966-6

Typography by Dana Fritts
19 20 21 22 23 PC/LSCH 10 9 8 7 6 5 4 3 2 1
❖
First Edition

To Leo, Spencer, Calvin, and Max
for always reminding me of the magic in
"Just one more chapter, *please!*"

～ 1 ～

Charlie O'Reilly *was an only child.* It therefore made everyone uncomfortable when he talked about his little brother.

Liam. The kid who sang incessantly, left his dirty socks on the floor, and messed up Charlie's carefully arranged comic books. The one who both drove him insane and made him laugh until his sides hurt. *That* little brother.

But Liam didn't do that stuff anymore, because he didn't exist. And according to nearly everyone in Charlie's life, he never did.

"Please, Charlie," his father would say, removing his reading glasses and tipping his head to the ceiling. "Not again."

After a year of seeing that look on his father's face, Charlie learned to keep quiet. At home, anyway. But he had to talk during his visits to Dr. Barton's office, session after session, perched on her couch, the cushions dented by him and countless other troubled kids.

Dr. Barton had spent months explaining—in that tone that made Charlie feel like he was four years old instead of almost twelve—that his "imaginary brother" was a perfectly normal psychological response to "all the stress at home."

All the stress. The code words every adult used for Charlie's mother.

"People don't just vanish from everyone's memory, Charlie," Dr. Barton had said at their first session. "And your parents could *never* forget one of their own children."

But Liam had. And his parents did.

Charlie understood one important thing from his weekly sessions: no one was listening.

Today, however, was different. There was nothing Dr. Barton or his dad could say that would ruin Charlie's good mood. The next twenty-four hours held too much promise and hope for Charlie to let the doubters get him down.

"It's nice to see you in good spirits," Dr. Barton said over her cup of tea. She was tucked into her overstuffed leather chair, a perpetual electric waterfall burbling beside her. The

2

sound of the waterfall was supposed to be soothing, but all it ever did for Charlie was make him need to go to the bathroom.

"Well, it's a big day tomorrow," Charlie said with a smile.

"I know—it's your birthday," she said.

"Yup. And one year to the day since Liam disappeared."

Charlie's father, sitting awkwardly beside him on the sofa, wilted at these words. Dr. Barton drew in a slow, deep breath.

Charlie knew what these sessions were about: to coax him into finally uttering, "Liam isn't real." Those three little words held the power to stop all the appointments, frustration, and hand-wringing. And as such, these sessions were pointless. Charlie would sit on this couch until he was eighty before he would say those words. Charlie's loyalty was stronger than whatever force had taken his brother away and wiped him from everyone's minds.

Just think of what we could accomplish if we spent this time acutally looking for Liam instead of sitting here blabbing, Charlie thought.

"As you know, Charlie," Dr. Barton said, "your father and I believe *something* happened last May. We just don't understand what, exactly. Why don't you tell us about that day one more time?"

Charlie stared at the bowl of fidget balls on the table between them. They had dissected his eleventh birthday countless times in Dr. Barton's quest to figure out what had "really happened." The truth, apparently, wasn't good enough.

He sighed. "When I went to bed the night before my birthday, Liam was there, in the bunk above mine. When I woke up the next morning, he was gone." Charlie recounted every detail: how the top bunk had vanished; how Liam's Legos and stuffed animals and posters and clothes and favorite cereals had disappeared from the house as cleanly as his existence had been scrubbed from everyone's minds. Charlie told the story slowly; they had an hour to kill, after all.

In each telling, Charlie offered up everything he could remember about that terrible morning and the days that followed. Charlie's dad would rub his back reassuringly as Dr. Barton ticked through her usual probing questions, most of them about his mom.

But she never asked about the night before, about what happened between him and Liam before they went to bed. Which was convenient, because Charlie was never going to tell her. That was none of her business. Only Ana, Charlie's best friend, got to know about that.

The fact that Liam's disappearance was Charlie's fault.

Finally Dr. Barton brought the session to a close with an

unsatisfied sigh. "Well, our time is up for today. I'll see you both next week."

Not if I can help it. Charlie popped up and headed down the hall, giving the adults the space they needed to whisper about him in the office doorway.

"Have a happy birthday tomorrow," Dr. Barton called after him.

"Oh, I will."

"Good work today," his dad said with a forced smile, the thud of the car door punctuating his last word. "I'm proud of you."

"Thanks," Charlie said, pretty sure the look on his dad's face five minutes ago hadn't been pride.

"Have you made all your birthday wishes, bud?"

I only have one, Charlie thought, but said, "Yup," instead. His dad thought all he wanted was a Nerf gun and a few comics.

They pulled onto the highway and Charlie watched the town of Kingsberg, New York, slide past in the purple early-evening light—new condos and shops mixed with old industrial buildings and warehouses, all under the ever-watchful eye of the old abandoned orphanage on the highest hill. *It's going to work,* he repeated to himself until they pulled into their driveway, past the crooked and sun-bleached invisible fence sign that no one had bothered to remove in the ten months since their Australian shepherd, Dipsy, had passed away.

"Can you get the door for me, Charl?" Dad said. "I still can't find my remote."

Charlie grabbed his backpack and hopped out. As he flipped up the plastic cover of the garage-door keypad, a fat, icy drop of water splattered on the tip of his nose. He looked up and almost caught the next drop in the eye. A blanket of blackened leaves clogged the gutter, dispensing yesterday's spring rain in little dive bombs. Green shoots stretched skyward from the eaves, having found a fertile home in the choked roofline. The weeds in the gutter mirrored those that were taking over the yard. Overgrown plants that Charlie's mother would never have allowed in her meticulously tended flower beds now thrived. The woody reeds of last year's lilies lay in a thick mat over the soil, and nothing but a few meager tulip shoots struggled toward daylight.

Charlie followed the car into the garage, stepped into the dark house, and immediately stumbled over something heavy in the mudroom. With a flick of the lights, his heart sank. Sitting by the door was his father's suitcase.

"It's just for a week, bud," his dad said, reading Charlie's face. "We're getting an exhibit on loan from the Smithsonian, and they need me in Washington, DC."

"You're not going to be here on my birthday?" Charlie said. He didn't care about parties or gifts, but he worried his father might need to be home for his plan to work.

His dad gently lifted Charlie's chin. "I hate it too, bud. I did everything I could to get out of this one, but there was no changing it. It's kind of a key part of the job."

Charlie looked at his dad and nodded.

"You know I'd be here if I could."

Charlie did know that. He knew a lot of things: that his dad's promotion at the museum of natural history meant a lot of trips out of town; that the raise that came with the new job was necessary to replace some of Mom's income; that he should be thankful they hadn't moved out of their house in Kingsberg to be closer to New York City. Knowing all of this, however, didn't make it easier. It seemed like his dad was gone more than he was home these days, and the geodes, T-shirts, and sharks' teeth that filled Charlie's room from museums around the world did nothing to make it feel less empty.

"As always, Ana and her folks are right across the street if you need anything," his father said, as if Charlie had forgotten where his best friend lived. "And I told Mrs. Gleason I'd be gone too, but I asked her not to check in on you this time without calling first."

Charlie grimaced. There was no catastrophe that could

inspire him to turn to their seventy-year-old neighbor. Even if she didn't smell like cigarette smoke and look like a bespectacled crested crane, she seemed just a little *too* interested in what happened in the O'Reillys' house. Apparently some people got pleasure from the misery of others.

"The exhibit should be pretty cool," his dad said. "It's a forty-eight-foot fossilized snake skeleton they found in Colombia. We'll go see it together when I get back."

"Dad. I hate snakes." Charlie pressed his lips together to stop himself from adding, "Liam loves snakes. You should take him."

"It's not like it's *alive*, bud. It'll be fun!"

Charlie wondered if his dad ever got tired of being so upbeat, the light that kept trying to penetrate the ever-present darkness in their house. It seemed exhausting.

"Anyway," his dad said, "I have the usual list of things to do while I'm gone. Why don't you go say hi to Mom while I grab some stuff from upstairs, and then we can go through it before I take off?"

Charlie nodded and walked into the family room.

Josie O'Reilly sat in her cave on the couch, staring at the television that hadn't been turned on in days. Her morning coffee was still on the end table, half full and capped in a skin of cold cream. Charlie clicked the lamp on and lowered himself beside her. He moved a clump of hair behind her ear and gave her a soft kiss on the cheek. Buried deeply under the musty odor of the unwashed hoodie she wore every day was the distant but comforting scent of Mom: Aveda shampoo, Dove soap, and something that always reminded Charlie of grapefruit. Even on her worst days—when everything seemed upside down—this fragment of the past calmed him. It gave him hope that his vibrant, adoring mother was right there, just under the surface, ready to spring back to life any day now.

A faint smile lifted the slack in her cheeks at his touch. "You're home?" she said. She was half under a blanket, her fingers tangled in the edge.

"Yup." He leaned in to her and wiped at his eyes. If it were years ago, she would ask him about his day, tell him she loved him, and throw her arms around him. Now, she sagged slightly under his weight. Charlie closed his eyes, knowing the ache in his chest would pass. It always did.

"Do you need anything?" he asked. "Want me to warm up your coffee?"

She shook her head.

After a few silent minutes, Charlie rose. "Love you." Her silence chased him out of the room.

Dad was a whirlwind of activity in the kitchen, packing up his carry-on and adding final notes to his list for Charlie.

He handed Charlie the scrap of paper, most of which was familiar at this point:

Drag the trash and recycling to the curb Monday morning
Do the dishes every night
Bring the mail in after you get home from school
Lock the doors and make sure all the lights are off before bed
Remind Mom to shower
Try to get Mom out for a few walks together

"What do these last two say?" Charlie asked, pointing at the bottom of the list. Despite inheriting his father's horrific handwriting, Charlie was no better at deciphering it than anyone else.

Dad looked over his shoulder. "Oh, the first one says pick up Mom's prescriptions on Tuesday. They can't fill them until then, but Lindsay and Donna at the pharmacy know you have permission to get them." He squeezed Charlie's shoulders and kissed him on the forehead. "And the last one says, 'Have fun on your birthday!'"

Charlie nodded and let himself be brought in for a hug.

"I'll see you next Sunday, okay? This should be the last trip for a little while, I promise." He waited for Charlie to nod. "Love you, bud. Take care of your mom."

And, with one last squeeze, he was off. Charlie watched

out the window as their ancient sedan backed out of the garage and his father tooted the horn in three short bursts as he drove away.

Dinner. Charlie's stomach growled as he crossed to the kitchen cupboard. He reached up to grab a box of spaghetti but found the shelf empty. He closed the cabinet and turned to the kitchen table, where he'd left the grocery list he'd made that morning.

"Mom!" Charlie hollered. "I thought you were going to get groceries today?" He tried to keep his tone light.

"Oh, Charlie, I'm sorry. I didn't get to it."

He knew Ana's mom could pick up groceries for them— she'd done it before—but he was tired of asking her when he could just do it himself; the store was a bikeable distance away. He wrote "groceries" at the bottom of his list of duties. He thought about adding birthday cake to the list on the table, but he couldn't bring himself to do it.

"I didn't get the laundry folded, either." Now his mother's voice rose in pitch, threatening tears.

"That's okay, Mom," he said brightly. "I'll do laundry after I eat, okay?"

Charlie was glad to hear nothing else from the family room. Silence at least meant no crying. Mom had been dealing with depression since before Liam left, but since he'd disappeared, it had gotten even worse.

Maybe she'll start to get better tomorrow, he thought. *When Liam's back.*

Charlie turned to the largely empty cabinet. Cereal again.

The clink of his spoon and the crunch in his ears was the soundtrack of dinner as Charlie leaned against the kitchen counter, bowl in hand. He turned the cereal box around so the Trix bunny would stop smiling at him, and a few minutes later he was putting his dish in the sink and heading down to the basement. He ignored the unwrapped Nerf gun in a Target bag on the floor of the laundry room, put his earbuds in, and got to work folding.

He emerged twenty minutes later, grunting from the weight of an overloaded laundry basket, to find all the lights out on the first floor. Mom had gone to bed. Charlie climbed the stairs and set the basket down quietly by his parents' bedroom door.

It was time.

He took down the New York Yankees poster from his bedroom wall, clearing the space Liam's Mets poster had once occupied. He then cleaned his clothes out of Liam's half of the dresser drawers. On top of the dresser, next to a stack of comics waiting to be sorted into Charlie's meticulously organized collection, was a photo encircled by a Yellowstone National Park picture frame. Three happy people beamed at him: Mom, Dad, and his own round eight-year-old self.

Liam's gap-toothed grin had once been in the photo too, but a bison's butt now occupied that space. Charlie had made Liam laugh so hard on that trip, he had shot juice out his nose and all over the back seat of the rental car. His parents had failed to see the humor.

Charlie grinned. He was totally going to make Liam snarf tomorrow.

When he happened upon the pair of pajama pants he had worn the night Liam vanished, Charlie stared at them for a moment. *It can't hurt, right?* He hurried to put them on, only to find they were at least three inches too short. His heart sank at the sight of his bony ankles. He wasn't the same person as he had been a year ago. He was taller, older. Sadder. *Not everything has to be exactly the same,* he tried to reassure himself.

As he brushed his teeth, he stared at the shelf where Liam's dumb baby shampoo used to sit. Somehow, despite being nine years old, Liam still hadn't figured out how to keep soap out of his eyes. Charlie scooted his own half-empty shampoo bottle over to make room. He glanced at the hallway mirror on his way to bed, his eyes catching on the spot where Liam had cracked it years ago during a tantrum involving a launched Matchbox car.

The glass was perfectly smooth. Like everything Liam related, it was as if he'd never existed.

Charlie's phone buzzed in his back pocket. A text from Ana glowed up at him.

What if it doesn't work.

He typed back: **It's going to work.**

If all it took was a wish, every one of my brothers would have vanished *long* ago.

Charlie smirked. **But did you ever wish it for your *birthday*?** ☺

It took a while for Ana's next text to arrive.

I get it -- if you could wish him away last year, maybe you can wish him back this year. But what if that dumb wish had nothing to do with it? Maybe it's not your fault.

Nice try, Charlie texted.

He knew what she was doing. Even though Ana, like everyone else, didn't remember Liam, she was the only one who believed Charlie. As such, she was also the only one who understood his disappointment and frustration every time he pulled a wishbone, tossed a penny into a fountain, or saw the first star of the evening. Each time a wish failed, it crushed him.

But none of those wishes was a birthday wish. The one that had made Liam disappear.

His phone vibrated again.

Just promise me you won't get all sad if he's not

back tomorrow, okay?

I promise. An easy promise to make, Charlie thought, since it's going to work. **It's going to be great!** he added, and then turned off his phone.

All he had wanted for his birthday last year was for his parents to move Liam into the guest bedroom so Charlie would have a room of his own. He had begged, pleaded, and whined about it for weeks, not asking for any other present.

"Don't get your hopes up," his dad had warned.

He got his hopes up.

Then, one year ago, sitting in this exact spot, at this exact time, Liam had charged into their room, swiping furiously at his red and watery eyes.

"What's wrong?" Charlie had asked.

"I don't want to talk about it!" Liam started kicking things around the room.

"Dude! Stop!" Charlie barely dodged an airborne shoe. "What's up?"

"Nothing!"

"Obviously."

"Just leave me alone!" Liam said, falling onto Charlie's bottom bunk with a dramatic flourish that sent his stack of comics tumbling. The sound of tearing paper came from beneath him.

"Jeez, Liam!" Charlie shoved him off the bed, causing

15

another comic on the floor to rip under his foot as he landed.

"Why are you pushing me?" Liam yelped.

"Look what you did!" Charlie held up the two halves of the most recent Avengers cover.

"Oh, I'm sorry one of your beloved comics got ripped. Boo-hoo."

"Get out of here!" Charlie shoved his brother again, this time with his foot.

"Don't kick me!"

"GET OUT!"

"IT'S MY ROOM TOO!"

That was when Dad had torn into the room, looking as bent out of shape as Liam, and demanded a silent but seething treaty for the night. Lights out, Charlie glared up at the underside of his brother's mattress until his eyes watered.

Over and over, he had wished he had his own room. He had wished his brother would go away. Disappear.

And the next morning, he had.

Now, alone in his bed, Charlie felt his breath catch at the memory. He clicked off the lamp, rolled onto his stomach, and reached between the bed and the wall. The threadbare edge of his baby blanket met his hand. He had crammed it into this recess on his seventh birthday, the day his dad had said he was too old for a blankie. Charlie would deny, even to Ana, that he knew it was there. He never pulled it out—

he wasn't a baby, after all. He rolled its seam between his thumb and index finger and closed his eyes.

"Whoever out there makes birthday wishes come true, I hope you're listening. Could you bring my brother home, please? For my birthday, all I want is Liam."

❧ 2 ❧

Charlie awoke with a jolt in the middle of the night. The wisps of a nightmare—hunger, a house on fire, anguished cries—slipped from his mind even as he tried to hold on to them. He stared into the dark above him and reached his hand into the air. Still no top bunk. The bright light of his watch told him it was 2:43 a.m.

It's okay. There's still time.

He rolled over, trying to force himself back to sleep, sure he was doomed to lie awake for the rest of the night, but mere moments later, the orange glow of sunlight through his eyelids announced morning had snuck up on him.

This time, he kept his eyes clamped shut. His fingers played nervously with the piping on the mattress edge. When he opened his eyes, he was going to see the top bunk hovering over him. He was going to kick the bottom of it just like he used to, and Liam was going to be so mad Charlie had woken him up early on a Saturday. He was going to yell, "What'd ya do that for?" before throwing a pillow down at Charlie's head. Then his mom was going to come to see what all the noise was about.

And later, Charlie might even make it up to Liam by helping him build the world's biggest pillow fort, and he'd even sleep in it with Liam if Liam asked him to. He'd let his brother call him Booper, an irritating nickname that lasted years after a game they'd made up when Liam was two. Liam would push Charlie's nose like a button, and Charlie would yell, "BOOP!" in a way that always made Liam laugh.

Summoning his courage, Charlie hummed a few bars of the happy birthday song in preparation to opening his eyes. He took a huge breath. He did it again. He tried to block out Ana's text replaying in his mind. **Promise me you won't get all sad.**

One, two . . . two and a half . . . two and three quarters . . . three.

He looked.

Ceiling.

He covered his face with his hands as his eyes filled. He buried his head in his pillows so no one would hear.

Charlie found a slice of cinnamon-sugar toast and a Nerf-gun-shaped package sitting on the table when he came down some time later.

This was where it had started. This was the spot where, one year ago, he had bounded into the kitchen howling, "Thank you! Thank you!" and had wrapped his arms around his mother where she sat warming her hands around her coffee mug.

"For what, honey?"

"For my own room!" he had said, squeezing her even tighter. "How'd you guys get all his stuff out of there without waking me up?"

His mother had squinted briefly at Charlie before taking a sip. "I don't know what we're talking about."

"My room. It's all mine!" Charlie searched the kitchen. "Where is he, anyway?"

"Who?" she asked, putting down the mug, her forehead creased.

"Liam." Charlie looked pointedly at his mom; she looked pointedly back. He tipped his head quizzically; she did the same. "Li-am?" he said, stretching out the syllables.

Her pinched eyebrows softened. "Okay, I give up. Liam who?"

His father marched into the kitchen, bellowing "Happy Birthday" and brandishing a small present. He finished singing with a flourish and placed the box in Charlie's hands. "Go ahead! Open it, bud!"

Three Yankees tickets lay in the box.

"Just like you wanted! They're for tonight's game!"

Charlie had never asked for Yankees tickets. He looked up slowly and asked, "Are these for you, me, and Liam?"

"They're for you, me, and Mom. . . . Who's Liam? Is he on your baseball team?"

That was the moment Charlie's world had tilted sidewise, permanently.

The conversation had degenerated quickly from there—Charlie insisting he had a brother his parents knew nothing about; his parents exchanging increasingly troubled looks. Each, at times, laughed at whatever joke the other was playing. Each got angry. Everyone yelled. Eventually, everyone cried.

His mother hadn't stopped crying since.

Now Charlie walked past the toast and the present and out the door to the garage, his feet so numb they seemed to belong to someone else.

Ana had tried to warn him. She had tried to save him

21

from himself. He should have known better. Hadn't he learned yet?

Charlie grabbed his bike from the garage, ready to ride until his legs burned more than the hole in his chest.

But as he turned toward the street, he found he wasn't alone. Ana was at the curb, bike at the ready. She stood in the same place Charlie had first seen her five years ago, the day she had moved in and bitterly disappointed Charlie by being a girl. Her crinkled eyes and forehead asked a question she already knew the answer to. Charlie thought he might throw up if he opened his mouth, so a blank stare was all he offered.

She blinked wordlessly, as if to say "I'm sorry," and grabbed her handlebars. Motioning with her head, she led Charlie away.

They rode west, toward the Hudson River. Ana and Charlie. The freaks. The figment chasers.

Charlie and Ana's well-known search for Charlie's nonexistent brother was a common source of gossip at Westmore Middle School. "They used to be normal," their fellow sixth graders whispered behind their hands. Their social schedules, previously chockful of birthday parties and sleepovers, had emptied dramatically in their year-long, relentless quest to find Charlie's little brother, or anyone who remembered him—who recalled he was in Mr. Sheldon's class, did Minecraft club after school, and was the third-grade record holder in the fifty-yard dash.

Despite their alienation, however, Ana's support of Charlie never faltered. She stood by his side and shouted down anyone who teased or mocked him. She searched with him for the boy with a Star Wars obsession, an infectious belly laugh, and a mop of auburn hair.

Which amazed Charlie every day, since she didn't remember Liam either.

"Where to?" Ana yelled over her shoulder.

"Power plant," Charlie answered. His favorite.

They left behind the heart of Kingsberg, with its coffee shops, craft beer pubs, and bookstores, and headed for the shoreline. It was a place time had forgotten, left to decay in the pollution of its industrial past. Charlie and Ana dodged potholes and scrub bushes sprouting from each crevice beneath their tires and passed the relics of the city's history: the crumbling, graffiti-covered train roundabout, the boarded-up mine entrance, and the old mill. They had explored every broken window and crumbling cement surface over the years.

All, that is, except the orphanage on the hill above the industrial side of town. Neither of them liked the idea of exploring where people had died.

Charlie used to worry that his mother would freak if she discovered their pastime, which probably qualified as breaking and entering, but since Mom had stopped caring about anything, he decided not to worry about it either.

They ducked multiple NO TRESPASSING signs and climbed up the power plant's four flights of stairs. Charlie dangled his feet over a huge circular ledge where the machinery had been torn out and sold for scrap twenty years earlier. Panting, he launched chunks of cement into the air, watching them tumble and spin. Free one moment, shattered the next.

Ana swung her feet in time with Charlie's, her tube socks brushing against his leg. "Happy birthday, by the way."

Charlie snorted and plowed his fingers through his thick black hair. "I'm an idiot."

She rocked sideways and bumped shoulders with him. "It was worth a shot. Besides, this proves it's not your fault. Liam would be back this morning if it was." She waited a beat before asking, "Was your mom up to wish you happy birthday this morning?"

"She wrapped a gift and made me toast, but I think she went back to bed." Charlie picked up a rusty bolt that was beside his thigh and turned it over in his hands. "You know, I don't know who I miss more. Her or Liam."

"At least your mom's here."

He let out a sad laugh. "Kinda." Charlie felt a familiar surge of anger. Unfortunately, it was an emotion that was always blended into a messy slurry with guilt and shame. Being furious at his mom was like being mad at a wounded puppy. Didn't she have enough problems without him wanting to shake her by the shoulders and yell, "Snap out of it!"

Charlie threw the bolt as hard as he could into the void—too hard, and he pitched forward. Adrenaline flooded his body as he tried to right his balance before falling off the ledge. His arms windmilled—

Ana snagged the back of his shirt. The *plink plink plink* of the bolt bouncing below accompanied Charlie's crablike skittering away from the precipice.

"Dude! If you splatter yourself all over the floor down there, I swear I will *never* forgive you."

Charlie flopped onto his back. "I'm so . . ."

"Tired?" Ana finished. And she was right. He was tired. Tired of hoping Liam would come back, tired of not being believed, tired of missing his mom.

"My dad brought home cupcakes a few nights ago," Charlie said, "the ones Liam always begged for every time we went to the store."

"Which ones?"

"These monster cakes with the green frosting hair and

25

the googly eyeballs. I stared at them and just started crying. My poor dad just stood there, wondering what he'd done wrong." Charlie gently shook his head, but stopped when all it accomplished was grinding gravel into the back of his scalp. "I went up to my room, but that place is even worse. I just stood there, looking at everything, just the way I'd left it. Neat and organized. Liam's junk used to be everywhere. I never thought I could possibly miss his stupid crap."

"Let's trade: I'll take your room, and you can come live with Lily and all her stupid crap." Ana tossed a small chunk of cement onto Charlie's belly. Ana and her sister shared a bedroom, a situation Ana bemoaned regularly. Lily was the biggest slob in the family, but it was a title she earned against fierce competition with their three brothers. Their home teemed with clutter, chatter, and barely controlled chaos. Surprisingly, Charlie loved it. Of course he didn't have to live there.

"At least Lily doesn't mess with your stuff on purpose," Charlie said.

"Seriously? She takes my stuff all the time."

"But because she likes your stuff," Charlie said, leaning up onto his elbows. "Liam stole my things just to bug me, like it was a game. He'd swap two posters on our wall, or rearrange my baseball cards or my comic books, because he knew it'd drive me crazy." He was surprised to find himself smiling. "Sometimes I want to tear my whole room apart—sweep everything off my desk and dump my drawers on the floor—just to make it feel like he's here. Maybe that would bring him back."

Ana said the only thing she had to offer. "I'm sorry, Charlie."

Somehow, it helped. It always did. Ana was Charlie's closest friend, and yet he had despised her when she had moved in five years ago. He closed his eyes and remembered how completely obnoxious he had found her from the moment she beat him in a game of horse the first day she arrived on the block.

"I promise I'll take it easy on you," Charlie had said with a proud flip of the ball before his first shot.

Ana had smirked and said, "Sure. You do that."

She proceeded to pound him. And not just in those four games of horse they'd played—for the next six months, Ana systematically outplayed Charlie at any opportunity: soccer, baseball, tetherball, it didn't matter. Charlie came to hate her knee-high socks, her post-win celebratory cartwheels, and her stupid Oakland Raiders jerseys.

"She could at least wear some New York gear!" Charlie had complained to his dad.

"Bud, Ana's lived all over. The Finches were in California last year, Denver and Phoenix before that."

"Why?"

"Mr. Finch's job has moved them every year."

This was the best news Charlie had heard since her arrival. Twelve months of Ana was more than enough. Then Charlie's dad dropped the bomb.

"But this time, they're here to stay," he said with a double thumbs-up. "Mr. Finch has been assigned permanently to New York."

"What?" Charlie said, slack-jawed. "Why?"

"Be nice," Mr. O'Reilly said. "Ana and her brothers and sisters have bounced around a lot. They haven't had much of a chance to make friends before."

"That would explain why Ana's so bad at it."

His father leveled a stern stare at him. "I said be nice."

Tell her that, Charlie thought. It didn't help that everyone else in their families got along. Liam and Lily were already best friends, making drawings for each other and screeching around their yards playing tag.

Charlie and Ana wouldn't become friends until later. Until he broke her arm.

"I need to be back for lunch," Ana said, her words echoing slightly in the cavernous expanse of the power plant. "You should probably check on your mom."

"Yeah." Charlie sat up. He tossed one last cement piece through the hole. "Liam's coming back someday, right?"

Ana met his gaze but didn't speak. Her hesitation made Charlie's heart beat faster than his brush with death a moment before. If she stopped believing him, he was sure he would collapse into himself like a black hole.

"I don't know," she said finally.

Good enough. Charlie rose and dusted himself off. "Maybe tomorrow."

ᴐ 3 ᴈ

The nightmare returned that night. And this time, Charlie remembered everything.

It started with a gnawing in his stomach. Next came the loud rustling of hay beneath him and the pelting of sleet against the thatched roof. It was uncomfortably hot, so he sat up lazily and reached down to pull off what he was wearing: a thin linen nightshirt. That was when Charlie became aware he was not himself.

A quilt slithered off his legs, pulled to the other side of the cot by the mumbling redhead lying next to him. *She needs the blanket more than I do anyway,* he knew, somehow. He didn't need to see his sister's thin shoulders and cheekbones to know how they poked out beneath her skin. It was dream knowledge: those details that simply *are*, without explanation, like accepting that a gorilla is driving your taxicab, or that you can fly. But none of the knowledge in this dream was fun: Charlie knew he was in Ireland, it was 1846, famine was draining every farming family that worked this land, and an unusually bitter winter was threatening them all.

How can I be so hot? he wondered. He hadn't felt warm in months.

Then the details he remembered vaguely from the night before began to unspool: the sting of smoke in his nose, stronger and sharper than the scent of the burning peat that kept their home warm. Then the thick and soupy air catching in his throat. Next, the crackling.

He turned. The wall was on fire.

Then came the screams.

"Kieran! Nora!" his mother called to him from the other side of the flames.

He was Kieran. She was yelling to him and his sister.

"Mother!" Charlie shouted back. He rose and took a step forward but was instantly repelled by the smoke and heat. The door connecting their two rooms was invisible within the inferno.

He backed toward the door leading outside, though

every part of him wanted to find a way through the flames to his parents. The sound of breaking glass announced his father had punched out the tiny window in their bedroom, opening their one path to escape. The blast of fresh air fueled the fire, and flames surged between the thick layers of straw overhead. Falling embers turned to a downpour, and Nora was now awake, screaming as a cinder grazed her cheek. She looked to Charlie with a dawning terror. She wriggled under the blanket, using it as a shield.

Get her out, Charlie's mind screamed.

A curtain of fiery thatch swung down between him and Nora, unbearably hot. He stumbled back through the door, coughing, out of his home and onto the snow. His parents rounded the hut in their nightgowns, covered in soot and dirt, the blood on his father's hand glinting in the firelight. They looked nothing like Charlie's parents.

"Kieran!" his dream mother cried, her ivory features flooded with relief as she pulled Charlie to her chest, moving him away from the flames. Her arms were warm and safe, an immediate solace. Charlie buried his face in his mother's chest, her thick red curls like a curtain over his face as he gulped clean, fresh air.

"Oh, a stór, a stór!" she cried. *My treasure.*

She clung to Charlie with such force, he felt they might merge into one. The ferocity of her embrace almost made the horror and pain of this nightmare worth it. It took Charlie's breath away. He couldn't remember the last time his own mother had held him so.

Then panic rose from her like smoke. "Where is Nora?"

Charlie pointed at the house, unable to speak. He watched his dream father race toward the engulfed hut, arms up to shield his face. Before Charlie could utter a word of warning, however, the entire structure fell in with a quiet sigh, releasing a wave of heat and light that blew his father back. The flash of light blinded him, and his mother's cry of agony faded away.

Charlie then found himself transported, standing in a graveyard. His breath rose in front of his eyes, a white cloud that temporarily fogged his view. His mother stood ten yards from him, before three small headstones. One mound of fresh brown dirt scarred the landscape. *Nora's grave.* Charlie watched the bitter wind whip his dream mother's hair into a scarlet tornado, lashing at her lips and her cheeks, a few strands glued in place with tears.

Charlie knew the story of each grave: three sisters, now gone. He had been too young to remember Siobhan, but he knew she had been found two farms away, carried facedown in the swollen stream at five years old while his mother nursed newborn Nora. He had vague memories of Kaitlyn, who was wracked by seizures a year later. Her convulsions worsened for months, until the day came they didn't stop. She was buried next to Siobhan that spring. His mother had stood on this same spot, clutching him and baby Nora to her shaking body.

"Mother," he whispered now behind her. "Please, come in. It's too cold to be out so long."

She didn't move. "How can I continue to live when my heart is frozen, a stór?"

"Please." Taking her to warmth was the only thing Charlie had to offer. He turned her from the graves, leading her on the long walk to their neighbors' home, where a small corner had been cleared to accommodate Charlie's family after the fire. Charlie gently stroked the back of his mother's icy hand with his thumb. Surely a seat by the hearth and a mug of tea would help.

He shepherded her through the door and onto a stool. The tang of burning peat rising from the flames was a comfort of home, even if it wasn't theirs. Charlie encouraged his mother to warm her hands and nodded to Mr. Sheehan and his father at the nearby table. They were deep in conversation, however, and barely noticed his arrival with his mother.

"You and I both know Mr. Walker is no longer making money on this land," Charlie's father said. "He pays more in taxes for each of us than he makes back in rent or crops. He wants nothing but to be rid of us!"

"So what if he does, John?" Mr. Sheehan said. "It's a wonderful opportunity, all the same."

His father sighed and laced his fingers. "The land of opportunity, yes?"

"There is nothing left for you here. Look around you, man. Your home's gone. You have no food and no money. You pulled half the potatoes from a year ago, and most of those reeked of blight. If we had the means, we would leave Ireland too. And Kieran . . ." Mr. Sheehan said with a quick glance at Charlie before lowering his voice. "He's aging ten years for every one he suffers here. Get out while you can."

His father's gaze swept over Charlie, appraising him without meeting his eyes.

"You'd be a madman to turn down Mr. Walker's offer," Mr. Sheehan said.

"What offer?" His mother's voice cracked.

Charlie's father pushed himself up from the table slowly, crossed to the hearth, and placed a hand on each of his wife's shoulders. "My love, Mr. Walker has kindly offered us passage to America on one of his ships."

"America?" She blinked and shook her head. "John, we have no money for such things."

"We have no money for staying here, neither. And the famine here is only getting worse. I believe Mr. Sheehan is right. We'd be fools to turn Mr. Walker down."

"And you are a fool to even consider it. What would we do in America? How will we live?"

"There are jobs there. Real jobs. Real money, and real food." With this final word, John tipped his head toward Charlie. "I don't think we have a choice."

Charlie knew the reason his mother would never want to go to America, or any other country, for that matter. She would never put an ocean between herself and her three daughters. How could his father not know this?

Two fresh tears tracked down his mother's wind-chapped face. She lowered her head and whispered, "No, John. We must put flowers on their graves in the spring."

His father closed his eyes and tipped his head back before reaching down and gently raising his wife's chin. He wiped the tears from her freckled cheek with his thumb. "If we don't leave Ireland, we may be tending four graves by spring."

Charlie looked at his own hands. The skin between the bones sagged the same way his grandmother's had as she lay dying. A gnawing, rumbling hunger tore through his middle.

As if feeling his pain herself, Charlie's mother stood and embraced him, smoothing the hair on the back of his head with a gentle hand. The weight of deprivation, grief, and cold that threatened to crush each one of them became tolerable with her touch. She would do anything to protect him.

That's when he awoke, back in New York, gasping, his dream father's last words echoing in his ears.

"I'll make the arrangements."

~ 4 ~

Ana wasn't impressed when they met up the next morning.

"I don't get it," she said as she threw a seven-skipper across the surface of the Hudson. "What does a dream about a fire in the 1800s have to do with you or Liam?"

Charlie had been a whirlwind of excitement ever since blowing into Ana's house that morning. "You don't think it's a sign?"

She scrunched her face up in a look of bewilderment. "Uhm, no. I don't."

"Okay, so you don't think it's weird that on my birthday, one year after Liam disappeared, I got an incredibly detailed and vivid vision of a family torn apart by the loss of a kid, leaving only me behind? Not to mention the fact that I'm Irish!"

She threw another stone, this one bouncing an impressive nine times. "First of all, it was a dream, not a *vision*. And second, even if it is a sign, whoever's sending it needs to work on their communication skills, because I'd need a lot more than that to go on."

Charlie had to agree with her there—intrigued as he was by the dream, he had no clue what it could mean.

"Hey, is that Coach Jonathon?" Ana asked after watching Charlie's rock sink into the depths after only three meek hops. On the opposite bank of the bay stood their assistant baseball coach, expertly throwing stones of his own.

"Looks like him," Charlie replied, and waved. Jonathon lifted a friendly hand in response.

"Alone again," Ana noted.

"Keep your elbow in, Charlie!" Jonathon hollered across the water. Charlie picked up another stone and did as he was told. He was rewarded with an eight-hopper.

"Whoa!" he said with pride. "Thanks!"

Jonathon tapped his baseball cap brim, tucked his hands into his pockets, and walked downstream.

Charlie and Ana didn't know much about Jonathon; in fact, they didn't know anyone who did. He was new to their school baseball team's staff this year; they guessed he was around eighteen years old, but he didn't attend Kingsberg High, and he didn't have any other job, for all they knew. Every time Charlie and Ana had seen him around town, he was by himself, always wearing the same clothes he wore to practice. None of this, however, kept him from being their favorite coach. He was basically Coach Kemp's complete opposite. Whereas Kemp could hardly clomp his 260 pounds to the mound without turning into a sweat ball, griping at them between labored huffs and puffs, Jonathon could chase them down for a tag out and rocket a throw to home plate from the outfield, all with a joke and a smile.

"If he could only fix your throws to second so easily," Ana said, shaking her head. Charlie made like he was going to throw a rock at her, and she laughed.

The two friends stayed outside the rest of the day, throwing rocks and exploring the abandoned buildings. Any time Charlie broached the subject of the dream again, Ana gave him a look that said, "You're killing me, Smalls." They made a pit stop at home for lunch and to check on Charlie's mom. Ana even managed to coax Mrs. O'Reilly out on a walk with them after lunch. They only went around the block once, but it was something. If nothing else, getting her out helped replace some of her pallor with a touch of the color she used to have in her cheeks.

By the time they were making their way home Sunday

evening, long shadows led their way. Ana put out her hand for a low-five between their bikes before turning up her driveway.

"Sure you don't want to come bunk with Lily?" Ana shouted as she opened her garage.

"Not tonight!" Charlie yelled back with a laugh. He walked into his house and closed the door behind him with a soft click. After a day of sunshine, movement, and fresh air, it was like walking into an alternate universe.

"Mom?"

He found her in the kitchen. She was sitting at the table, showered, dressed, and holding what smelled like a fresh cup of coffee before her. She had something resembling a smile on her face. Maybe the walk had helped.

"Hey!" he said, cautiously optimistic. "How are you doing?"

"Good," she said with a vigorous nod, like she was trying to convince herself too. "I made you dinner." She nodded to a bowl set before an empty seat.

"Thanks, Mom." Though Charlie didn't particularly like mac and cheese, the fact that she'd actually cooked made him forget all about that. He sat and lifted the spoon, only to have the entire orange mass rise like a bowl-shaped pasta lollipop.

"Oh," his mom sighed. "I guess it got cold. I'm sorry. . . ." She reached to take it back, but he turned both himself and the bowl away.

"No! It's fine, Mom! I actually like it better this way." He bit off a mouthful from the pasta-sicle and swallowed with a smile.

"Are you sure? I could make something else."

"It's perfect," Charlie said. He would have eaten a bowl of rocks if it kept a smile on her face.

"I'm glad," his mom said, relaxing back into her chair.

His mother's upbeat mood gave Charlie an idea. He set down the pasta glob.

"Mom? Could we make some cinnamon rolls tonight?" A breath seemed to catch in his mother's throat, but he pressed on. "It'll be fun!" He stood and moved to the cabinet to assess how much flour, sugar, and yeast they had. "Like a baby's butt, right?"

"Like a baby's butt . . . ," she repeated faintly.

Baking cinnamon rolls was an O'Reilly Christmas-morning tradition, one that Charlie, Liam, and Mom had started five years ago. That Christmas Eve, she had shown them how to knead the dough—*"Push down with the heel of your hands, fold it over, rotate, repeat."*

After what seemed like an eternity, Liam had whined, "How long do we have to do this?"

"Until the dough feels like a baby's butt," their mom had said earnestly.

Liam lost himself to giggles while Charlie jokingly

recoiled. "Mom! Gross! This is food we are talking about!"

She had laughed and poked the top of the dough with one finger. "Nope! Not a butt yet!"

Charlie, mostly to make Liam cackle more, had said, "Exactly how many babies' butts do you think we've touched, anyway, Mom?" She had then started chasing them around the kitchen, poking flour fingerprints onto their pants. The game only stopped when Liam slipped on the fine dusting of flour that now coated the kitchen floor, falling on his own baby butt and howling with a blend of laughter and pain that made Charlie grin where he now stood, alone by the cupboard.

They didn't have any yeast. They had hardly a half cup of flour. There would be no cinnamon rolls tonight. But it didn't matter, because before he could say anything, his mother stood and said, "Oh, Charlie, I don't think I'm up for it today. I'm going to head to bed, okay?" She looked much more tired than she had just moments before.

"Okay," he said as she headed for the stairs. "Don't forget to take your pills!" He tried to keep his tone light and chipper, masking a familiar bloom of frustration and anger that rose as he looked around the empty first floor.

Where are you, Mom? Where did you go?

If Charlie could pinpoint the moment everything had changed, it would be a year before Liam's disappearance. Charlie and Liam had come home from school to find their

43

mother crying inconsolably. She couldn't tell them why—said she didn't know—but from then on, life just seemed to have become too hard for her. She stopped playing in her Thursday soccer league. Her mountain bike sat in the garage untouched. Friday movie night was forgotten.

Their father was just as confused as they were. He tried to figure out what had happened. He took them all on a vacation, but it did no good. He planned date nights, only for Mom to cancel them. Charlie and Liam tried to help—they made her art projects and breakfast in bed. But none of it had any effect. And soon after Liam was gone, the bad days started to outnumber the good. Then came doctors' appointments, scans, and pills. Dad even had the house checked for poisonous carbon monoxide levels. Six months ago, the garden center had fired her for missing too many days.

All along, the only thing she could tell her family or her doctors was "It feels like there's a hole in my heart."

Once she had had to go to the hospital. Charlie's dad had taken her maybe six months ago, and after two weeks, she had returned, more her normal self. She had curled up with Charlie that night and told him, "You know, bud, *you're* the thing that keeps me going." It was like she had finally come up for air, finally broken free from the monster that pulled her underwater.

That respite, however, was short-lived. She descended

again over the next many weeks; returned to the depths of her silent and almost unreachable world. It was his fault. If Charlie was the thing that kept her going, he was obviously doing a terrible job.

He cleared his bowl; the noodle brick made a loud thud as it hit the bottom of the trash can. "Granola bar it is," he said quietly, and grabbed two packages on his way upstairs.

Tipsy the turtle seemed to smile at Charlie as he entered. "Hey, little guy." Charlie dropped a few pellets of food into the tank.

When Charlie and Liam had found the wounded, three-legged turtle, their dad had warned them that he probably wouldn't make it through the night. But Dad was wrong. Within the week, Charlie had fashioned a peg leg—a bent paper clip glued to his shell. So whenever Tipsy hid, he looked like a car with three flat tires—tipsy. Dipsy the Dog and Tipsy the Turtle, the dynamic pet duo.

Charlie and Tipsy nibbled their respective meals. "Family dinner," Charlie said.

Tipsy smiled again.

Quiet lay like a blanket of snow around Charlie as he did his homework. He crumpled the granola bar wrapper and drummed his fingers on his desk simply to make noise, then spent the rest of the evening sketching. Flying men and invincible women. Superheroes. People who could save the day.

He finally stretched and glanced at the clock. It was 9:30 p.m. He yawned and traded his sketchbook for a comic from his shelf. After pajamas and toothbrushing, he clicked on the bedside light and got under the covers.

Almost immediately, Charlie's eyelids began to droop. Each time his head bobbed, he was faintly aware of something tickling the back of his mind. He gave up on reading and flicked off the light, but a thought knocked on some distant door of his consciousness. Something was wrong. Had he forgotten some homework? Had he filled Tipsy's water dish? Sleep almost won out, but then, like water in a heating pot, realization came to a boil. It bubbled over the edges, hissing and splattering on the fire, jolting his brain to attention.

Charlie sat up and fumbled to turn on his light. He darted to the bookshelf so quickly he stumbled over his own feet.

It was exactly as he thought.

His Avengers issues were shelved after Batman. Watchmen was farthest to the left. His Bone books were scattered throughout, half of them upside down.

His comic books were completely disorganized. Clearly, and deliberately, out of order.

Liam.

᠊ 5 ᠊

Charlie scoured the house well past midnight. He checked the once-broken mirror, the shampoo shelf in the shower, and the Yellowstone photo, frantically searching for any other signs of Liam. *No one else would do that to my comics!* his mind yelled. *He's been here!* But nothing else had changed.

He paced for hours, staring at his bookshelf. By three o'clock in the morning, however, exhaustion won out. Like a toy draining its batteries, Charlie slowed, then stopped, and finally flopped into bed, asleep almost instantly.

"Stay close, a stór."

Charlie's hand ached from his dream mother's tight grasp. Beggars pawed at his thin coat, and a colony of seagulls screamed overhead as his father steered them along. The wharf was thick with rats, and the stench of rotting fish, sewage, and sea mist forced Charlie to cover his nose.

The *Randolph* bobbed in the distance. Charlie thought it looked like a gigantic piece of rotting fruit, maggots crawling on every surface. Only as they neared the ship that would take them to America did he see that it was swarming with dock hands, shipmen, and passengers on its every inch.

"You sure you don't want to stay here with me, pretty lady?" A man in filthy rags took a step out from an alleyway and into the light. Charlie's mother recoiled and reflexively grabbed at her neck, clasping her intricately carved stone pendent. It was the only thing of value she still possessed, a gift passed from mother to child for as many generations as they knew. Charlie realized in that moment that it would be his someday, since he was the only child left.

"You will do well to not speak to my wife!" Charlie's dream father barked.

"Don't get yer dander up, friend." The man chuckled. "Didn't mean no harm. Gonna try your luck on a coffin ship, are ya?"

John said nothing but pulled Charlie and his mother closer, pressing forward.

"What does he mean, coffin ship?" Charlie asked.

"He's a fool, Kieran," his father replied. "Ignore him."

Charlie looked to his mother for comfort. Though she appeared stricken by the man's words, she wrapped a strong arm around him. "Let's get aboard, darling." As it had been in last night's dream, her touch was like a warm cup of tea. Charlie leaned against her and drank it in.

Three enormous wooden masts, which had looked like toothpicks from afar, now loomed taller than any tree Charlie had ever seen. They reached skyward, tethered to the boat by a complex web of sails, lines, and ties. The wind whistled an eerie tune through the ropes and repeatedly beat them against the masts. The sails were rolled tight, awaiting the moment they would be unfurled to take his family out to sea.

"There's no room for us," Charlie said from their spot on the gangway. "The ship is already full."

"They will get us aboard, son," John replied. "There will be space for each person with a ticket." Charlie looked behind them in line. At least a hundred people stood waiting. He wasn't one to speak back to his father, but anyone with eyes could see there was no way to fit all these bodies on board.

In front of them, an elderly man leaned so heavily on

his young raven-haired companion that Charlie thought they would both topple over. He was unmistakably ill; flushed cheeks, sweaty brow, and a moan of discomfort with each step.

At the top of the gangway stood a man in the finest suit Charlie had ever seen. The man inspected every passenger: peered into each mouth, felt each neck, and listened to each chest with an ear trumpet. Charlie felt bad for the sick man—surely he would be found unfit. The time the doctor spent with him, however, was a farce. Neither man spoke, and after going through the motions, the doctor stamped the elderly man's ticket and stepped aside.

"Next!"

After Charlie and his parents had also been touched, prodded, and proven to be in excellent health, a man in a dingy uniform shouted at them, "Proceed belowdecks! Come on now, move along! We set out in an hour." He jabbed his finger toward the stairs.

John had to tip his head to clear the low ceiling. Charlie slowed to adjust to both the darkness and the unbelievable stench that assaulted them. It was the unmistakable scent of human filth. The stream of people from above shoved Charlie roughly along. He steadied himself on the post of a bunk.

"Don't just stand about," said a surly voice from above.

"Move on now!" Charlie regained his footing and reached for his mother's hand. They flowed in a wave of bodies along the aisle of bunks—three tiers of wood planks loosely secured to worm-eaten posts. Hay atop each was flattened by the weight of the previous passenger and was hardly cleaner than the floor. The smells made Charlie immediately long for the comparatively delightful aroma of the pier.

At the end of the corridor, they found the final three bunks on the left empty.

"You'd best be on top," Charlie's mother said. She sat on the lowest with their small satchel.

"I'll sleep on the bottom," his father said. "I can catch you both if these bunks collapse in the night!" He laughed, dimly.

A voice rose from the darkness of the opposite bed. "Pick the one you like the best. But only one."

"Pardon me?" John squinted to see.

"I'm afraid the rule is one bed per family." An older woman with a kind face peeked out. "Be glad you know each other. My bunkmate's a stranger."

"You must be mistaken. It's not possible for us to fit onto one," his father said, pointing to the narrow bed as if for proof.

"No mistake. A deckhand quarreled for quite some time with that family," she said, tipping her head back the way they'd come. "Gave them a choice. Take the one or leave."

"But we have tickets. Three of them."

"A ticket buys you passage and daily water, but not a bed of your own. It ain't much, but at least it gets us out of this cursed place."

After a moment of stunned silence, John said, "Thank you. We don't want to cause a stir." He grabbed their satchel and put it on the lowest bunk.

Charlie's mother turned to him. She must have seen the look on Charlie's face—a mixture of despair and fear—because she forced a smile and put her arm around him and his father both.

"Let's see if we can find some fresher air on deck, shall we? We won't see land again for a month."

6

"Whoa. What happened to you?" Ana asked.

Charlie sat down and looked furtively at the other kids on the bus. He kept his voice down. "He was in my room yesterday."

"Who was in your room?" Ana asked, her head cocked. "Have you slept?"

The bus revved into motion, and Charlie whispered, "You know exactly who! My comics were all scrambled up when I went to bed last night. It was like someone had thrown them all on the floor, then shoved them back on the shelf. *And* I had another one of those dreams."

Ana put her hand on his left knee to stop it from

53

bouncing rapidly up and down.

"Hold on. You told me *you* messed up your comics the other night, to make it feel like he was there."

"No! I *thought* about messing them up, but I didn't. I know for a fact they were alphabetized yesterday morning. I swear, Ana." Charlie felt a grip in his chest. *She has to believe me.* "I wanted to call you last night, but your mom would freak if I bugged you after ten o'clock. I went through the whole house. He's not there now, but *he was*."

"Maybe your mom moved your comics?" Ana didn't appear eager to begin another ride on Charlie's never-ending emotional roller coaster. "Or your dad?"

"My dad's out of town. And my mom never goes in my room. Even if she did, why would she touch my comic books? She's not exactly a Marvel fan."

Ana leaned back in her seat and chewed her bottom lip. "Was it the same dream again?"

"No. It was, like, the next chapter of a story." He told Ana about the pier and the ship. When he was done, Ana stared forward, her face screwed up in concentration.

The bus stopped and the chatter of boarding kids wafted over them. Charlie watched other kids load on—the kids who got up each day with their normal families, went through their normal days, and were tucked in each night next to their normal siblings.

The engine revved up again and Ana spoke. "Charlie, I believe you, about Liam. You know that. But this doesn't make any sense. I don't understand how these dreams connect to Liam's disappearance."

"But they must have *something* to do with it," Charlie pleaded. "These aren't normal dreams, I promise. Someone's trying to tell me something. And what about the comics?"

"Okay, let's say you're right about those. Let's say Liam was in your room. What are we supposed to do now?"

"I don't know. But we have to keep looking. He's out there, Ana, I know it."

Ana nodded, her own leg now bouncing up and down next to Charlie's.

"I told my mom I was going to stay after school until baseball practice. Meet me in the library and we'll keep digging. We're going to figure this out. We're going to find him!"

Ana didn't say anything for the rest of their ride. When the bus came to a stop behind the school, Charlie grabbed his bag and sprinted out the door, a wave of energy emanating from him. He didn't notice that Ana was walking slowly, far behind him.

Charlie was surrounded by books when Ana joined him in the library after seventh period. Many of the titles were familiar. Charlie glanced back and forth from a computer screen to a page in *Strange Mysteries of Time and Space*, a book they had both read many times. The only new book in the stacks was *The Great Potato Famine: The Story of Irish Immigration*.

Ana sat beside him, glancing at the national missing children website Charlie had pulled up. They'd searched these images regularly for Liam, but they both knew something was very different about these missing people. They were actually being *missed*. They had mothers and fathers, friends and family, avidly searching for them, spending time and money to find them. Liam did not belong in such company.

Over the past year, Charlie and Ana had formulated all sorts of theories about what had happened to Liam: magic, curses, time travel, alien abduction. Mostly, they learned there were a ton of loopy people in the world. After memorizing his mother's credit card number, Charlie had ordered a forty-nine-dollar online spell to bring back the dead, figuring it was worth a shot even if Liam wasn't dead. As a result, he now knew two things:

1. His parents didn't pay attention to their credit card statement.
2. Some scam artist was now forty-nine dollars richer.

"Find anything new?" Ana pulled out her notebook and pen and tried in vain to read Charlie's notes. She was constantly telling him it looked like he wrote with his feet. "What does that even say?"

"*Randolph.* That's the name of the ship in my dream . . . but when I Google it, there's like a thousand boats by that name in history. I think we need to check out the David Lang disappearance again." Charlie scribbled more notes.

Ana put down her pen. They had long ago dismissed the story of David Lang, a Tennessee farmer who reportedly vaporized in front of his family midstep in his cornfield in 1880. It was said that the plants around where his feet had been withered and died, and that patch of land stayed forever brown. But the whole thing had turned out to be a prank, a story concocted by a newspaper writer. No David. No family. No field. It was a spooky story, but only a story.

"Charlie, David Lang never even existed, let alone disappeared."

"That's why it's perfect! Just like Liam. He disappeared as if he never lived!"

"Right. But his wife and kids never existed either. It's a hoax."

"I think we've missed something." He turned back to his notepad.

Ana stared at him, unmoving. "You're torturing yourself."

Charlie looked up from his work. "What?"

The librarian sitting at the other end of the room cleared

her throat. Ana gave her a little "Sorry!" wave. Charlie, however, didn't lower his voice.

"Ana, we finally have a sign! We've been waiting a full year for something like this. We're close, I know it."

Ana didn't move. "I believe your comics were jumbled and I believe you've had some weird dreams, but . . . I just can't get my hopes up over a random mess in your room and some super-obscure story about Irish immigrants. You're just . . . desperate for some kind of clue after the birthday wish didn't work."

Charlie stared at her in disbelief. "Well," he said, his words crisp, "I'll be sure to tell Liam that you didn't think the signs he gave us meant anything when we see him again!" He turned back to his screen, muttering.

Ana closed her notebook and pushed out her chair. "I can't watch you keep putting yourself through this. I'll see you at practice."

೨ 7 ৬

By the time Charlie walked onto the practice diamond at five o'clock, the adrenaline that had fueled him all day had run out. Wide-eyed enthusiasm was replaced with bleary-eyed exhaustion.

"O'Reilly! Wake up!" Coach Kemp yelled when Charlie dropped an easy pop fly that Jonathon hit out to center field. "You look like you've been dragged around by a dog!" Charlie tried to focus, but even the simple seemed impossible. Ana ended up coming over from left to catch most of his flies after that, but they didn't say a word to each other.

Dante Jackson waited up for Charlie at the end of practice as he walked in slowly from the outfield.

"Lovers' spat?"

Most of the seventh grade had moved on from Charlie and Ana—even the most gossipy kids seemed to finally believe they were just friends—but Dante never tired of picking at Charlie like a scab.

"Did Ana finally realize you just aren't her type? Maybe she likes your 'brother' better?" he said, making air quotes.

"Dante, can you just shut up? For one day?"

"Oh, come on! You and Ana are the best entertainment in town. Beauty and the Freak. I can't wait to see what kind of weirdo kids you two have."

"I said shut up!" Charlie rounded on Dante, his fuse clipped down to a nub. He reared back, fist clenched, ready to smash Dante's leering grin, but found his arm stuck in midair. He was so focused on Dante that he hadn't noticed that Coach Jonathon had come up behind him.

"Whoa there!" Jonathon said, a firm grip on Charlie's arm with one hand, the other around Charlie's waist, pulling him back. Charlie's eyes were still trained on Dante, whose smile had dropped when he realized how close he had come to tasting Charlie's fist.

"Let go!" Charlie said, wriggling to get free. He strained and struggled, but Jonathon was much stronger than he was.

Dante's sneer returned. "Be careful, Chuck. It'd be such a shame if you had to *disappear* from the team." He wiggled his fingers, moved his hands in circles, and let out a laugh.

"Watch it, Dante," Jonathon said, still holding Charlie fast. "Unless you want me to tell Coach Kemp you're taunting your teammates, I'd recommend you get your gear and head out."

Dante turned to go, but not before giving Charlie a wink and a smile. Only after he had left the field did Jonathon completely loosen his grip.

"Dude, you can*not* punch him. Even I can't save your butt from Coach Kemp if you get in a fight."

Charlie looked down at the dirt. His rage had drained, replaced by regret and exhaustion. Jonathon was right— Coach Kemp would have kicked him off the team on the spot. Charlie had fantasized about pounding Dante so many times in the past, but he never thought he'd actually act on it. He'd never hit anyone before.

"I'm just so tired of him." Charlie worried he sounded like a baby as he spoke.

"Dante's a jerk. Don't let him get into your head."

Charlie eyed a scar over Jonathon's eyebrow. "Is that how you got that? By just ignoring it?"

"We're not talking about me now, are we?" Jonathon said with a wink. He put an arm around Charlie's shoulder and eased him toward the dugout. "Come on, let's head in."

Ana was leaning on the dugout fence, bag slung over

her shoulder, a fascinated grin brightening her face. She had always been far more likely to slug someone than Charlie, and her joy at witnessing his near-scuffle lifted his spirits. He returned her smile before grabbing his gear.

"I'm going to give you one chance to let me pretend that never happened, O'Reilly," Coach Kemp said. "One! Don't let me down."

"Got it."

Coach lumbered up the small hill between the field and the parking lot. Charlie, Ana, and Jonathon followed a few minutes later.

Charlie knew better than to look for his mom's car, but he still felt a pang of disappointment that the parking lot was empty. She used to pick him and Ana up after practice, dragging Liam with her in the back seat. Whenever he saw Charlie coming, Liam would smash his mouth up against the glass and puff out his cheeks in a way that let Charlie see all the way to his tonsils. It left a nasty smear of spit on the glass that would make their mom yell, but it always made Charlie laugh.

"You guys walking?" Jonathon asked.

"Looks like it," Ana said, clapping her hands together, "which is awesome, because that'll give Charlie plenty of time to tell me what just happened out there. Ooooh, I wish it'd ended differently!"

"Well, I don't," Jonathon said. "We need Charlie on the team, not in the ER." He surveyed the bags under Charlie's eyes. "I'll be honest with you, man—you look terrible. Go home, take a hot shower, and get some sleep."

"Yeah, that sounds pretty good," Charlie said through a yawn.

"And just steer clear of Dante. He wants to get under your skin, so don't let him. If you ever just need to talk . . ." Jonathon patted his chest.

Charlie nodded. "Thanks. Nothing a good night's sleep can't fix, right?" he said, repeating a quote of his dad's that he usually found ridiculous.

Jonathon's mouth twisted. "I don't know. Some things take more than sleep." He held up a hand for a high-five from them both and headed in the opposite direction.

Charlie leaned down to fish a pebble out of his shoe. When he stood, he turned to Ana, ready to apologize for what he'd said earlier. Instead, he saw Ana glancing at Jonathon's receding silhouette with a silly smile on her lips and a half-glazed look in her eyes.

"And here I thought you'd stayed at the field for me," Charlie said, playfully poking her in the back.

Ana snapped to attention. "What do you mean?" She adjusted the bag on her shoulder and took several purposeful steps toward the walking path, away from Charlie. "Who else would be I waiting for? Come on, let's go."

Charlie smirked and took a few quick steps to catch up with her. "Ana and Jonathon, sitting in a tree . . . ," he began. Ana glared at him.

If Ana had ever liked anyone more than a friend before, she'd never told Charlie about it. She was always more interested in bikes, one-on-one, batting practice, and slug bug (which always left a bruise). She laughed at fart jokes and found the popular kids, with their popped polo shirt collars or seventy-dollar yoga pants and lip gloss, repulsive. Charlie didn't find the girls in particular quite so revolting— more like epically confusing and a little fascinating—but he and Ana both ended up in fits of laughter whenever she did her dead-on impersonation of Monica, the most popular girl in the class. *Like, can you believe he said that? I mean, I know! Right? Do you think he likes me? OMG!"*

"Stop" was all Ana mustered to Charlie's playful taunt. She looked tired too. "Tell me what Dante said."

"Well, he was blabbing about *our* supposed love affair. Again. It just got to me. I would have knocked him out if Jonathon hadn't been standing right behind me."

Ana burst out laughing. "Dude, Dante weighs like forty pounds more than you! Someone would have been knocked out, but it ain't Dante!"

"Well, I think my first punch would be the last," Charlie

said, puffing out his chest, but he knew she was right—
Coach Jonathon had not only saved his baseball career but
his face too.

*What would happen if I did come home with a black
eye and a missing tooth? Would Mom even notice?* Charlie
immediately felt guilty for wondering.

"You know, you'd think Dante'd be tired of messing with
me by now. I don't even talk about Liam anymore. Not to
anyone but you."

"Yeah, well, you'd think he'd stop asking me, 'Where's
your skirt?' But that hasn't happened yet either."

Charlie was once again reminded that as bad as he
thought he had it on the team, Ana had it worse. Dante just
couldn't seem to wrap his feeble mind around playing with
a girl. Thankfully, the rest of the team had happily learned
to live with Ana's .470 batting average in the lineup. No one
else's numbers were even close.

Charlie's next yawn was so large, he thought his jaw
might get stuck. "You know, if you'd give me a piggyback
ride the rest of the way home, I'd really appreciate it." He
grabbed Ana's shoulders from behind and jumped in the air,
pretending to leap on her back.

"Don't you dare!" Ana yelped, pulled off-balance
backward. "I might—*might*—carry your bag. *If* you forgive
me for not getting all excited about the comics."

"Well, consider yourself forgiven." Charlie held out his bag with a huge, goofy grin, his frustration from the library melting away. Ana mock-begrudgingly took the bag, and Charlie stretched out his arms like she had taken the weight of the world from his shoulders. "Ahhh, you should be a jerk every day so you always carry my stuff."

"I never said I was being a jerk," Ana said, slinging the strap over her head. "But seriously, I'm sorry. You're right, the comics could mean something. I just don't know what."

"I don't know what either, but I know I can't figure it out without you."

Ana smiled, and they walked in silence until their homes came into view.

"What's your homework like tonight?" Charlie asked.

"Not too bad. Some English and a math worksheet. You?"

"Just the math. I may even do it in the morning so I don't end up sleeping on my desk. Here, I can take my bag back," he said, his hand out. "I didn't really mean for you to carry it all the way home."

Ana pulled both bag straps over her head and handed him his gear. A white scrap of paper the size of a cookie fortune floated gently to the ground. He couldn't tell if it had come from his bag or hers.

"You dropped something," Charlie said.

Ana bent down to scoop it up, and Charlie took a few more steps before realizing she hadn't moved. He turned back to find her frozen, staring at the paper.

"What is it?" Charlie asked. "You okay?"

She looked at him with wide eyes.

"What?" Charlie said again, and returned to where she stood. Ana held the slip out toward him. Charlie took it and read, freezing in place just as she had.

"Did you write this?" she asked.

Charlie shook his head vehemently. "Absolutely not!"

"Well, it's O'Reilly handwriting. And your dad is out of town. So if you didn't write it, then who did?"

The words, written in nearly undecipherable scrawl, read: TALK TO JONATHON.

8

"You look like I did yesterday," Charlie said over the hum of the bus the next morning. He was back to his old self, having slept deep and dreamless sleep. Exhaustion had won out over all the excitement.

Ana gave him a bleary, sideward glance. "I couldn't sleep. First I was trying to figure out who could have slipped that note into your bag if it *wasn't* Liam. Then I gave up on that and spent the rest of the night trying to figure out what the heck we're supposed to say to Jonathon."

"Well, we've got all day to think about it." Without a last name, phone number, or address, neither Ana nor Charlie had any idea how to contact Jonathon outside of baseball.

They would have to wait until after practice to talk to Jonathon alone. "But you'll be thinking about Jonathon all day anyway, won't you?" He elbowed Ana gently in the ribs.

"Very funny," Ana said with the slightest hint of a smile as the bus bumped over the railroad tracks. The same tracks that had turned them from enemies into best friends.

It had happened on a damp and cool spring afternoon three years ago. Charlie had been escaping his annoying little brother by riding to a friend's house on the bike path approaching the tracks when he saw her. Ana Finch, on her irritating candy-apple-red bike, wearing a stupid Denver Broncos jersey, casually pedaling toward some unknown destination. Charlie stood on his pedals and picked up his pace.

"Beat you to the crossing!" he yelled as he blazed past her, startling her. He glanced over his shoulder to see her leaning forward over her handlebars, ponytail whipping side to side.

"Not happening!" she spat.

They were off. The finish line, where the tracks curved slightly and crossed the bike path, was a half mile ahead. Charlie tried to pick up speed, but his wheels slipped on the wet pavement. He looked forward. Coming from the right, fast and loud, was a freight train. Charlie hesitated slightly to reconsider, but in this moment of caution, Ana pulled even with him, pumping her legs as hard as she could. She wore a huge, infuriating smile on her mud-speckled, freckled face. Charlie put his head down and found a burst of speed, but Ana pulled slightly in front of him, keeping her eyes trained on him to gloat.

With painful clarity, Charlie saw the reality of their situation. They had both miscalculated. They were going too fast to stop on this side of the train, but not fast enough to beat it to the other.

The train conductor blew his warning horn loud and long.

"Ana! LOOK OUT!" Charlie screamed.

He did the only thing he could think of. As Ana finally faced forward, he turned his handlebars hard to the left, sweeping Ana's back wheel off course.

The scream of the train muffled the sounds of tumbling bike frames, cracking helmets, and thudding bodies. They came to rest in the grass only a few feet in front of the tracks, the hammering wind of the cars slapping them again and again.

It was only when the roar of the engine faded that Charlie heard another sound—the cries of the girl who never cried. He lifted himself onto bloodied elbows to see Ana writhing in pain in the grass a few feet away. Her right forearm didn't make sense; it bent in a way it never should.

Charlie made a frantic 911 call from the home of a little

old lady with too many cats who kept saying, "Oh! Oh my, oh my, oh my!" after he knocked furiously and begged to use her phone.

That night Charlie's mind raced as his parents told him and Liam that doctors had put a metal plate in Ana's arm to hold the broken bones in place. *What did she tell her parents? Do they know it's my fault?* Ana's dad was huge—he'd been heading for a pro football career before he blew out his knee—but Charlie hoped the fact that he'd become a minister instead would keep him from murdering Charlie.

Liam had tried to cheer him up by sneaking an ice-cream sandwich into their room, grinning and whispering, "Don't tell Dad!" Liam always worried about getting in trouble with Dad. Their mom had tried to comfort Charlie with "Don't blame yourself, honey" and "It wasn't your fault." But it was. Charlie knew why he'd done what he had, but in the days following the accident, he replayed the scene endlessly in his mind. *Would she have made it across the tracks? Could she have stopped?* He also worried about how strong Ana's now-bionic arm would be and how much it would hurt when she bludgeoned him with it.

Ana returned to school a week later. Just as he feared, she cornered him in the hallway after the final bell. He tried not to cower as she came at him; her cast appeared ominously weaponized.

"Hey, Charlie," she said.

"Hey," he replied, his voice lifting at the end, more a question than a statement.

"Did you tell your parents what really happened?" she asked.

Was she nuts? "I told them you slipped," he said, hands at the ready to shield himself.

"Good," she said with a nod.

"Really?" Charlie's shoulders relaxed. "So . . . you're not mad that I almost killed you?"

"No, dummy. *I* almost killed me."

"Huh?"

Ana checked to make sure no one was listening. "Look, I couldn't let you beat me. It was stupid. And I also know I'd be dead if you hadn't done what you did." A pained, twisted expression gripped her face, like she was sucking on a lemon. Charlie was pretty sure she was breaking into a sweat. "Thank you . . . and I'm sorry."

A week of pent-up tension burst from Charlie. He began to cackle. "You should see your face!"

"What? Why are you laughing?"

Charlie couldn't stop. "It really kills you, doesn't it? You are the most stubborn person I've ever met! Say it again. Come on, say 'I'm sorry' again!"

Ana put her hands on her hips, but the corners of her

mouth curled upward. "I will not. In fact, I take it back!"

"No no no no. You can't take it back!" By this point, Charlie was leaning against the wall giggling.

"You're such a jerk," Ana said, but she started laughing too.

They missed the bus. They walked home together, talking about sports, school, and annoying little siblings. After two years of blocking each other out, they heard each other for the first time.

Ana's injury ended her baseball season, but she sat in the dugout and pointed out things Charlie had never seen. She taught him to see when a pitcher was throwing consistently high and outside; she showed him how Matt couldn't catch above his head, so Charlie needed to throw low to him; she saw that a player on another team only had power to the opposite field, giving Charlie a jump on where to stand. With Ana's help, Charlie didn't just play better—he played smarter.

In short, she showed him how she had always beaten him.

Once Ana's arm healed, they practiced together for hours, both getting stronger.

They were better together.

So, together, they would talk to Jonathon. Together, they would find Liam.

The bus's brakes squealed as they pulled up to school. Ana, who had been nodding off a moment before, jerked to attention with a gentle nudge from Charlie.

"Wow," she mumbled, and rubbed her eyes. "This is going to be a long day. Is it time for practice yet?"

"I wish," Charlie said with a snort. They both shuffled down the bus aisle, dragging their bags over the seats, willing the clock to move faster.

9

Coach Kemp cut practice short so they could get home and rest up for their game tomorrow. The team happily poured out of practice into spring's warm embrace, but Ana and Charlie stalled, packing up slowly and deliberately. Charlie was also having trouble managing the zipper of his bag with nervous, trembling fingers.

"Don't be late tomorrow, okay?" Coach Kemp said.

"Got it," they both answered. *Yup. Whatever. Just please leave!* Charlie thought.

Coach Kemp nodded and heaved his way to his car.

"Nice job today, guys," Jonathon said as he locked up the supply closet. "You look like a new person today, Charlie. I guess sleep *was* all you needed!"

"Thanks." Charlie hadn't figured out where and how to begin. "I got a note from a boy who doesn't exist anymore telling me to talk to you" didn't seem like the best approach.

"Jonathon . . . ," he finally began, "you know how you said I could talk to you about stuff?"

"Yeah. Of course." Jonathon glanced toward Ana, one eyebrow up.

Charlie waved a hand in Ana's direction. "Oh, Ana's cool. This is actually something we both need to talk to you about."

Jonathon sat on the bench and clapped his hands. "Okay, then. Shoot."

"Sooooo," Charlie began, "Ana and I have this little . . . secret."

"Okay . . . ," Jonathon looked concerned.

"Well, not a secret *exactly*. It's more like something we don't talk about. Not in public, anyway. It's about my little brother, Liam." Ana had come up behind Charlie, standing close to him, backing him up. "It's just that he . . . well, he disappeared a year ago."

"Disappeared?" Jonathon repeated slowly. "Was this what Dante was talking about yesterday?"

"Yeah."

"So your brother was, like, kidnapped?"

76

Charlie felt Ana's hand on his shoulder. This was the stepping-off point. This was the ledge where Charlie jumped into the thin air of Cuckoo Land, hoping Jonathon wouldn't just watch him fall. Every time he had said these words to anyone besides Ana, he had tumbled into a canyon of regret and isolation. Charlie liked Jonathon; he didn't want to add him to the list of people who thought he was unhinged. Maybe better to pull up now, keep the crazy to himself. Charlie looked over his shoulder at Ana, trying to get some sense of what to say next. She just gave him a nod.

"Well . . . we don't really know what happened to him. No one does."

"Oh, Charlie. That's terrible. I'm so sorry."

Jonathon wasn't getting it. Charlie was going to have to spell it out.

"So here's the thing . . . he vanished into thin air. Completely. And I'm the only one who remembers he even existed."

"What's that?" Jonathon's expression morphed from sympathy to confusion. He looked rapidly back and forth between the two of them.

"And," Charlie said, now determined to finish what he'd started, "for reasons that are even harder to explain, we're apparently supposed to talk to you about it."

Charlie immediately felt sick. Why had he let himself

hope? Why didn't he just stay in his room for the rest of his days and accept the fact that nothing was ever going to change? He'd wished his brother away, sunk his mom into a deeper depression, and dragged Ana into social no-man's-land. Maybe locking himself away was the answer. Ana could slide food under the door and give him updates on the outside world. It sounded much better than a lifetime of this.

"Are you serious?" Jonathon asked.

Charlie closed his eyes and tipped his head back. This was going to end as poorly as his sessions with Dr. Barton. Here he stood in front of another person who thought he was nuts. Charlie turned to get his bag, wanting nothing more than a quick exit. "You know, forget about it. Forget I said anything."

That's when Ana grabbed his arm. "Charlie . . ."

"Come on, Ana." He tugged at her grip, but she didn't move.

"Charlie!"

"What?" he shouted back, but he was surprised to see Ana was not looking at him, nor was she annoyed. Charlie reluctantly followed her gaze to Jonathon, expecting the familiar look of doubt or pity. What he saw, however, was him nodding and . . . smiling.

"Incredible," Jonathon finally said. "This is unbelievable."

"What do you mean?" Charlie said.

"I can't believe it, but yes, Charlie, I'm exactly who you should talk to about this."

"You are?" Ana said.

"Yes," Jonathon said. "You're not making this up."

"I'm not? I mean, yes . . . I'm not!" Charlie felt like his feet had abruptly found solid ground after a year-long freefall. "But how do you know?"

"Because," Jonathon said, "I'm just like Liam. I disappeared too."

ᴄ 10 ᴄ

"**W**hat?" Ana and Charlie said at the same time.

Charlie searched Jonathon's face to see if he was joking. This was supposed to be the point in the story when Jonathon told him he was mistaken or confused. No one had ever believed him, let alone taken a step even further down Crazy Avenue.

"Just what I said," Jonathon replied, his grin gleaming. "I'm one of those kids. One of the disappeared."

The most articulate question Charlie's mind could formulate was *Huh?* Jonathon couldn't have vanished like Liam. He was clearly right there. Suddenly, the ground Charlie had been so happy to find beneath him felt dreadfully unsteady.

"I don't think you understand what he said," Ana said, as if reading Charlie's mind.

"Oh, I understand perfectly." Jonathon tossed a baseball up and snatched it back out of the air. "Unbelievable!"

"Actually, I'm pretty sure you don't," Ana said, a crease of confusion between her eyes. "Liam's *gone*. Poof. He's not here. No one knows he even existed. You distinctly *are* here."

"That's because I came back."

Charlie's tongue felt like concrete in his mouth, heavy and unable to move, but that was okay, because Ana had plenty to say.

"Came back? What does that even mean?" she asked.

"I went away, vanished just like Liam, and then I came back."

These words sent Charlie's mind spinning. *Does that mean Liam could come back? Is he somewhere right now? Is he okay?* Questions tumbled in his mind like clothes in a dryer, but none were able to find their way out of his mouth.

"Back from where?" Ana said.

"From a place kids can go to disappear."

"Aha!" Ana sighed sarcastically. "You disappeared to a place where people *disappear*? Very informative, thank you!" She turned on her heel and slung her gear bag's strap over her shoulder. "Look, Jonathon, if you're going to mess with

Charlie, we're not interested! He told you something real and important, and you come back at us with some vague circular nonsense? Let's go, Charlie."

But Jonathon's look was not that of someone messing with them. He was serious. His eyes were pleading.

"Ana," Charlie said without breaking eye contact with Jonathon, "everyone we've ever talked to about Liam has called *us* crazy, right? What's the harm in hearing what Jonathon has to say?" Slowly Charlie took a step toward the bench, dropped his bag, and sat. Even the birds had stopped their spring revelry to listen in.

"Give me ten minutes, Ana," Jonathon said softly. "I promise you won't regret it."

Ana pierced Jonathon with a "So help me, if you hurt him . . ." glare, but she sat down cautiously beside Charlie.

"Thank you," Jonathon said. "What I'm going to tell you will be hard to believe, but no more so than what you told me." He looked at Charlie. "Your brother was here and then he was gone, right? Liam, and every trace of his existence, disappeared?"

"Absolutely," Charlie said.

"That was my story too—vanished completely. Forgotten by all."

"Except I remember Liam even though no one else does," Charlie said. "And this week, someone messed up my room and left me the note to talk to you. I know it's him. He's trying to tell me something."

Jonathon shook his head. "I don't understand why you remember him. . . . It's not supposed to work like that. And it's not just me—there are dozens of us, hundreds over the years. All erased. All forgotten. Plucked from our lives, while everyone else moved along without us. Sound familiar?"

"But how?" Charlie asked.

Jonathon stopped. He nodded a few times, appearing to weigh his every word. "It's because. We all . . ." Each of his words was like a small step into a cold swimming pool— painful and unnecessarily prolonged. "Well, we all have one thing in common."

Ana was always the sort to just jump into the deep end. "Jeez, Jonathon! Just say it!"

"Okay . . . we wished we'd never been born."

Charlie blinked.

"And . . . ?" Ana said.

"And we got our wish."

"What? And some magical fairy came by with a wand?"

"Well, it's a bit more complicated than that. But basically, yes."

While Ana was mired in skepticism, Charlie considered the implications of what Jonathon was telling them as it applied to Liam. *Never been born? Wished his life away?* "But

Jonathon, Liam would never have wished that. He was—is—a happy kid!"

"Yeah, Liam didn't leave. He was taken," Ana stated as fact, despite having no proof. She wasn't always right, but she was never in doubt.

"Well, someone did take him," Jonathon agreed. "Kind of. But not the way you think."

Ana leaned across Charlie and poked Jonathon in the chest a few times, testing to see if her finger would pass clean through. "So, what? You were never born? You're telling us you're some sort of ghost?"

"Ow," Jonathon said with a playful grimace, grabbing her hand to stop it from striking him a fifth time. "No. Not a ghost. To be a ghost, you have to die. I didn't die. I just left my life." He held her fingers and looked at her just kindly enough for a slight blush to creep up Ana's neck. She snatched her hand back before the crimson overtook her face.

"How could you leave your life?" she said. "That's not even possible."

"You're right. It's not. But neither is Liam vanishing."

It makes sense, Charlie thought reluctantly. *Never been born. Never born, never had parents, never been to Yellowstone, never broke a mirror or used baby shampoo.*

Someone who was never born could never be missed.

It fit.

But if what Jonathon was telling them was true, then he'd given up his *life*? Just quit? Like that? Charlie—who wouldn't quit something as simple as a game of Monopoly—found this concept incomprehensible. "Why?" he asked. "Why would anyone wish to never be born? Why would Liam do that?"

A shadow of emotion darkened Jonathon's face. "Well, that gets at the *real* thing we all have in common: our regret. A mistake so big that forgiveness is off the table. When we were offered the chance to leave everything we knew behind, even if it meant setting sail into the unknown, well . . . we took it."

Setting sail? The words fell like a stone in Charlie's stomach. Tall masts floated before his eyes, and he could smell the stench of a pier. "What did you just say?"

Ana, however, asked at the same time, "What did these kids do that was so bad? What did you do?"

Jonathon shrugged evasively. "We all have our own story. Some are worse than others."

Focus, Charlie told himself. "But Liam was nine. What could he possibly have done to make him want to leave his life forever?" Sure, Liam was a pain in the butt sometimes, but he had never done anything truly bad. Nothing worth this.

"What if . . . what if what happened to you has nothing to do with Liam?" Charlie said.

Jonathon stared solemnly at him and said, "Charlie, the last kid to arrive before I escaped last year was a nine-year-old boy. I didn't know his name but . . . he looked just like you."

A loud boom filled Charlie's ears, and he wondered if there was an actual sound that came with having your mind blown, but then he realized it was a car door slamming. Coach Kemp barked at them from the parking lot, "What the heck are you three still doing over there?"

They all jumped and looked back at him blankly.

"Jonathon!" he called into their stunned silence. "Practice is over. These kids need to get home and rest up." One of his eyebrows tipped so severely downward, it looked like it might slide off his face. Charlie felt like he was somehow in trouble, despite the fact they weren't doing anything wrong.

"We were, um, just talking about the lineup for tomorrow's game," Jonathon answered with as much conviction as one could give a fake excuse. He stood. "Did you forget something, coach?"

Coach Kemp walked past each of them very slowly, crossing to the far end of the bench, his suspicious eyes sweeping all around Jonathon like a police dog sniffing its subject. "I forgot my wallet," he finally said, reaching a hand into the helmet rack. "I think that's enough talk about the game. Charlie, Ana, you two need to head home. If I leave and something happens to you, it's going to be my problem." When they didn't respond with anything other than gaping mouths, he snapped, "Go on, now!"

Charlie wanted to scream, "Please! Just five more minutes!" But the look on Coach Kemp's face silenced him. Ana rose, defeated, and tugged gently at the shoulder of Charlie's shirt. "Come on, Charl. We'll see you tomorrow then?" she asked Jonathon. "At the game, right?"

"Yeah," Jonathon said, grabbing his own bag. "Hey, let me write down the name of that bat I was telling you about. If your folks are willing to spring for it, it really hits like a dream." Jonathon fished a scrap of paper from his pocket, grabbed the pen from a nearby clipboard, and slowly scribbled a few words. He handed it to Charlie, who stuffed the note into his pocket, not daring to look at it. "See you guys tomorrow. G'night, Coach." Jonathon jogged across the grass, into the parking lot, and out of sight.

Ana led the way out of the dugout and toward the path home as Charlie followed, picking up the pace as they moved farther from the field. The minute they turned behind the trees lining the path, Charlie pulled the paper out of his pocket so quickly that it snagged and tore in half.

"Careful!" Ana said. "What does it say?"

Charlie held the two pieces side by side. In meticulously printed words, it read:

Palace Diner, 7:00 a.m.

Charlie's hands dropped to his side, and one of the paper halves fluttered to the ground. "I guess our questions will have to wait until morning."

⍦ 11 ⍦

Staring up at the darkened ceiling of his bedroom that night, Charlie found himself hoping he'd be back on the *Randolph* in his dreams. He told himself it was because there might be a connection to Liam, but that was only part of the story. If he was being honest, he wanted to see his dream mother again. To feel her hug, to see her caring eyes. He glanced at the wall separating him and his real mother and immediately felt guilty for thinking this. But it soon passed. It was only a dream, after all; what was the harm?

And as he drifted to sleep, the sound of waves carried him away from Kingsberg.

It was Charlie's job to flick the weevils from the rock-hard, stale biscuits they'd brought aboard; soaking each in a small cup of rationed water was his mother's job. The water came from reused vinegar barrels, so swallowing the nearly inedible lump was a chore for anyone who attempted it. Today, however, Charlie was glad to at least try, having finally found respite from the gut-twisting seasickness of the last six days. He tipped his face toward the sun, thankful for the open air.

"Are you sure you don't want one, Mother?" he asked.

"No, thank you, a stór." She took his hand in hers and warmed it by rubbing gently against his skin. The warmth spread through his whole body. "Kieran, why don't you check on your father? See if he wants a biscuit, then we can keep reading."

"Yes, Mother." They had read every page of *New Fairy Tales* already, but he never tired of listening to his mother's voice. He gave her hand a squeeze and went belowdecks, the sound of his footsteps mixing with the symphony of moans and retching sounds. Charlie had never seen typhus before, but he was now too familiar with the fever, crushing body aches, and disorientation that consumed its victims. He passed a mother and child halfway down the aisle, both perched on the edge of their upper bunk, the woman cooing words of comfort to the feverish girl. He felt a wave of relief that his family had escaped the fever, but this sensation was immediately replaced with remorse. He knew better than to take pleasure in another's suffering.

He sat on the edge of his family's bunk and reached out for his father's shoulder to wake him. Before his hand even made contact, he could feel the unnatural heat.

"Papa . . . ?" Charlie said, shaking his dad before rolling him onto his back. The sight was horrifying.

His father's handsome face was a mask of agony. He moaned as Charlie touched his flushed forehead, and his eyes looked right through Charlie. Rivers of sweat flowed down his brow. His shirt was drenched.

His father bolted up. "We have to get Nora! Kieran, get your sister!" he cried before collapsing back onto the bunk with a crushing wail of pain. It was a suffering like nothing Charlie had ever seen.

Then, in an instant, his father and the bunks around him melted to white before his eyes. For a moment, Charlie was suspended in a sea of white dream space—not asleep, not awake, not on the *Randolph* and not in Kingsberg. Then he found himself back on deck, days later. He was with his mother again, her face creased with worry.

"He'll get better. Papa's strong." Doubt seeped around the edges of every word.

"I want you to sleep up here from now on," Charlie's

mother said, placing her head on his shoulder. Even this close, the wind snatched her words and carried them away.

"I don't know that they'll let me," Charlie said.

"They will have to let you. The bunks are a hospital ward, not a place of rest."

Dozens of their fellow passengers were ill; many had died. For the past three evenings, there had been a burial at sea, when anyone strong enough to come on deck had gathered to say goodbye to a countryman who would never see his or her new home.

"We'll find you a place to sleep," said Mrs. Clery, shifting some of her blanket to better cover Charlie's legs. Mrs. Clery, the woman who had helped them navigate their bunk selection and much more—water, toileting, rules on deck—now felt as close as family in Charlie's heart. Her nighttime lullabies for the children helped everyone forget where they were and what they were enduring. Charlie had never known his own grandparents, and he hoped they could live near Mrs. Clery when they landed.

Tired of talking about the sick and the dying, Charlie said, "Mother, Mrs. Clery was telling me about New York earlier. Her daughter wrote that there is a store in Manhattan that goes up *five* layers. All on top of each other! And every one of them has windows."

"I don't believe that's even possible, Kieran," his mother said.

"That's what she wrote," Mrs. Clery said. "Five stories tall, all marble and glass. But I agree with you, dear, I won't believe it until I see it."

"Well, it's only a matter of time before it collapses in on itself," his mother said, taking Charlie's hand. "I would certainly never walk into such a thing."

"Oh, I would," Charlie said. "It sounds beautiful. And she said that anyone can walk right in, isn't that right, Mrs. Clery? Anyone! I want to go there every day."

Mrs. Clery laughed and patted Charlie's knee. "I think your mother will have better things for you to do than walk around Mr. Stewart's store all day. And though they do let anyone who wishes to come in, they expect you to buy goods, not just wander about."

"What else did your daughter tell you?" Charlie asked.

"She read in the newspaper that the cross atop the new Trinity Church is eighty-six meters up. That's as tall as twenty-five floors!"

Charlie stared at Mrs. Clery with his mouth agape, the corners of his mouth upturned in a fascinated smile. He finally whispered, "Unbelievable."

Again, all went white, and the energy, excitement, and

possibility of that moment evaporated.

The fog cleared from his eyes, and the ship reemerged under a dark evening sky. The bugle of a trumpet filled his ears, and he found himself at the rear of the *Randolph*'s deck. He and his mother stood huddled at the front of a moderate-sized gathering of thin and disheveled travelers. A large bundle lay on a plank perched on the rail, held steady by the same man who distributed the water each day. He gave a solemn nod first to Charlie, then to his mother.

"We still have each other," she whispered.

Charlie didn't know if she was soothing him or herself. He pulled her even tighter to his side. "Always, Mother."

"Always," she repeated.

"For as much as it hath pleased Almighty God," the man boomed, "we therefore commit his body to the deep."

And with that, he hefted the plank upward, sliding the bundle overboard. Charlie's father's body splashed into the ocean, and his mother slid through Charlie's grip, collapsing on the deck.

Charlie startled awake with a cry, gulping for air in the dark. Though relieved to exit the nightmare, he simultaneously yearned to return to his dream mother, scoop her into his arms, and rock away their shared pain and heartbreak. But he was in his room, alone.

Upon quieting his breathing, he was surprised to hear voices coming from downstairs. He tiptoed into the hall before realizing it was the TV.

Why would his mom be up? She slept soundly at night now because her new sleeping medicine was—

Charlie felt another, sharper, pang of guilt. He had promised his dad he'd pick up her prescriptions today, but he'd forgotten with everything that happened after practice. Here he was, yearning to comfort a mother who didn't exist, while failing to care for the one who did.

But it's not as if Mom remembered my dinner tonight. Or most nights.

The thought was there before he could stop it, and all it did was make him feel worse. "I'm sorry, Mom," he whispered to the night. "I'll go tomorrow, I promise."

ও 12 ৬

Ana had told her parents she and Charlie were heading
to the Palace Diner before school to get ready for a test.
This wasn't a complete lie—there was a test. Next week.

Charlie, on the other hand, didn't have to tell anyone
anything.

On the ride over, Charlie strained to remember every
detail of his dream in order to present it to Ana for analysis.
"I hope I have another one tonight," he told her. "Every bit
of information helps, right?"

"I hope you do too," Ana said, "because you'll need
about thirty more dreams for me to have the faintest clue
what they're about."

He knew Ana doubted the dreams mattered, and he didn't really know how to explain why he thought they did, so he left it at that. It conveniently allowed him to stay silent about how he craved the company and affection of his dream mother. That part sounded stupid even within his mind. Besides, it was no one's else business.

A bell on the door announced their entry at the Palace Diner. Jonathon was already waiting in a corner booth. Charlie and Ana slid onto the cracked plastic seat across from him. The waitress took their drink orders—two OJs and a coffee—before leaving them in peace.

"What I *don't* understand," Jonathon said without prelude, "is why you remember Liam. He's supposed to be forgotten by everyone."

Charlie felt a bit knocked on his heels by this reversed perspective. "Um, I guess I've always been more concerned about why everyone else *forgot* than why I remember. I mean, aren't I supposed to remember my brother?"

"Well, yeah," Jonathon said, "but not after he got his chain."

"Whoa, whoa, whoa," Ana said. "Back up, both of you. We left off with you telling us that kids who make mistakes can wipe themselves off the face of the earth by wishing they were never born, that you did this BUT you're back, and Liam *might* be one of those kids. Which is all great, except I don't understand any of it."

Charlie knew what was happening. Ana was already in protective mode, trying to defend him from his false hope and enthusiasm.

Jonathon laughed and put his arms up. "All right, all right. Sorry. Let's take it from the top."

The waitress returned with their drinks, sloshing some from each cup onto the glittering Formica tabletop. She tossed a couple of straws onto the table from her apron pocket and stood over the three of them, pencil perched above a tiny spiral notepad.

"Pancakes," they all said at once.

The waitress, appearing tragically bored, pocketed the notepad without writing a word and turned away. Charlie mopped up the mess with a napkin and nodded for Jonathon to continue.

"Maybe . . . it would be easiest to explain how this all works if I tell you what happened to me."

Of Charlie's vast list of questions, Jonathon's past wasn't in the top ten, but this made sense. It also might be nice to know if he was a murderer or something.

Jonathon put down his coffee and rubbed his mouth. "My mistake was that I hurt my brother. Bad."

Neither Charlie nor Ana said a word. Their silence was

awkwardly punctuated by giggles from a clutch of teenagers across the room.

"You hurt him bad, like . . . *how*?" Ana persisted.

"Ana—" Charlie started, but Jonathon put up a hand.

"No. It's fine. Besides, it's not like I don't think about what happened every day. So . . . two years ago, my family was at my grandparents' cabin. Our parents kicked us kids outside one morning, telling us to go enjoy the sunny day— you know, while they sat like lumps on the couch drinking coffee. We were throwing the football around and one sailed past me and into my grandpa's shed, and when I went in to get it, I found a big bag of fireworks—sparklers, bottle rockets, Roman candles, the works."

Charlie knew exactly what he was talking about. His family loved to set off huge fireworks displays at his grandparents' place in Minnesota on the Fourth of July. He also knew that he was forbidden to touch them.

"I wasn't supposed to play with any of that stuff, but I'd seen my grandpa set off enough fireworks to know what I was doing. I ran inside, pretending I needed a glass of water, and took the lighter Grandma kept in the kitchen."

Ana shifted nervously.

"Pancakes." The waitress clattered three plates between them.

"Ah, breakfast," Jonathon said. They all awkwardly doctored their stacks with butter and syrup as the waitress topped off Jonathon's mug and asked them if they needed anything else. Once she was out of earshot, Jonathon continued.

"There's an empty lot across the road, and I thought my parents would just assume the neighbors were setting off fireworks. We did the sparklers first, dancing and giggling as they sprayed sparks all around. My brother and I hadn't enjoyed doing much of anything together for a while, but something about breaking the rules together made us buds again. When we moved on to the Roman candles, I staked the first one in the ground, the way my grandpa always had, and stood back as four flaming balls shot into the air, screaming fifty feet before exploding. I held the second one, aiming it like a gun toward the sky. My brother wanted to hold one too, but I told him he wasn't old enough."

Charlie was starting to think he didn't want to hear the end of this story. Ana's fork stopped in front of her mouth, and a drop of syrup fell to her plate.

Jonathon slowly shook his head. "I, of course, knew exactly what I was doing," he continued sarcastically. "*I* was fifteen, after all. I had just lit the last Roman candle when I heard my dad shout my name. We hadn't fooled anyone by crossing the street—he'd started looking for us the minute he heard the first crack. He came at me, face red, eyes crunched up . . . so furious. I dropped the Roman candle, like, if it wasn't in my hand, I didn't do anything, right? And that's when it went off. Four fireballs, all shot straight toward my brother standing ten feet away."

Ana raised her hand to cover her mouth. Charlie's chest burned from holding his breath without realizing it.

"It blew him off his feet. His shirt burst into flames. I don't know if the screams were from the fireworks, my dad, or my brother."

Jonathon's face changed. Previously, he had been telling them a story. Now it seemed he was talking to himself, reliving it, his head bowed. "I watched, paralyzed. My dad ran toward the fireball that had been my brother two seconds earlier and tackled him. They barrel-rolled over and over, my dad trying to put out the flames. When they were out, and I heard my dad yelling at me to call 911, all I could think was *I don't have a phone!* He yelled it again, telling me to run back to the house. I remember a loud honking noise, so I must have run in front of a car, but I don't remember seeing one. My mom watched me streak to the phone, looking up from her book, about to tell me not to run in the house. When I pleaded into the phone that we needed an ambulance, she got this terrified look on her face. I'd never seen her look that way before—it's all I see every time I think of my mom now."

He paused and used the sleeve of his shirt to wipe at his wet eyes. "Sorry," he said, giving them a small smile before continuing. "I actually don't have any other memories from that day. My mind skips to visiting him in the burn unit. They had to keep him knocked out for over a week because the pain was so bad."

Jonathon stopped making any effort to sop up tears that now flowed freely down his cheeks. "I only saw his chest and arms once without bandages. They looked like a red-and-pink checkerboard because of the skin the doctors took from his legs to graft over the burns. I cried every night, trying to block out the sound of my mom weeping in the next room."

Charlie felt like his throat was on fire as he fought against tears as well. He wished Ana had never asked.

"Jonathon . . . ," Ana said, "I'm sorry. I shouldn't have—"

"No, it's okay. So one night, right before my brother finally came home from the hospital, I overheard my parents wondering whether I'd"—his words seemed to catch in his throat—"done it on purpose. They thought maybe I hated my brother for being the good kid, since I was . . . well, a bit of a screwup. But it wasn't true. My brother made a career of driving me nuts, but I really did . . . *do* love him. I would never hurt him. It was an accident. I may have been a horrible big brother, but I'm not a monster."

Monster? Even the description of "a horrible big brother"

didn't fit the person Charlie knew. Jonathon seemed more like the awesome big brother Charlie had always wished he'd had.

"It didn't matter, though," Jonathon said. "Nothing could change the fact that my brother was never going to be the same, that my parents could hardly bear it, and that it was my fault. All I could do was wish that it had never happened. I lay in bed begging for some way—any way—to take it back. I wished . . . I'd never been born. And that's when she came and granted my wish."

"Who?" Charlie said.

"A woman. She was the one who helped me make the world Jonathon-free. She erased me and everything I've ever done."

What woman? Charlie wanted to ask, but the words wouldn't leave his brain.

"But you're not erased." Ana said. "You're right *here*."

"Right, but that's not the point. The old Jonathon—my previous *life*—is gone."

Gone. Just like the crack in the mirror and the shampoo bottle. The bigger picture of what Jonathon was saying dawned on Charlie. "Your brother's okay now, isn't he?"

Jonathon nodded slowly. "Without me, the accident never happened. No scars, no pain." With those final words, a sad smile appeared on his face.

Charlie pushed his uneaten pancakes away.

"Is every mistake that terrible?" Ana asked in a voice that was impossibly small.

"Every kid's story's different. Some are like mine. Some are worse. And some kids probably shouldn't even be there at all. Like this one girl, Amanda, she was arguing with her grandpa when *boom*, he died of a heart attack, right in front of her. Like, gone before he hit the floor. She didn't really have anything to do with it, but she thought she killed him and wished herself straight out of her life."

Jonathon set to the task of eating his pancakes, leaving Ana and Charlie to chew on all he had told them.

If this was the world Liam now occupied, Charlie wondered, what was his story? What terrible thing had he done that vanished with him?

Ana spoke with a newfound compassion. "But I still don't understand . . . why are you here? In Kingsberg, coaching baseball, eating with us at a diner? Aren't you supposed to be gone, off to wherever the never-borns or whatever go?"

"Yes, but . . . I escaped."

"So you tell us that you wished to leave your life. Now you're saying you escaped *from* the place you escaped *to* in order to return to the life you left?"

Jonathon let out small laugh. "I know, it sounds backward, but yes, that's basically right. Leaving solved one problem, but it created another: I was so lonely and I missed my family so much. So after a year, I found a way out. Kind of. I mean, I was able to come back into the world, but it doesn't matter."

"What does that mean?" Charlie asked, his tone kind.

"I'm still forgotten. No one remembers me. They look right through me."

"Wait, some people can't see you?" Ana asked.

"No. I don't mean like that. Everyone *can* see me, but nobody *knows* me. I'm a stranger to everyone I knew in my old life. The day after I returned, I went to the coffeehouse my dad walks to every morning and stood right in front of him. He said, 'Excuse me,' and sidestepped me on the way to the cream and sugar."

"He didn't even recognize you?" Charlie said.

"Nope. I went to my house and rang the doorbell. All my mom said when she answered the door was 'Can I help you?' I asked, 'Is Jonathon home?' hoping my name might snap her out of it. She got a weird look for a second, but then she said, 'Nobody by that name lives here.'"

Charlie swallowed, thinking back to the weird look on his own mom's face a year ago, when he had asked where Liam was. One kid missing, one kid back. Both moms had no idea.

"It's like I'm the opposite of a missing person," Jonathon

continued. "I'm here but no one misses me. They don't make milk carton pictures for dudes like me."

"And your brother?" Charlie asked tentatively.

"Well, at least that's good news. I went to his bus stop that first afternoon, nervous as hell, but I had to see him. He was *completely* back to normal. Not one scar. Looked just like he did before the fireworks. Even with me standing there, the accident was still wiped clean." Jonathon balled up his napkin and put it in the puddle of syrup on his plate. "So this is my life now. It's not perfect, but at least my mistake stayed erased."

"Wait," Ana said, "so that's it? Your family still doesn't know you?"

"Nope. I started drinking coffee every morning to go see my dad, and I walk by the house every once in a while, but they never recognize me."

Charlie tried to imagine it. No parents, no home. The isolation sounded awful, even compared to his meager situation. "But where do you live? How do you eat? You *do* need to eat, right?" Charlie asked.

Jonathon pointed to his empty plate. "I'm still a person. I just don't have a past. It's like I dropped out of the clouds— no family, no history. No friends. I needed money, so lied about my age and got a job working for a lawn-care company that pays cash and doesn't ask any questions. They don't care

106

who I am as long as I show up and do the work, and by next week, I won't even have to lie about being eighteen anymore. My boss, Mr. Cutter, rents me a one-room apartment over his garage."

"Mr. Cutter? Seriously?" Ana said with a laugh.

"I know. Funny name for a guy who mows lawns. I'm pretty sure he thinks I'm a runaway with a shady past . . . which, I guess, is pretty much true, but not in the way he thinks. I'm more of a run-to."

"A run-to?" Charlie said.

"Yeah. I keep trying to run *to* home."

"Sounds like baseball," Ana joked.

"Ha!" Jonathon smiled. "You know, the baseball field is the one place I can go to forget it all. I loved playing Little League so much when I was your age." He picked at his thumbnail, and even though he smiled, crinkles around his eyes belied his true mood. After a few moments, he took a deep breath and rubbed his hand over his face, wiping sadness and regret from his features. "Helping coach the team lets me kind of pretend that I still have a normal life."

"You kids need anything else?" The waitress plinked the plastic tray with their bill on the table. Charlie checked his watch, alarmed at the time. He was never tardy, but leaving seemed unthinkable.

"No. Thank you," Jonathon said, pulling out his wallet.

Charlie felt guilty Jonathon was paying for their meal on a lawn mower's income, but he hadn't thought to bring any money.

"You guys get out of here," Jonathon said. "You need to get to school."

"Wait, what?" Ana said. "We haven't even talked about where you went, or who this woman is, or how she has the power to erase people!"

"We're not doing ourselves any favors rousing people's suspicions by missing work or school. And trust me, you *want* to stay in school. Mowing lawns for a living ain't where it's at. Don't worry. I'll tell you everything I know tomorrow."

"Tomorrow?" they both repeated.

"Can't we talk more tonight, after the game?" Charlie pleaded.

"I don't think so, man. Kemp's watching me like a hawk—I think he thinks I'm selling drugs or something. You guys are off from school tomorrow for teachers' conferences, right? Let's meet at the mill, nine o'clock, and I'll tell you everything I know." When neither of them moved, Jonathon nodded and scooted out of the booth. "See you guys tonight."

13

Charlie was thankful for the hour he had between the end of school and warm-ups for the game. It gave him the chance to run home and get some chores done. He quickly emptied his backpack, thrilled that he could put homework out of his mind for the remainder of the four-day weekend, and grabbed the grocery list and the hundred-dollar bill his father had left. He would have preferred to do the shopping tomorrow, but he couldn't wait another day to hit the pharmacy. He was halfway to the garage when his mom's voice rang out from the other room.

"Where ya going, Charlie?"

"Store," he shouted back.

"Hold on. . . ."

Charlie looked at his watch. When he looked up, his mother was standing before him, dressed and showered for the second time in a week.

Though she had deep bags under her eyes from her long night, her purse was slung over her shoulder. "How about we go together?"

"Um, yeah, sure! That'd be awesome." Charlie couldn't recall the last time he and his mother had gone to the grocery store together, and having a ride would speed things up beautifully. He tossed his backpack back into the house and held the door open for her.

"How was your day?" she asked after backing out of the garage and turning down the road. She sounded like someone reading awkwardly from a script, but he appreciated the effort.

"It was . . ." What? Supernatural? Vindicating? Hopeful that he might actually find the brother she doesn't believe exists? "Good."

A little bit of the light in her expression dimmed. He tried again. "My day was busy. I had that test to study for, and then at school there was a fire drill. Oh, and a kid in my class twisted his ankle so bad during recess that they called an ambulance because they thought he might have broken it. He was back for seventh period, though, with crutches and an Ace wrap." Charlie could babble on about nonsense forever if it kept his mom's eyes bright. He pulled the smallest details from each one of his classes, chattering all the way to the grocery store.

As Charlie grabbed a cart and led the way into the produce department, he decided to risk it. He swallowed hard and asked, "And how was your day, Mom?"

"It was . . . okay!" she said with the first thing resembling a real smile Charlie had seen in as long as he could remember. She seemed to find her own answer a little surprising. "I felt . . . I don't know . . . hopeful, today? Maybe that's the wrong word. I don't know how to explain it, but . . . I guess it was just a good day."

Charlie nodded and smiled back. He said nothing, not wanting to risk ruining the mood.

His mother reached out and took one of his hands in hers. She rubbed it between hers, warming it, and looked at him lovingly. A sense of déja vu rocked Charlie to his core. He blinked hard and shook his head before checking to make sure he wasn't back on the *Randolph*, dreaming.

Her expression changed. "What is it? Are you all right?"

"No! I mean, yes. I'm fine. I just . . . it's . . . nothing." He grinned with enthusiasm to try to keep the moment alive, but, like trying to hold on to a wave on the beach, it was gone.

His mother let out a long breath, and the deep crease that was usually between her eyebrows returned. She looked around, seeming a little confused as to how she came to be standing between the apples and the ugli fruit. "Wow, I forgot how big this place is!"

"I got this, Mom. Just follow me."

They cruised every aisle, even the ones Charlie knew they could skip, grabbing not only essentials from the list but treats Charlie didn't even realize he wanted: cookie straws that changed white milk to chocolate, Double Stuf Golden Oreos, Chex Mix with Flavor Blast. He lost track of time, not caring if he was late to the game.

"These look good!" his mom said, picking up a package of string cheese wrapped in thin slices of fancy ham.

"Those are so good! Ana's mom buys them all the time."

"Oh . . . ," she replied quietly. She started to put them back, but Charlie took them from her and put them in the cart.

"You are going to love them. We'll eat them on the way home."

His mom nodded but looked away.

"Hey! I know," Charlie said, scooting her along beside him. "You pick for tonight!"

He directed her to the frozen foods section, aka the Land of Dinner, with a cart as full as Charlie had ever pushed.

Other than spaghetti, Charlie's meal preparation was limited to microwave-safe cardboard trays that slid out of boxes.

"What looks good? Lasagna? Enchiladas? Chicken-fried steak?" He pointed each one out as he listed it, imitating a game-show model, showcasing his prizes.

His mother just looked befuddled by the options. "Oh, I don't know, Charlie. You pick."

"I know. Let's just get one of each." He started rapidly pulling boxes from behind the cold glass doors. "Then you can pick when we get home!"

"It looks like we are shopping for a family of five instead of the two of us . . . ," she said.

At least that's what Charlie thought she said. The last few words were garbled as his mother's composure finally crumbled, apparently reaching its expiration date right there in the middle of the frozen-food aisle. She covered her face with both hands and started to sob.

Charlie stood, hands and arms frozen, clutching the boxes he'd pulled out. What was he supposed to do now? He dumped the boxes into the cart and put his arm around her. "It's okay, Mom . . . it's okay." He deflected the stares of two other shoppers; one asked if she was all right.

He waited a few minutes, murmuring, "We're okay," and "We just got some bad news," to those whose leers demanded comment, before realizing there was no end in sight. There would be no groceries or baseball tonight.

"Come on, Mom. Let's go home." He gently escorted her to the front of the store, their cart left for some poor stock clerk to discover later. Only after he managed to get her tucked back into the car did he bolt back inside, find Lindsay at the pharmacy, and make the only purchase of the night.

At least he'd done one thing right.

ᴗ 14 ᴗ

"Ana!" her mother called after her. "Where are you going? We have your sister's soccer game in an hour."

"I'll meet you guys at the park, okay?" Ana didn't wait for an answer before pedaling up next to Charlie, who had rolled out of his driveway at exactly 8:45 a.m., as planned.

She recounted the team's win to Charlie as they took the path that led to the mill at full tilt. She didn't ask for any follow-up on his one-word text from the night before: **Mom.**

Their bike tires crunched as they passed a boarded-up entry to the old salt mines, a source of many legends in Kingsberg. More than once, Charlie had read in the paper about curious fools who ignored the huge red STAY OUT—

STAY ALIVE! signs, only to require rescue after falling or getting lost. In all their explorations of Kingsberg, Charlie and Ana left the salt mines alone.

They pulled up in front of the mill, its once-whitewashed walls now a patchwork of peeling yellowed paint, bare cinderblock, and black mold. The river was slowly snacking on the portion of the building that jutted over the water. This landing, where boats used to cozy up for their fill of flour, looked only a few nibbles away from complete collapse.

"You know," Ana said, catching her breath, "if what Jonathon told us is true, it was never your fault. Your birthday wish had nothing to do with Liam's disappearance."

Charlie didn't reply and instead searched for any sign of Jonathon. He would need more proof before letting go of the guilt he'd been carrying with him for the past year. "There!"

A bike was propped against the far wall, beside a pile of rubble whose summit served as a welcome mat to one of the gaping first-story windows. Charlie and Ana made their way to the heap and crawled through the opening. They landed on a swath of broken flooring tile, and cool, damp air wrapped its arms around them. The scent of mold, oil, and wet cement crawled into their noses.

"Jonathon?" Charlie called.

"Up here," the answer echoed from above.

Charlie and Ana ducked beneath one of the innumerable rusty grain pipes that wove a complex maze above their heads like a crazed hamster track, and moved toward a staircase in the corner. The steps were so steep that Charlie had to hold on to both handrails, hoisting with his arms as much as his legs.

They popped through the cutout in the floor. Jonathon sat perched on an abandoned dolly, rolling slightly side to side, a welcoming smile on his face. "Morning."

"Hey," Charlie said, face flushed.

"Where were you last night?"

"Oh, you know. Family stuff."

Jonathon nodded. He looked like he wanted to inquire further but decided to take the hint. He handed them each a note card. "I want to give you guys my address. I can't afford a phone, but you'll have this if you need to reach me." Written in the same meticulous script as his diner note, Jonathon's address card placed him on the "wrong side of town," as Charlie's parents referred to it.

"Well, have a seat," Jonathon said. "No coaches, waitresses, or giggling kids to interrupt us this time."

Charlie and Ana cleared a spot on the dusty floor with their shoes and sat down in front of Jonathon like kids at storytime. "Can we recap for a second?" Charlie asked with a nervous laugh.

"Of course," Jonathon granted.

"Okay, so you hurt your brother, then got whisked off by some woman who granted your wished that you'd never been born."

"Correct."

"And when she took you away, your entire life was erased?"

"So far, so good," Jonathon said.

"And even though you tried to come home, your life's still wiped out?" Ana added.

"You guys are batting a thousand so far. My whole prior existence lives in here," he said, pointing to his head, "and in here." He pulled from his shirt collar a chain that was around his neck. Dangling off it was a key. It looked like something that would open the door of a medieval dungeon.

"What do you mean? What's up with the key?" Charlie asked.

"Well, each kid who disappears has the memory of their mistake held for them, right here," he said, pointing to the clover-shaped hole in the handle. "It's a constant reminder of why we can never go home. The key holds our past—all we have to do is look through the opening." He placed the key to his eye like a monocle. "And voilà."

Jonathon's face shifted, any trace of a smile melting away. Only a few seconds passed before he closed both eyes and dropped the key to his chest. "It never changes, and it never gets any easier."

"Can I look?" Ana said in a whisper.

"Ana!" Charlie gasped. Why would she possibly want to watch that?

"What?" she said, palms to the sky. "We're all being honest with each other now, right? If all this is for real, I want some proof!"

Charlie shook his head. Jonathon, however, didn't seem bothered by the request at all. "You can look," he said, holding the key away from his chest.

Ana walked over to the dolly, bent at the waist, and pressed her eye up to the cloverleaf handle of Jonathon's key. She stood back up a moment later.

"All I see is your shirt," she said with a disappointed frown.

"That's because only those *in* the memory can see it," Jonathon told her.

Ana screwed up her face suspiciously. "Interesting." She sat back down. "So where did you go? What is this place that holds all you never-borns?"

"Well, I didn't bring you guys up here solely for the posh accommodations," he said with a wink and a sweep of the arm at their surrounding rubble. "Come with me." Jonathon rose and went to one of the few windows that hadn't been shattered over the years. The glass was hazy and their view was obstructed somewhat by a web of vines that had taken up residence on the other side. It did not, however, obstruct one of the best views of their hometown that Charlie had ever seen.

"To answer your question, Ana, I went up there." Jonathon pointed toward the top of the highest hill of Kingsberg.

Charlie didn't need to follow Jonathon's outstretched hand to know he was pointing at the burned-out landmark that overlooked their city. "The orphanage?" he said incredulously.

"The Asylum," Jonathon said.

"The what now?" Ana said.

"The Asylum. Or rather, the New York Asylum for Orphaned Children. At least, that's what the plaque on the door says. But these days, we just call it the Asylum."

Ana shook her head slightly side to side. "You're telling us you escaped from a mental ward?"

"No, no," Jonathon said, hands out in front of him like he was stopping traffic. "It's not a mental institution. The word 'asylum' never used to mean that, specifically—it just means shelter, or refuge, or in this case, orphanage."

"Jonathon! A rat would have trouble finding shelter in that old thing!" Ana said. "There's no roof. No windows. It's a gaping hole of a building."

"Yes and no." Jonathon turned. "Charlie, what do you know about that building?"

Charlie shrugged. "Just that it burned down."

Stories varied wildly about what had sparked the inferno that had gutted the children's home over a hundred years before, but everyone knew that people had died—many of them kids. In one version of the tale, an angry white mob burned the orphanage to the ground when it started taking in children of color. In another, a teacher torched it after the headmaster broke her heart. But Charlie thought the most likely story was also the most boring: soot buildup in a chimney had caught fire and spread. Legend had it you could hear the cries of the orphans' ghosts at midnight, echoing within the remaining walls. It was all a bit too creepy for his tastes.

"Well, it was built almost a hundred and eighty years ago," Jonathon said, "by the rich, old New York family who owned the salt mines, the Ketterings. The widow left it to the state when she died, requiring it be converted into an asylum for orphaned children. It burned down only six years later, and that ruin is all that was left. That's all I ever saw, until I got this." He touched the chain around his neck.

"So what do you see?" Charlie asked slowly.

"I see a beautiful old home with lights flickering in the

windows and smoke coming from the chimneys. I see the place I lived for a year after I disappeared from my life."

"You see that right now?" Charlie said, his voice thick with doubt. Jonathon nodded.

"You see things that aren't there?" Ana said, her voice flat.

"I wouldn't say they aren't there, Ana, just that *you* can't see them." Jonathon smiled. "The Asylum's still up there, and this"—he tapped the key around his neck—"and its many copies open the door."

"There is no door!" Ana insisted, walking away from the window, exasperated. "Nobody needs a key to get into that old thing. Every window's a gaping hole."

"To you, yes," Jonathon said. "But I'm telling you, Ana, the Asylum is still open for business up there. It's undamaged and full of kids who need shelter."

Full of kids.

"Are you saying Liam is up there right now?" Charlie asked. "He's been this close to home this whole time?"

Jonathon nodded solemnly.

Charlie walked over to Ana, took her arm, and moved them both out of Jonathon's earshot. "Ana, I need you to stick with me here. I know everything he's saying is hard to believe, but we have to trust him. He's all I've got."

"I think he needs an asylum, all right. A modern-day one."

"I can't do this without you. Please. We have to see this through to the end, wherever that may be."

Ana stared hard at Charlie for a solid ten seconds, a war of doubt and loyalty battling behind her eyes. Then, with a crisp nod, she turned away from Charlie and marched back toward Jonathon. He was seated on the dolly again, chewing on his nails.

"So," Ana demanded, "who is this woman who took you away?"

Jonathon gestured for them both to take a seat again. "Her name is Brona. She's the housemother—the governess, basically—of all us lost souls."

"What is she?" Ana asked. "Like, a witch? A sorceress?"

"Well, a ghost is my best guess, but she's not see-through or floaty or anything like that. It's just that she's been in the Asylum for as long as the stories go back. At least a hundred and fifty years."

"A child-snatching ghost," Ana summarized.

Jonathon shook his head and laughed. "Kinda. To you, she probably seems like some creepy kidnapper, but remember, she's the one who saved us from our mistakes. We asked to be taken away from the pain we caused. She's more like a savior to kids like us. At least that's how many kids see her."

Charlie wanted to ask more about Brona, but the name

caught in his throat. Instead he said, "But you changed your mind, right? You wanted to come home. What kind of savior keeps a person against their will?"

"Well, that's complicated. Take me, for example. Sure, I missed my family and friends, my real life. But I didn't want to return to what I'd done. Brona believes the real world is nothing but a stage for mistakes and pain. And . . . she's not wrong. I still don't want to go home if it means the accident comes home with me. I wanted them both: no accident *and* a family standing there with open arms. But it doesn't work that way. Brona knows this, and for all the kids who need a place to be after their lives have been erased, she takes care of them."

"Jonathon," Charlie said, "there's something else that still doesn't make sense to me. Why doesn't your family remember you now? You left the Asylum. Why didn't your life come back with you, mistakes and all?"

"Well, Charlie, that brings us back to the chain," he said, pointing to his necklace. "This thing does a lot more than hold a key. The key gets you into the Asylum and serves as a constant reminder as to why you're there, but the chain is also what erases you from everyone's minds. As long as this thing is around my neck, I am, literally, within its magic. No matter where my body is, I'm still forgotten."

"So why don't you take it off?" Ana said.

Charlie snorted. "Okay, queen of the obvious, I'm guessing he's tried that. It's not that simple, right?"

Jonathon bowed his head toward Ana, like he was awaiting an Olympic medal. "Go on. Try it."

"Try what?" she said, hesitating.

"Try to take it off."

"Is it going to hurt me?"

"Nope," Jonathon said, his key swinging gently back and forth. "Give it a try."

Ana started to reach for the chain but then pulled her hand back. "What are you not telling me?"

"You'll see." He held Ana's gaze. "You both *need* to see what happens."

Ana turned to Charlie, and though he was as unsure as she was, he nodded encouragingly. Slowly Ana's hand advanced, but the rest of her leaned away. It looked more like she was preparing to pick up dynamite than a necklace. Charlie held his breath. Ana pinched the chain, and both she and Charlie flinched.

Nothing happened.

Jonathon swiveled his head upward. "Ana, you're just touching it. You have to take it off."

"Give me a second, will ya? This whole thing's freaking me out." Ana took a breath and lifted the chain off the nape of Jonathon's neck. She let out a scream.

Charlie scuttled backward. "What! What is it?"

Ana stumbled away from Jonathon, a look of bewilderment mixed with disgust on her face. She wiped her hand on her pants. "That thing's alive?"

"Only when you try to take it off." Jonathon sat up and cleared his throat a little.

The key, which had previously hung in the middle of his chest, was pressed so firmly against his Adam's apple, it dented his skin. The necklace was now as tight as a dog collar. Jonathon looped a finger under the chain the way Charlie had seen his dad yank on his shirt collar and necktie.

"Are you okay? Why did you have me do that?" Ana asked, coming closer to him. When she saw how tight the chain had become, she turned away. "That thing's strangling you!"

"I'm fine."

Ana paced and Charlie sat frozen, staring at Jonathon's neck.

"Guys, really, I'm fine. Trust me, I've made this thing tighter than this before. You can't imagine how many ways I've tried to get it off. It's like the world's most frustrating finger trap." He cleared his throat again.

Charlie felt helpless seeing Jonathon's obvious discomfort. "There has to be a way to lengthen it again, right?"

A wry smile crossed Jonathon's face. "Good behavior,"

he said. "As long as I leave the chain alone, it'll be back to normal by morning. Do you believe me now, Ana?"

Ana nodded vigorously. "What would happen if you tried to take it off again?"

"I've only seen a few desperate kids try that," Jonathon replied. "They aren't at the Asylum anymore. And they aren't back home either."

⌒ 15 ⌒

The midmorning sun streaming through the window struck Jonathon squarely in the face, making his pale skin glow. After all he had told them, Charlie's mind was spinning with questions, but in the end, there was only one that mattered. "So how do I get Liam out?"

"I don't honestly know," Jonathon said, "but I'm pretty sure you can't do anything from out here. We need to get you and Liam together. I think you have to go in."

Into the Asylum. Charlie had already come to this conclusion but had hoped Jonathon had some alternatives to offer. He swallowed hard.

"The good news is I know I can get you in," Jonathon

said. If this was the good news, Charlie thought, he was pretty sure he didn't want to hear the bad. "The tricky part is getting you out."

"Let's start with getting in," Ana said. "How does that work?"

"Well, that's easy. Any Asylum kid can create a new key and chain for a newbie. Brona shows us how when she takes us out on gatherings."

"Gatherings?" Charlie asked.

"That's what it's called when we pick up new kids. She takes each of us out with her at least once in our first year. She says it makes things easier for the kids who she's trying to help, to see another kid there."

"Isn't there any way to skip the whole chain thing?" Ana asked. "I mean, as fun as that whole slithering, choking thing seems, couldn't someone just sneak in without one?"

"There's no sneaking in. Without a chain, you can't even see the Asylum. You'd just be walking into the burned-out shell."

Charlie did not relish the idea of placing what amounted to a noose around his neck with no idea how to get it off. "Okay, so you can get me in. Couldn't I get out the same way you did?"

"No, I just got lucky. Brona leaves the Asylum every day by a door only she can open, and she's always careful to close it. But one time, she didn't. And I took my chance."

"Well, that doesn't sound like a very reliable getaway plan," Charlie said.

"Agreed. And even if it was," Jonathon said, "you and Liam would have the same problem I have—still chained, still forgotten."

Charlie sat quietly, replaying all that Jonathon had told them. There was something paralyzing about being so close to the answer; so close to Liam, but not close enough. Without the knowledge of how to get the necklaces off, they were effectively no closer to bringing Liam home than they'd been before they'd first spoken to Jonathon. It was like discovering the end of the rainbow only to find that the leprechaun's pot held no gold.

"There's something about all this that doesn't make sense," Charlie said. "If Liam's stuck in the Asylum, how did he get into my room to mess up my comics or leave me that note?"

"I was wondering that too. My only guess is that Brona took him on a gathering near your house, and he was somehow able to slip away and lay those clues. I agree with you—I don't know who else could have known that messing up your room would tip you off *and* known that I could help you, as an Asylum kid myself."

Once again, Charlie tried to imagine what would push

his brother to wish his life away without ever even talking to him about it. Surely, no matter what Liam had done, they could have figured out a better solution than this. Even if he had done something as awful as Jonathon, Charlie would have forgiven him.

Wouldn't he?

"So . . . what did he do?" Charlie asked the question so quietly, the others almost didn't hear.

"I don't know, Charlie." Jonathon appeared truly apologetic. "I wish I could tell you more, but I left right after he got there."

"And no one's ever figured out how to get the necklaces off?" Ana asked.

Jonathon tilted his head side to side, scratching behind his ear and measuring his words. "Well, not no one. All the kids say that one girl did it, like fifty years ago, and was able to escape and return to her life, but no one knows how. Honestly, I always just thought it was a myth, the sort of story someone made up to keep hope alive, and it just stuck. As far as I know, there's only one surefire way to get your chain off, and that's to be—" He suddenly froze, midscratch and midsentence, and stared right at Charlie.

"What?" Charlie said. "What way?"

"Okay, hang on." Jonathon ran his hands through his hair and closed his eyes as he spoke. "Brona tells every kid who comes into the Asylum that there's only one way to get the chains off. The problem is that it's effectively a catch-22."

"What's a catch-22?" Ana asked.

"It's like . . . a paradox," Jonathon said.

"That doesn't exactly sound promising," Ana said with a frown.

"Bear with me. So Brona says that the chains aren't permanent, but there's only one way to remove them. *Forgiveness.* All we need is forgiveness for what we did. The person who was hurt by our mistake has to forgive us, and that person alone can then remove the chain."

"But your brother can't forgive you," Charlie said. "He doesn't even remember you."

"Exactly. You can't be forgiven by someone who has no clue who you are, right? Also, my brother can hardly forgive me for burning him to a crisp, because it never happened. Not anymore. And of course, the only way he could remember it is if I took off my chain, which I can't do without his forgiveness."

Charlie struggled to follow the logic of it all. "That makes my head hurt."

"Exactly." Jonathon laughed sadly. "That's why it's a catch-22! You can't do one without the other, so neither is attainable. Anyway, it's not like I'd let my brother forgive me for what I did, even if he did remember me. Taking off my chain would bring back the past, and there's no way I'd let him get injured again."

"Hold on!" Ana said, gripping Charlie's arm as she said it.

Charlie startled. "What?"

"Maybe that's it!"

Jonathon nodded at Ana with a knowing grin and said, "Exactly."

"*Exactly?*" Charlie said, feeling left out of the loop. "Exactly what? What am I missing?"

Ana's eyes were wide. "That's how Charlie could get Liam home, right? I mean, he's already halfway there. He knows who Liam is, even if he doesn't know whatever it is that Liam did. If Charlie can get into the Asylum, he can forgive Liam for what he did and take Liam's chain off."

Jonathon nodded. "Bingo."

"And once his chain is off," she continued, "Charlie can bring Liam home *remembered*!"

Jonathon rubbed his hands together in thought. "There are a lot of ifs, but . . . there might be a plan in here."

Charlie stared at Ana, stunned. She was the only person he knew who could, in the blink of an eye, go from bald-faced skepticism about Jonathon's story to now laying out a plan based on it. This was not the first time he had envied her decisiveness. So often, he felt mired in the mushy gray matter of life. How could he be understanding of his mom's depression while also being so frustrated with her? How could he appreciate all his dad was doing to hold them together while still fuming at him for leaving all the time? How could he be so eager to save Liam while remaining clueless about why Liam had apparently left him behind?

Ana's plan, despite her immediate certainty, felt very shaky to Charlie. There were too many unknowns. "Guys," he said, "all we have to go on is a kid in the Asylum who looks like he *could* be my brother. It might be Liam, but we don't even know that for sure. And even if it is Liam, we have no idea what mistake he made to wish his life away, and we *certainly* don't know if I'm the one who needs to forgive him. What if his regret has nothing to do with me, or even with our family?"

Ana smacked Charlie's chest with the back of her hand. "Are you serious? We're this close and you're chickening out *now*?"

"No one said I was chickening out, Ana! But if we're wrong about any of these assumptions, I could get stuck in there forever with a kid who isn't even my brother."

"Charlie's right." Jonathon nodded slowly. "It's too big of a risk."

"What? You guys! This is what we've searched for, isn't it?" Ana countered. She looked between them pleadingly.

"Jonathon, tell us more! *Anything*. What else do you remember about the kid who arrived a year ago?"

Jonathon crossed his arm and screwed up his face in concentration. "Like I said, he arrived right before I left. Another kid showed him around, and I didn't get to talk to him. He was pretty upset, crying mostly. I think I remember him saying, like, the bonker or the booper will never understand. Something like that. It was weird."

The Booper. Charlie's throat tightened and his vision blurred as his eyes welled with tears. He could feel Liam pushing his nose like a button; could hear his peal of baby laughter as he yelled, "BOOP!"

It's him.

Liam was in the Asylum, and he needed Charlie's forgiveness.

Ana screamed and punched the air above her head. "I *knew* it! It's him! It's totally him!"

It took a moment for Ana to explain the Booper to Jonathon, her excitement growing by the second. As she did, the gears of Charlie's mind now spun so rapidly, he thought they might break free and sail out of his skull.

"So let's say this is all true," Charlie said. "Jonathon can get me in, I can forgive Liam and get his chain off. . . . I still have to have a chain to get in there, right? So who takes *my*

135

chain off? How do I not end up stuck?"

"Simple!" Ana said, like she'd anticipated this question. "When you wish you'd never been born, just think of something you did to Liam—something he can forgive *you* for! Then you can take off his chain, he can take off yours, and violà!"

Like wishing for my birthday that I'd never see my own brother again? Charlie thought. He'd carried that guilt around every day for a year. Surely it qualified. Charlie turned to Jonathon. "Do you really think this could work? That we could get him home *remembered*?"

"Yeah. I think so. Once the chain is off, it'd be like he never left." A sad expression crossed Jonathon's face, but he quickly recovered with a forced smile.

That look, as fleeting as it had been, hit Charlie in the chest. Nothing about this plan helped Jonathon. Here he was, offering information to help Charlie every step of the way, but once all was said and done, Jonathon would still be family-less and forgotten. Surely there was some way to get his life back—one that didn't include him living alone and mowing lawns for all eternity. One without all the pain.

Charlie offered him a smile and said, "Maybe, when my family's back together, you can come live with us?"

Jonathon's face softened and he nodded his head appreciatively. "Thanks, Charlie. But for now, let's just focus on getting Liam home."

Charlie agreed but vowed silently, *We'll figure something out, Jonathon. I promise. Somehow I'll fix your family too.*

∾ 16 ᦸ

Charlie biked home alone, unable to spare even a sliver of his brain to the heap of trouble Ana was in for being so late to her sister's soccer game. Instead, his mind was a tangled knot of questions and doubts, fears and hopes, all topped with a big dollop of joy. Ana had wanted to throw a chain around Charlie's neck right there in the mill, but he needed a day to digest all Jonathon had told them. They planned to meet again tomorrow to go over every detail again.

Could there actually be a happy ending to all this? Was Charlie really going to find Liam *and* bring him home? And not just to their house, to their *home*—the one with a dad who didn't travel so much and a mom who baked and gardened and went to work. They had been happy before. At least, happier. Surely bringing Liam home could get them back to how they used to be.

There was just one last question—one that Charlie had pushed away and ignored ever since the Palace Diner. Here, alone, it finally burst out of the shadows of his mind, refusing to be ignored for another second.

What if Liam didn't want to come home?

What if his wish that he'd never been born was something he'd never take back, unwavering and immutable, just like Jonathon's? What if what he'd done was truly horrible? Unforgivable, even?

Charlie shoved these questions back into the darkness.

He felt like he was standing at a massive fork in the road without a compass, a map, or even a clue. Turn left and go to the Asylum on a hope and a prayer that he could get them both out. Or turn right, and stay home waiting for . . . for what? Another idea? Another plan? While his dad kept leaving and his mom didn't get any better? If they had more information about the Asylum, or about this Brona person, could they come up with a more reliable plan than this?

Charlie rounded the final corner toward his house, and what he saw drained every thought of Liam, Jonathon, and the Asylum from his mind. Flashing red and blue lights danced on the trees and over the walls of his house; diesel fumes hit him in the face as he skidded to a stop in the driveway. He left his bike in a heap and ran past an ambulance and up to the door.

"Mom?" Charlie entered the family room to find his bulge-eyed, birdy neighbor, Mrs. Gleason, standing over the couch, where two paramedics huddled. A bright yellow stretcher stood behind them, blankets and straps hanging open.

"Mom?" Charlie repeated quietly, fear in his voice. He looked to Mrs. Gleason for answers, but she was too enraptured by what was happening on the couch to hear him. One of the paramedics spoke in a soft voice to his mother.

"Josie, is this your son?"

"Yeah, I'm Charlie." He was stuck to his spot, not sure he wanted to get closer to all the medical gear. "What's going on?"

"Charlie?" his mother said.

Relief flooded through him, allowing him to move closer to the couch. "Mom. What's going on? What are they doing here?" He inched around the stretcher. "Did you fall or something?"

Rounding the couch, he saw she was pale and sweaty, cocooned in a blanket and holding a bloodstained wad of gauze to her forehead. A plastic tube started at the back of her hand and ended in a bag of liquid hanging from a pole on the stretcher. She didn't speak but instead stared at a spot on the floor, her eyes puffy.

"We need to take your mom to the hospital, Charlie," the second paramedic said, her hand resting on his mom's thigh. Charlie wanted her to stop touching his mother.

"No, it's okay," Charlie told the paramedics. "I'm home now, so we're all good."

They exchanged a glance. The man spoke first. "Charlie, she's not okay right now. Your mom needs a couple stitches and some time with the doctors."

"Well, okay, but hang on. Let me call my dad." Charlie turned from them to Mrs. Gleason.

"Your mom already called your father," Mrs. Gleason said, "and told him she needed to go to the hospital. He called me and them." She pointed at the medics. "He tried to get a flight home, but there are terrible storms in Washington, and the best he could do was a flight first thing tomorrow morning."

"Let me talk to him," his mom whispered, so quietly Charlie wondered if he had even heard her correctly. "Alone, please."

Again, the paramedics spoke to each other with only their eyes, and after a few nods and some shuffling, Charlie was left alone with his mother. The shadow of their boots darkened the light at the base of the closed door.

Charlie sat on the couch and a queasy feeling filled his stomach as she started to cry. He reached out to take her hand, but pulled back, scared to touch the tubing and tape. He didn't want to hurt her. "Mom, what happened?"

"I fell and hit my head on the coffee table when I tried to go to the bathroom."

"You fell? Why?" He searched the room for clues as to how a grown woman could topple over so badly that she needed the paramedics. The answer came when he saw the basket that held his mom's medicine bottles. There were multiple identical containers, all full.

"Wait. Mom, did you stop taking your meds?" Charlie knew her doctor had told her she could have balance troubles if she suddenly quit taking them. "Is that why you fell?" A hot flare of anger filled Charlie's chest. Just yesterday he had beaten himself up about being a day late with her refill, feeling terrible that he'd let her down. Now he could see she hadn't been taking them at all.

"See," she sobbed, reading his face, "I ruin everything I touch. I can't even walk to the bathroom right. You and your dad shouldn't have to take care of me like this. I used to know how to do this—how to be a good mom—but it's like I forgot." She looked at him, her eyes pleading. "I don't know how to remember." Her final word cracked in half. "You deserve a normal life."

This was where he was supposed to say, "We have a normal life," but he couldn't bring himself to say the lie. Why should he play the role if she wasn't going to hold up her end of the deal?

"I'm sorry. You deserve so much better," she said, letting out another sob. "You deserve a better mother."

Charlie shook his head vehemently.

"You are so good, Charlie." Tears flowed down her face in a constant stream, catching on her chin momentarily before dropping down into two expanding, darkened spots on her pajama top. "I don't deserve such a good family."

"Stop it!" Charlie yelled. "Just stop talking!" His voice was so shrill he hardly recognized it.

The paramedics were back at her side before Charlie's protests had echoed off the walls. "Josie, do you want help getting on the stretcher?" the woman said, offering her hand. The other paramedic gently pulled Charlie away. "Charlie, I need you to let us do our job, okay? We're here to help your mom."

Charlie sat, paralyzed with rage as they each supported an elbow and his mother stumbled the two steps to the stretcher, her balance wildly off. How could she do this to him? To herself?

His mother tilted onto the pillow and allowed the medics to swing her legs up. Charlie watched helplessly as they wrapped their blankets around her like a mummy.

With the press of a button and a whirring sound, the stretcher rose to chest height, and the paramedics rolled his mother toward the door. "All I ever wanted was to be a good mother," she said softly as they pushed her away, her face unmoving.

That was when something in Charlie turned. Something awful and ugly swelled and ruptured within him, unwilling to be pushed down and ignored one minute more.

"How can you be like this?" Charlie shrieked. His voice found the strength that his body lacked. "What is *wrong* with you? Why can't you even try to get better? Why can't you just be there for me? For dad? Have you forgotten that I even exist? Just like you've forgotten Liam?"

"Charlie . . ." Mrs. Gleason started to cross toward him.

"No! You want to be a good mother? Then be one!" He stood and choked on a blend of tears and words that spilled from him uncontrollably. "*Get up! Be* my mom. Snap out of it!" Mrs. Gleason was now physically restraining him, as if his body was the problem. "Let GO of me!" Charlie struggled, wanting his mother to look at him. He wanted to see the effect of his words—to see *anything* on his mother's face other than that horrible blank stare.

She didn't turn.

How could she quit? How could she quit on *him*? "You're right! You *suck* at this. If you leave now, I swear, I will *never* forgive you!"

The pillow crunched as she finally lolled her head toward him. "I know," she said, agreeing with his accusations. "I failed you."

Charlie stopped struggling against Mrs. Gleason's grip as the paramedics rolled his mother through the door and out of sight.

The emotions inside him, raging just a moment ago, drained completely, leaving him numb. All that was left was a question.

Did you fail me, or did I fail you?

❧ 17 ❧

Mrs. Gleason was supposed to stay with Charlie until the Finches came home. She was then supposed to hand Charlie over to them until morning, but escaping her proved extremely easy. Once the ambulance was gone, he assured her he was calm and just wanted to get something to eat from the kitchen. He then bolted out the back door and tore furiously across town on his bike, the card with Jonathon's address clutched firmly in his hand.

Twenty minutes later, Charlie was racing up the rickety staircase to Jonathon's garage apartment. The tired old door didn't appear much sturdier than the stairs; his knock was a damp thud instead of a crisp beat. *Please be here.*

Jonathon opened the door. "Hey! What are you doing h—"

"We need to go to the Asylum," Charlie blurted. "Now."

"Whoa." Jonathon stepped aside to allow Charlie in, but Charlie didn't budge. "Slow down, man. What's going on? Where's Ana?"

"This has nothing to do with Ana." Charlie's face burned. He wanted to leave and never come back. He wanted to rescue Liam and return, making his mom never need an ambulance. He wanted to vanish forever and deaden the horrible feeling in his heart. He wanted all these things and none of them, all at the same time.

Jonathon put an arm around Charlie's shoulders. "Come in."

He offered Charlie the one place to sit: a twin-sized mattress on the floor in the corner. Charlie shook his head, preferring to pace.

Jonathon lowered himself onto the mattress instead and waited.

"How could you do it, Jonathon?" Charlie said. "How could you just give up on your family and your life? Didn't you think about anyone else?"

If Charlie's words hurt him, Jonathon didn't show it. "Charlie, what's happened?"

Charlie raked his hair with both hands. How could he

147

recount the stretcher, the tubing, the medics, his mother's words, his own words? It was impossible. "I need to get out of here, Jonathon. I need to get Liam. To bring him home. Or not. Whatever. I just can't be *here* anymore. You know how to make me vanish too, right? You can erase me."

Erase this pain. Erase what I said to my mom.

"I can," Jonathon said slowly, "but you should tell me what's going on first."

Charlie shook his head. He had to move forward, not back. Surely bringing Liam home would do *something* for his mom. She had been sick before Liam vanished, but not like this. Add Liam, subtract the ambulance.

Subtract his words.

But even this plan made his pain flare hotter. Like a devil sitting on his shoulder, a voice chirped, *But why does it have to be Liam? Why aren't you enough? Like Kieran is for his mother?*

A knock at the door caused Charlie to jump.

"I wondered if we might see you," Jonathon said, moving aside. Ana stepped into the cramped space, looking worried and a little scared.

"Hey," she said to Charlie.

"Hey," he replied, forced to stand still, his pacing strip now occupied.

"Mrs. Gleason called my mom. She thought I might

know where to find you."

"You brought Mrs. Gleason here?" Charlie peered out the window.

"Of course not, you doof. I lied and said I had no idea, and then snuck out and biked here. She said there was an ambulance at your house. Is your mom okay?"

"Nope!" Charlie said. "My mom is definitely *not* okay, Ana. None of the O'Reillys are okay."

"Wait. What happened to your mom?" Jonathon asked.

"Oh, nothing really," Charlie said with an exaggerated shrug. "She had my dad call 911 to cart her away, apparently forever, because she doesn't want to be my mom anymore. Just another day at the O'Reilly house!" His breaths were coming in great, heaving gasps and his nails were digging into his palms. He wanted to simultaneously run screaming out the door and lie down forever. He wanted to punch something; to cry; to laugh uproariously at the absurdity of it all. Simply *being* seemed impossibly difficult.

Ana turned her eyes to the floor. Jonathon turned away with a hand over his mouth.

It was the hurt on Ana's face that pulled Charlie back from the brink. Ana wasn't the enemy. Jonathon wasn't the enemy. He took a huge breath. They were his team. He needed them.

Slowly, he told Jonathon and Ana what had happened:

the medics, the ambulance, and his mother's words. Ana listened, shaking her head. Jonathon kept his hand over his mouth. Charlie didn't mention his own horrible, unforgivable words. No one needed to hear those.

He felt a fraction lighter when he finished. Sharing the truth felt better than sharing his anger. The act of retelling also allowed Charlie to see his two possible paths stretching out ahead of him. He didn't know which he would ultimately take, but he knew they both started in the Asylum.

He kept silent about Plan B: to alter everything that had happened today by simply vanishing from it, forever. Just like Jonathon, disappear and take the pain he'd caused with him. If he stayed in the Asylum, at least he and Liam would have each other.

He only spoke Plan A aloud. "We have to go get Liam. Once he's back, Mom will be better, just like she was before he left. She needs him. . . ." He choked out the last words. "It's pretty obvious I'm not enough for her."

"Come on, Charlie, don't say that," Jonathon said.

"At least your mom has a magical excuse to forget about you," Charlie snapped. "Mine's given up on me when I'm standing right in front of her!"

Jonathon's face turned stony and his eyes cooled. He opened his mouth to speak a few times, pursing his lips after each false start. Finally, in a measured and monotone voice, he said, "Charlie, leave my mom out of this."

Charlie deflated. Couldn't he just keep his big mouth shut? "I didn't mean—"

But Jonathon cut him off by moving to the door. He opened it and turned to Charlie. "Meet me here in the morning, seven a.m. I'll take you to the orphanage. But I think you'd better leave now."

"Jonathon, I . . ."

After a long silence, Ana took Charlie's hand. "We should go." She pulled him out the door.

"See you tomorrow, then," Charlie said, trying to catch Jonathon's eye.

"Yeah" was Jonathon's only response before the door clicked shut.

At the bottom of the stairs, Charlie regarded his bike as if he hadn't ever seen one before. His brain was addled. He watched Ana throw a leg over hers and he mimicked her, before realizing he had nowhere to go. He planted both feet wide and sat down hard on his seat.

"I said some things I shouldn't have." The truth leaked out of his mouth despite him wanting to hold it in.

"He'll get over it," Ana said.

I'm not talking about Jonathon, he thought, both relieved and disappointed at Ana's misunderstanding. "Is this really happening? Am I really going to see Liam again?"

"It is. And we are."

It took a moment for Ana's words to register. "Wait. We?"

"Yeah."

"But, Ana, you can't—"

"I've come this far with you, Charlie. I'm not stopping now. We go in together and come out together. Both stuck or both free."

This was a horrible idea. Charlie had no idea if he held the power to take off Liam's chain, and even less of an idea about his own, but he was willing to risk it. "What if we get stuck? I couldn't live with myself."

"Neither of us is going to get stuck. I have a plan. We'll each think of something that we can forgive each other for when we make our wishes. You take mine off, I take yours off. Simple. I didn't come this far, listening to you all year while we tried to figure out what happened to Liam, to quit now."

"What about your family?"

"They won't even know I'm gone."

He had to talk her out of it. But, he realized, he didn't *want* to. He needed her. Her smarts, her friendship. Charlie couldn't do this alone. "Better together?" he said with a faint smile.

"Better together," she repeated, determined. "Get in, get the chains off, and get out. That's the plan."

They rode away, Ana taking the lead. All Charlie had to do was listen and follow. No matter what, they would stay together to the end.

18

"We are here to discuss the matter of the boy."

The cold, steely voice of the police officer was the first thing Charlie knew of his dream that night.

"Are you his grandmother?" the officer demanded of Mrs. Clery. They were standing at the open door, cold rushing into the already frigid room.

"If you are speaking of Kieran, no, I'm not his grandmother. I'm a friend. What is this about?"

Charlie was in New York City, in Mrs. Clery's daughter's apartment. The tiny one-room tenement seemed palatial in comparison to the accommodations of the ship, but its sole furnishings were a table and two chairs. The chairs were currently occupied by three young girls: Mrs. Clery's granddaughters. The oldest, who was only five years old, was feeding the baby on her lap from a bottle. A shelf, a black cast-iron stove, and a bucket of coal constituted the kitchen against the far wall.

Beneath Charlie's hands was the stack of blankets he was folding, one for each of the four adults who slept on the severely pitched floor each night, and two more to share among the children. His mother sat on the floor near the girls, having remained largely motionless in the three weeks since their arrival—not in illness, but in grief. This voice at the door, however, roused her like the crack of a gun. Her eyes cleared and she crossed to Mrs. Clery's side.

"I am his mother." Her voice sounded rusty from lack of use. Charlie crept behind her and took her hand. The two uniformed officers were standing on a rickety balcony, perched above a trash-strewn alleyway. Clothing on countless laundry lines stretched between buildings flapped like flags behind them.

"Is there a problem, officers?" his mother said. "Has Kieran done something wrong?"

The shorter man removed his cap and smoothed his hair and mustache. "Your son has been loitering at Stewart's all week, fingering the wares. He is up to mischief."

Charlie recognized the officer, though when they had

met yesterday, he had been dressed in plain clothes. The man had taken an unusual interest in Charlie at Stewart's, engaging him in what seemed like innocuous enough banter. Charlie's heart sank as he thought of all they had said.

"You misunderstand," Mrs. Clery said. "He admires Mr. Stewart and his store greatly. He would never do anything wrong there."

"Admires it so much he wants some of it for himself," the taller man barked.

"Did he steal something?" his mother said.

"He didn't have to." The shorter man straightened his sleeves. "Loitering itself is illegal. And let me be frank. Your son wasn't going to stop at loitering."

"You cannot blame Kieran for something he hasn't done!" Mrs. Clery said.

"Spare us your indignation," the man said tersely. A sneer lifted the upper lip of the taller officer, and his eyes traveled up and down Charlie's mother, taking in her gaunt face, tangled red hair, and thin clothes, stained no matter how many times she laundered them. "Did you send him to steal for you?"

"I beg your pardon, sir!" She collected her shawl around her neck and drew her shoulders back.

He let out a derisive chuckle and elbowed the short man in the ribs. "They're all the same, Lenny, ain't they?"

His partner did not appear to find any comedy in the situation. "We are here to discuss a more suitable environment for your son."

Charlie's mother blinked and gazed quizzically at Mrs. Clery, fear freezing both her body and her voice. Her only movement was to squeeze Charlie's hand so firmly he had to stifle a small gasp.

"Not the sharpest knife in the drawer, is she, sir?" the taller man said, letting out a booming laugh. Charlie felt a blush of anger in his cheeks. How dare he talk about his mother like she wasn't even there!

Mrs. Clery was the one who spoke. "What do you mean, exactly, by suitable environment?" The answer was interrupted by a cry from the baby, held by one of the two girls who had come behind them.

"Lord! How many urchins do they have in there?" the taller man asked, burly arms crossed atop his substantial chest. "Not enough asylums in all of New York to house them all!"

Charlie's mother ignored him and spoke to Lenny. "As Mrs. Clery asked, what do you mean by suitable environment?"

"Your son needs discipline. He needs an environment with morals, where he can learn skills that will make him a useful citizen in our proud nation."

Mrs. Clery took the wailing baby into her arms and bounced him up and down. "Are you suggesting that this home lacks discipline and morals, sir? I will have you know, my family may have little money, but we are good people!"

Charlie's mother placed a calming hand on Mrs. Clery's arm. "Sir, I have no money for formal schooling, if that is what you're talking about."

"No, no, not a school," he replied, shaking his head, his glasses sliding slightly down his thin nose. "He will, though, receive schooling as part of his daily activities. We're taking him to a home for orphaned children. It costs you nothing."

"Orphan?" His mother recoiled. "No one here is an orphan."

Oh, why had he spoken to this stranger?

"Kieran's father has passed, which makes him a half orphan. And this is not your home," Lenny said, gesturing to the room behind them, "making him a homeless, loitering half orphan. He is destitute. He is a problem of the state. Our job is to make him an honorable member of society, not another drunk Irishman stealing from the good people of New York."

Mrs. Clery let out a cry.

"We are not homeless, sir," his mother said, quietly but firmly. "We are not drunks, nor have we ever stolen from anyone. And I am Kieran's mother. His very much alive mother. We are not interested in your offer, and I will kindly ask you to leave."

The squat man's eyes narrowed. "I do not take orders from a penniless mick! You *are* homeless; being allowed to sleep on a friend's floor does not change that fact. This is not a request. We are simply informing you of the situation."

His tall partner's smirk broadened into a devilish smile.

Charlie felt a clutch in his chest as he absorbed this man's words. The small steps they had taken in the last few weeks, the beginnings of starting anew in the shadow of all they had lost, were all for nothing.

These men were here to take him.

Lenny replaced his hat. "He will come with us to the station, and the train will take him to the Asylum. Be thankful—you should see this as an opportunity. It's his one chance to stay out of jail."

Before Charlie could react, the taller officer had him by the upper arm. Despite his mother's cries and attempts to free Charlie, the hulk of a man shooed her off and lifted Charlie's thin frame as if he were a kitten. Mrs. Clery's efforts were even less effective. A high-pitched scream from the frightened baby filled the air.

Charlie's feet barely touched the steps as he was half dragged, half carried down to the street. "Let me go!" he yelled, but to no avail. Charlie turned his head up to see his mother clutching the balcony rail, her face a grimace of pain. She yelled, "How do I see him? What must I do to get him back?"

"Get yourself a husband and a home!" the tall officer yelled with a laugh. "If you can manage that, you can apply for his return." He kicked a pig that had trotted down the road behind them, sniffing at their pant legs. Its pained squeals were all Charlie heard as his tears fell into the dirt and the dream faded away.

ᔆ 19 ᕤ

Charlie's fingers were numb. He wasn't sure if it was from the cool morning air or his death grip on his handlebars as they rode to Jonathon's. He'd been awake for hours, addled and scared after bolting upright at three a.m on the Finches' couch, crying and unable to breathe. The grip of the tall officer's hands seared his shoulders long after the dream melted away.

"And you're sure he said *asylum*?" Ana asked.

"Positive! He was stealing me from my mother to take me to an asylum. In New York. How could this *not* be connected to Liam?"

"You know," Ana said hesitantly, "we all insert things

from real life into our dreams. Maybe after Jonathon—"

"Oh, come on, Ana!" he said.

"Okay, okay!" Ana said. "It's doesn't really matter anyway. I mean, we found out where he is, and it's not like it changes what we're about to do, does it?"

She was right. They were going to the one place they'd spent years avoiding because it was too creepy—and that was when they thought it was just an old pile of bricks. Now they knew it held missing children, a ghost headmistress, and serpentine necklaces that could imprison them forever. *What a wonderful time to drop on by!* Charlie thought.

"What do you think will happen to Jonathon when he goes back in?" Ana said, leaving clouds of breath behind her.

"I don't know. Will he be forgotten all over again?"

"Can you disappear twice?"

"Who knows?" Charlie said. "Honestly, I don't think many people are going to notice if he goes missing again."

"Jeez, Charlie. That's a horrible thing to say."

"I'm not trying to be a jerk, but it's true. I mean, maybe Mr. Cutter will miss him, but he probably won't do anything about it. I can see the headline now: 'Isolated Teen Doesn't Show Up to Mow Lawns.' Not exactly breaking news, you know? And, it's not like Coach Kemp cares."

They fell silent as they traveled the final block to Jonathon's place, staring at the hilltop orphanage as they rode. It looked the same as always, a crumbling, empty shell. One thing seemed undeniably clear: no one was up there.

Jonathon was descending the stairs of his apartment as they rolled up. The smile on his face melted when he saw Ana. A glob of jelly from his PB&J splattered onto his shoe.

"What are *you* doing here?" he asked.

"Seriously?" Ana said.

"Yeah, very seriously," Jonathon said.

"I'm going with you."

"Like, you're riding with us?"

"No. G*oing* with you. Into the Asylum."

Jonathon shook his head. "Oh no you're not. You can ride with us, but this is something Charlie and I have to do. I'm not dragging you into this mess."

"I've been into this mess way longer than you, Jonathon. I'm not stopping now."

"Sorry," Jonathon said, shaking his head. "There's no way I'm giving you a chain. No way."

"Look, I'll kick you in the shins, feel really bad about it, wish I was never born, and then you can forgive me later."

Jonathon rubbed the back of his neck and made a terribly ill-advised announcement. "Ana, I won't let you."

Charlie sucked in a quick breath and shook his head. If there was one thing he knew about Ana, he knew never to tell her "You can't do that." (Unless, of course, you secretly wanted her to do exactly that.) And you could never, *ever* tell Ana "I won't *let* you."

"You won't *let* me?" Ana leveled a stare at Jonathon that made Charlie shrink slightly into his shoulders. If her mind wasn't set before, it was now firm as concrete.

Jonathon began to launch into a doomed debate with Ana, but Charlie cut him off.

"Jonathon, Ana's coming. She has to."

"What are you talking about?" he said with pained frustration.

"I won't do this without her. We're a package deal."

"Don't be stupid, Charlie! What if she can't get out? Are you really going to be okay if you free Liam but lose Ana forever?"

Charlie had no answer for this. He knew including Ana was potentially disastrous. It was selfish and foolhardy and downright idiotic. But it was also still the plan.

"He's not going to *lose me forever*," Ana said. "We're going to stick together to the end. Either all stuck or all home. Charlie saved my life once—it's my turn to help save his."

Jonathon opened his mouth to speak, then shut it. There was no need to argue with him because it seemed he was silently bickering with himself. Ultimately, he said to Charlie, "Don't do this."

"Then it's settled," Ana said with a smile. She swung a leg over her bike and kicked off. "Let's go. We have an hour tops before my parents wake up and start to freak out that I'm gone."

Jonathon implored Charlie with his eyes. Charlie shook his head and said, nervously, "We'll find a way out."

Throwing his last bite of sandwich into the bushes, Jonathon grabbed the rusty piece of junk he called a bike from against the garage. In a defeated voice, he said, "Ana, no one's going to freak out. You won't even exist by the time they wake up."

Won't even exist. A torrent of butterflies took flight in Charlie's stomach. They were really doing this. What would happen to his mom? What would his dad come home to this morning? Would Ana's family be okay without her?

"Charlie!" Jonathon yelled. He and Ana were already halfway down the block. "You coming?"

It was time.

They rode for about ten minutes, Ana in the lead. Even from a distance, he could make out the faded yellow paint emblazoned across the third-floor bricks of the orphanage, proclaiming I LOVE YOU MAGGOT. It had originally declared I LOVE YOU MARGOT, but the spurned young graffiti artist had revised his thoughts after the Margot in question had eloped with his best friend. Charlie's mom had attended high school with all of them, and she loved to tell how the paint had lasted far longer than either relationship.

The blare of a car horn jolted Charlie. An old Oldsmobile zipped by them, passing far closer to their bikes than necessary. Ana veered into the gravel on the shoulder and screamed, "Share the road, you moron!"

Charlie rode up next to her. "Um, Ana. Since we're kinda runaways right now, you might not want to be all shouty at people."

"Charlie," Jonathon yelled from behind, "we'll vanish from that guy's mind within the next fifteen minutes. You could have been biking naked and he wouldn't remember you."

Ana laughed and smiled back at Jonathon. She immediately and resolutely looked back up the hill, however, when she saw Charlie watching her.

They rode the next many turns in silence, all of them breathing heavily from the climb. Then, after a burst of speed to take the lead, Jonathon abruptly brought his bike to a stop. "This is our turn. The path to the Asylum."

Charlie saw nothing different about this particular stretch of tree-lined road. He watched Jonathon dismount and push his bike through the ditch grass toward the trees and brush ten feet from the asphalt. With a heave, Jonathon pulled a cluster of branches aside, revealing a path.

Charlie and Ana exchanged a nervous glance, then pushed their bikes to where Jonathon stood.

"In you go," he said.

Charlie's feet sank slightly into the soft earth beneath him. Each step was silent, absorbed by the long-forgotten path. It smelled of composting wood and fungus.

Jonathon entered behind them and let the plants drop back into place, closing off their view of the road and the world beyond it. It was much cooler in this damp tunnel of greenery than on the road, and the sweat on the back of Charlie's neck felt like icy fingers.

Goose bumps prickled Charlie's arms as they walked farther, pausing beneath a stone archway halfway up the path. A bronze plaque hung crookedly from a single screw.

THE NEW YORK ASYLUM
FOR ORPHANED CHILDREN
Established 1843

"I'm kinda freaking out," Ana whispered.

Charlie was glad to know he wasn't the only one.

"What mistake are you going to think about when you make the wish?" she asked.

"Probably breaking your arm. That's the worst thing I've ever done, I think." He pushed away the chorus of his own words running through his mind: *What's wrong with you? You suck at this. If you leave now, I swear, I will never forgive you!*

"Well, that works nicely," Ana said, "because I was going to think about how sorry I was that I put you in the situation to have to break my arm! Perfect."

Perfect, Charlie repeated in his mind, wishing he had even a shred of Ana's confidence right now.

The trees thinned as they neared the top, and Charlie saw details of what he had called "the castle" when he was younger. The oversized red bricks of the outer walls were still blackened—scorched so thoroughly that 170 years of rain, snow, and wind couldn't wash the soot away. The seasons, however, had filed down the corners of the stones, softening the edges that remained. There were no floors, no stairs, no roof. And certainly no orphans.

Charlie laid his bike at the edge of the clearing and walked through the long grass. Ana and Jonathon came up beside him, and they all stared at the walls. Every window sneered down at them, baring its glass-shard teeth. Even in the full light of day, Charlie thought it was terrifying.

Charlie's eyes followed the leafy green tentacles of ivy that laced the walls and snaked into every opening. It had no regard for "in" and "out." He found it beautiful, in an eerie kind of way.

"Wow," Charlie said as he started circling the edges of

the property, taking in the side and back walls that were similarly decayed. He gathered the courage to poke his head into one of the rear window openings. A warm sensation washed over his face. It began at the tip of his nose and moved toward his ears as he advanced, like he was dipping his face into a warm tub of water. The same sensation washed over his fingertips as they curled around the window frame. It wasn't unpleasant, but it was certainly unnerving.

Within the walls, empty Cheetos bags, beer bottles, and cigarette butts littered the sun-dappled floor, a section of which had collapsed into the basement. A mini grill leaned crookedly against one wall. A filthy sleeping bag lay like a large green snakeskin a few feet away. The smells of urine, smoke, and trash poisoned the air.

Charlie stepped back, and the line of warmth receded. He removed his hands from the frame and could have sworn the tip of his nose and each finger made a small suction sound as he withdrew them.

A shadow seemed to dance past the opening, and Charlie took several frightened steps back, tripping over something hard protruding from the earth. He caught himself and turned to see a stone grave marker resting in the shade of an oak tree. One word was inscribed on its surface. *Son.*

Resisting a strong urge to run back down to the road, he returned to his friends.

"What are all those stone towers?" Ana asked. She was peering through the main entrance at the numerous columns that rose skyward within the building. With the door long destroyed, the opening looked like a yawning mouth, its cracked and weed-consumed stone footpath like a giant green tongue.

"Those are all the chimneys," Jonathon said. "No such thing as central heat in the 1800s."

"Do you know which one caused the fire?" Charlie asked, coming up behind them to peer through the arch.

"What do you mean?" Jonathon asked.

"You know, which chimney caught fire and burned the place down?"

"Ah," Jonathon said with a wry smile. "The popular theory as to the cause of the Great Asylum Fire. It's much tidier than the truth." Jonathon didn't elaborate, instead turning his attention back to the interior of the building. "You can't see them, but there are many eyes watching you as we speak."

"There are?" Ana and Charlie said in unison.

"Yup. So if you guys are ready, who wants to go first?"

Charlie and Ana stared at each other, immobile. They had spent so many years elbowing each other out of the way, always competing to be the first in everything, that their shared hesitation caused them both to burst into nervous laughter. Then, in a jumbled, simultaneous rush of words, they both said, "I'll go first. Okay. No, you go first. Okay, I'll do it."

"Okay, stop!" Ana said, hand out. "This is ridiculous. I'll go first." She turned to Jonathon and shook out her arms and legs the same way she did before a big game. But then she stiffened and stepped back. "Wait! Won't Charlie forget me the moment I put this on?"

Jonathon shook his head. "No. I once helped gather a brother and sister at the same time. If you make your wish together, you stay together."

Her shoulders relaxed again, and an easy smile returned. She stepped forward and said, "Okay, then I'm ready."

Ready for her key and necklace. Then Charlie would get his. And once they each had a key and chain of their own, they could open the true door to the Asylum, a door they couldn't even see yet. Jonathon hadn't told them much about this part, but he had promised them that it wouldn't hurt. This reassurance did very little to calm Charlie at the moment.

"Okay, both of you come over here," Jonathon said. Ana stepped toward him until they stood toe to toe. He looked down at her and said, "You know that I don't know how to reverse what's about to happen."

"Yup. I know."

"And you know that I think you shouldn't do this."

"I do."

Jonathon shook his head slightly. "Charlie?" he asked, clearly hoping one of them would stop him.

Charlie stayed silent.

"All right. Ana, give me your hands, palms up." He held out his hand for hers and grabbed his key with the other. He pressed the key firmly into the palm of Ana's right hand, closing her left hand around it. Holding her two hands in his one, he looped a finger of his free hand around the chain at the nape of his neck, waiting patiently for Ana's cue. "When you're ready, you have to say it."

Ana glanced quickly at Charlie, then at the surgical scar on her forearm, then back at Jonathon. Their foreheads almost touched as she said, "I wish . . . I'd never been born."

In that moment, Jonathon lifted the chain over his head and placed it over Ana's, pinning her ponytail to the back of her neck. Charlie's brow knotted. Hadn't Jonathon proved to them that he couldn't remove his chain? Why could he take it off now? But then he saw it. Even though Jonathon had placed a chain around Ana's neck, his own was still in place, undisturbed. Where there had been one chain and key, there were now two. Ana opened her hands, releasing the two keys that lay within, one connected to each chain.

"Whoa! How'd you do that?" Charlie asked, but quickly

realized that neither Jonathon nor Ana was listening to him. Jonathon was carefully watching Ana as her eyes grew wide, lifting from the ground and moving skyward, as if she were watching Jack's beanstalk sprout out of the ground right in front of her. She took a few steps back.

"Are you seeing this?" she said. "Oh my god, Charlie! Are you seeing this?"

"Seeing what?" Charlie asked, scanning the same unchanged brick walls. He didn't know whether to be frightened or excited. "Ana, what is it? What do you see?"

"He won't be able to see what you and I do until he gets his own chain," Jonathon said to her. "Ana, welcome to the Asylum."

ᴧ 20 ᴄ

Jonathon extended a hand to Charlie. "You're up."

Charlie stepped close. The sour scent of coffee on Jonathon's breath brought his mother immediately and unwelcomely to mind.

She'll be okay, he told himself. *She won't remember me. Maybe that will even help her get better. It's not like I could.*

"This is bonkers!" Ana yelled. She pointed up at the walls and waved toward one of the windows. "Charlie, you're not going to believe this."

There was no going back. Charlie put out his hands. "Let's do this."

Jonathon's brass key was colder to the touch than Charlie

expected. He sandwiched it between his hands, the edges pressing uncomfortably into his skin. He spread his feet wider to steady himself and awaited his cue.

"I'm ready when you are," Jonathon said.

"Can you promise me something first?"

"What's that?" Jonathon asked with a crooked smile.

"Promise you'll come back with us. After we find Liam."

Jonathon tilted his head slightly. He looked almost disappointed by the question. "Charlie, you know I won't let my brother be hurt again."

"I know that. But come back with us anyway—even if you still have your chain on. You could still live over your boss's garage, mow yards, and be our coach, right? It's just . . ."

Charlie dug a small hole in the dirt with his toe. "It's just that it's been really great, having you around."

Jonathon's eyes crinkled at the edges. "Charlie, you have no idea how much that means to me. And yeah, it's been great *being* around."

"So you promise?"

Jonathon nodded. "Yeah. I promise."

A grin blossomed on Charlie's face. "Okay. Let's do this." He closed his eyes and wrapped his hands around Jonathon's key.

Now was the time. He tried to conjure an image of the

bike path from a few years ago, the train, and Ana's cherry-red bike, but as he tried to focus on the feeling of regret he had felt in the days after their accident, all he could think of was the red flashing lights of the ambulance outside his house last night. He focused harder, before he could have any more second thoughts, and said, "I wish that I'd never been born. . . . Ow!"

The key doubled in his hand, the new edges cutting at his palm. He felt Jonathon place a chain against his neck, and he opened his eyes.

What he saw was impossible. Ten feet from where he stood, a thin ring of fire encircled the base of the ruined orphanage. It was frightening but beautiful. Its heat warmed Charlie, making him take a step back. He stared, openmouthed, as the halo of fire began to rise, scaling the sides of the building like a gold wedding band being removed from a finger, transforming everything in its wake. The thicket of thorny shrubs that had sprouted at the base of the wall moments before was now a grove of well-groomed bushes. The bricks became a brighter shade of red as the ring passed, their previously blunted edges now sharp and unweathered. A massive wooden door in the main entryway filled the void as if a child were coloring it in with a gigantic brown marker from the ground up.

"You see it now, right?" Ana said from beside him.

Charlie nodded silently as the flames progressed past the windows of the ground floor, glass flowing into place like liquid mercury. He clapped his hand over his mouth when he saw, behind each pane of glass, children peering out at him, waving.

A loud crack drew his eyes back up, where intricate ledges and balconies of wood sprouted from the stone, born of these flames instead of destroyed by them. Twists of ivy slithered like heat-charmed snakes, coiling around the window openings, entwining themselves in the exterior railings and pendants.

The ring reached the top of the stones and began to constrict, closing in on itself, leaving behind a steep roof of wooden shingles. The fire focused to a single torch at the tip of the central chimney, then shot down the flue with a flash.

The transformation was complete.

The scent of fireplaces and something Charlie would have sworn was bacon had completely replaced the odor of trash and human waste. The smoky warmth took Charlie back to lazy winter weekends at home, Mom reading to him and Liam in front of the fireplace while his dad made meals for the upcoming week.

"And now we're all here." Jonathon put an arm around Charlie's shoulder.

"Holy . . . is this what you always see?"

"Ever since I got my chain. It was pretty weird when you stuck your head through the glass back there," he said, tipping his head toward the rear of the building. He paused, put his hands in his pockets, and flashed Charlie a sad smile. This moment of melancholy reminded Charlie that this magical adventure had not come without a cost.

"I'm forgotten now, aren't I?"

"Yeah." Jonathon walked past Charlie and toward the door. "Yeah, you are."

"Don't feel bad! We wanted this," Charlie said.

"I know. Grab Ana. It's time to go inside."

They moved into the shadow of the great oak door, behind which Charlie could sense a crowd gathering. The air seemed unnaturally cool.

"Do we knock?" Charlie asked.

"Well, you could," Jonathon said, "but it won't do you any good. They can't open it."

"The door doesn't open?" Ana said.

"Oh, no. It opens, all right, but only from the outside. Your keys."

Ana and Charlie tipped their chins to their chests in unison. Charlie's brass key, with its chunky, square matrix of teeth and ornate clover-shaped handle, glinted up at him. He was afraid to wonder which of his regrets now lay inside it.

Jonathon swept his hand, palm up, toward the door.

"Do you want to do the honors, Charlie?"

Feeling he had already wimped out once today, Charlie nodded and said, "Yeah, sure." The door was almost twice as tall as he was, rising above his head beneath a stone arch. Three horizontal strips of iron bound the wooden slats, each with visible hammer marks from the tool of the blacksmith who had crafted them. The only other marking on the door was a large keyhole.

There was no knob.

Knowing better than to try to remove the chain from around his neck, Charlie bent forward slightly to fit the key in the keyhole. "Ready?"

"Yeah, we're ready," Jonathon said.

With a twist of his wrist, Charlie felt the heavy shift of a deadbolt, and a metal-on-metal screech met his ears. After one complete revolution, he withdrew the key, and stood back.

With a last glance at the world behind him, Charlie lowered his shoulder and pushed.

∂21∾

The sounds of the crowd were the first thing Charlie heard. An audience of twenty or so boys and girls stood in front of him, but sunlight from a bank of windows behind them made it difficult to see individual faces. Charlie sought any silhouette that could possibly match the boy who had left him a year ago.

"In ya go," Jonathon said with a gentle nudge.

The buzzing audience parted as Jonathon, Charlie, and Ana stepped into an immense mahogany entry hall that smelled of smoke and dust. It was the smell of Charlie's grandfather's attic, filled with ancient furniture, steamer trunks, and forgotten keepsakes left to marinate in a room never touched by air conditioning. The air was stagnant and thick in Charlie's throat, as though those same doors and windows that had materialized moments ago hadn't been opened in years.

In awe, Charlie stepped farther into the room. The clutch of people talked excitedly and stared at Charlie, Ana, and Jonathon. Though the Asylum was over a hundred years old, the clothing on each person was modern—jeans, shorts, and T-shirts. No one looked older than Jonathon. Charlie scanned each stunned child in the room.

No Liam.

He tried to calm himself. Surely Liam was just upstairs, or downstairs, or outside. He rechecked each face.

His eyes landed on a girl, maybe six years old, who was holding hands with another. It was hard to imagine each one of the people standing before him had done something so unforgivable they chose to leave their lives.

Charlie's eyes climbed the moss-green carpeted steps of a grand central staircase. He was so captivated by the grandeur of the vast room, he didn't see a curled corner of the area rug at his toe as he advanced one more step. He went down so fast he barely broke his fall with his hands.

"Charlie!" Ana said, coming to help him up. "Are you okay!"

"Yeah, yeah," he said, far more embarrassed than hurt. "I'm fine."

"Oh, your nose . . . ," she said, pointing.

Charlie put his hand to his face and drew it away. Red and wet.

"That's super weird," he sputtered as blood sullied his shirt. "It doesn't hurt."

"Just wait . . . ," Jonathon said.

Charlie was still looking at his hand as the blood vanished before his eyes. Similarly, his shirt, stained seconds ago, was spotless.

"I'll explain later," Jonathon said, helping Charlie up by the elbow.

Behind them, a booming sound made Charlie turn. The door had slammed shut of its own accord, and the back of the huge wooden slab was similar to the front—no knob or pull. But unlike the front, the inside had no keyhole. The dead bolt screeched back into place. Charlie swallowed hard.

Ana grabbed his arm and pulled his attention to the murmuring crowd. "Listen," she whispered. One word bubbled to the surface of the sea of chatter.

Jonathon.

A tall young man stepped forward, dressed in what looked to Charlie like a military school uniform. His creased white pants and jacket with gold buttons shone brightly, vividly contrasting with his dark skin and hair. Four long, crisp strides placed him nose to nose with Jonathon. His face was questioning, his mouth twisted. Charlie couldn't tell if he was going to punch Jonathon or burst into tears.

The crowd quieted. Charlie bent his knees slightly, ready to spring into action if Jonathon needed backup.

Then Sergeant Tall wrapped his arms around Jonathon. Charlie looked at Ana, making sure she was in agreement that this was a friendly gesture. She nodded, but her face mirrored his own concern.

Jonathon returned the hug, his face bright when they pulled apart.

"What are you doing here, you idiot?" the cadet asked with a smile that matched his military whites. He shook Jonathon by the shoulders.

"It's nice to see you too." Jonathon laughed as he tried unsuccessfully to wiggle free of the vigorous jostling. "Dude! Knock it off! You're going to break my neck."

"I *am* going to break your neck. For coming back here. What are you thinking?"

"I'll explain everything," Jonathon said, breaking free. "I promise. Let's just say being on the outside isn't all it's cracked up to be." He then turned to his silent companions. "Charlie, Ana, this is Michael. Michael, Charlie and Ana."

Michael turned toward them as if seeing them for the first time. There was an awkward pause as Michael stared at them, deep crinkles beside his squinted eyes.

Jonathon held out a calming hand, "Michael, be cool. Give me a chance to explain."

"Jonathon, what are you doing?"

"I've got my reasons. Please, you gotta trust me. I'll tell you the whole situation. In private. . . ." He cocked his head toward the crowd.

Standing with a posture so perfect it made Charlie wonder if his uniform was made of unbendable material, Michael nodded almost imperceptibly, putting the conversation to rest for now. He then slowly extended a formal hand to both Charlie and Ana.

"Nice to meet you." His voice was flat, betraying that he didn't find it nice at all. He turned back to Jonathon. "We need to *talk*."

"I know—"

"We asked Jonathon to bring us here," Ana said, coming to Jonathon's defense. "It's okay. We already know everything."

Michael looked at Jonathon, deeply quizzical. Charlie thought he saw Jonathon shake his head, but he couldn't swear to it.

After a long silence, a genuine and kind smile warmed Michael's face again. "I can't believe you're back, but it's great to see you."

His last words were clipped by a voice in the crowd. It

was a girl, pointing behind Charlie.

"She's coming!"

He followed the outstretched finger to a corner some fifteen feet to the right of the door. A seemingly ill-placed end table with an empty vase stood next to a blank wall. Before Charlie could wonder what the girl meant, something began to emerge from the stone. At waist level, a small bump rose, like a crocodile snout surfacing from a river. The protrusion darkened in color to a rich chocolate brown, and within seconds transformed into a polished, apple-sized, mahogany ball anchored to the wall by a bronze stem. A doorknob.

"Whoa," Ana said.

Then, near the baseboard, an image of a green shoot appeared as if painted on the wall by an unseen hand. Charlie blinked as the plant animated and began growing rapidly, sprouting leaves, twisting and flowering. Its stalk thickened and changed from new green to dark brown, the bark cracking as it expanded. Branches stretched upward. The tree grew feet higher with each passing second, growing beyond the edges of the room until it looked like a cropped picture of a fifty-year-old oak. Then, as quickly as it had come, much of the image faded away, bleeding like sidewalk chalk in the rain. However, a door-sized portion of the trunk intensified in color and a groaning noise—the sound of wood planks bearing too much weight—filled the room as the surface of the wall bubbled outward.

A towering solid-oak door now stood where there had been none moments before. The table that had seemed awkwardly placed now stood waiting beside it. The knob turned. Charlie and Ana both took a step back. With a heavy creak, the door opened.

A pale woman stepped into the room as if from another century. She wore a black bonnet and matching floor-length gown. The skirt of her dress ballooned from her tightly cinched waist, like something from a costume shop for princesses in mourning. Cradled in her arms like a child lay a bouquet of flowers—roses, lilies, and daisies. Their vivid colors stood in stark contrast to their black-and-white bearer. She placed them in the vase on the table beside her and closed the door with the air of someone returning from buying groceries. The door and the knob dissolved the moment her hand released them. She removed her bonnet and turned to the crowd.

Her bright red hair gleamed in the sunlight.

Every part of Charlie locked, unable to move or think. *That's not possible.*

"What are you all stand—" The words, delivered in a light Irish brogue, stuck in her throat. She stared at the three newcomers and uttered, "Is it really you? Can it be?"

Rustling crinoline and rapid footfalls filled the air as the woman, skirt in both hands, raced straight toward them.

Raced straight toward *Charlie*.

He took another startled step backward before the woman completely enveloped him, her hair splashing across his face as she held him tight.

"It happened! It's really you!" she sobbed from within her warm embrace.

Charlie relaxed involuntarily, as if he'd lost control of himself. Half of his mind was screaming to get out of this woman's grasp; the other half was blissfully calm, wanting this moment to never end. The familiar smell of peat smoke in her hair and the feel of her dress were intoxicating.

Her grip loosened, and the weight of her cheek lifted from the crown of his head. With her face inches from his, she cupped his chin and whispered, "I can't believe it. You're really here. You've been brought back to me." Curls of her hair tickled Charlie's cheeks as he looked up at her, transfixed by her adoring gaze.

It was Kieran's mother. *His* mother.

She was literally a dream come true.

"What the heck is happening?" Ana said from behind Charlie. When no answers came, she became more frantic. "Jonathon! What is going on?"

"I have no idea," Jonathon said, his voice weak.

"What do you mean? Who is that?" Ana asked. She pulled at Charlie's arm, trying to remove him from this woman's clutches. "Charlie, stop it! You're freaking me out."

"That's Brona," Michael said.

Charlie couldn't stop looking at her hazel eyes. They were just like his mother's—his real mother's—steeped in sadness even as she smiled. What was the woman from his dreams doing here? What did she have to do with this place? Charlie felt utterly disoriented as to where or who he was. He forced himself to break the trance. He gently took Brona's hands from his face and, with a respectful nod, turned away and stepped to Ana's side.

Brona's face fell slightly, but she said with a smile, "That's fine. All that matters is that you're here. You are finally here with me." She turned and reached out to Jonathon. He backed away. "Welcome back, Jonathon. Thank you for doing what I couldn't."

Jonathon looked back and forth between Brona and Charlie like they were playing a furious Ping-Pong match. "What is . . . ? How do you know him?"

She tilted her head serenely and said, "In all fairness, you should know that I wasn't entirely truthful with you before you left. I am grateful that you nevertheless performed your job, perfectly. And Ana! Welcome to you too, my child. I'm so glad you've joined us." She reached out for Ana's hand, but Ana stayed as still as a statue. Brona turned away.

Charlie could see Jonathon's chest rise and fall faster and faster. His face turned a blotchy red.

Brona gently looped her arm in the crook of Charlie's elbow, as if he were her escort. "Now, come with me. I'll take you to your room. I've had it ready for so long, Kieran."

Ana's head snapped to Charlie. *Kieran.* Her eyes went wide as Charlie watched her decipher that this was the woman from his dreams.

She pulled Charlie's arm. "Oh, no, no, no, no. Charlie's not going anywhere with you!"

Their plan to get in, get 'em off, get out was flying off the rails. His dream mother was never part of the arrangement. Loving embraces and long-awaited bedrooms were not on the schedule.

"Jonathon!" Ana demanded. "Help!"

But Jonathon didn't move. Charlie hadn't understood what Brona meant by his "job," but clearly Jonathon did. He looked horrified. He covered his face with his hands and shook his head.

"Ana, you are welcome to join us if you like? I can show you where you will sleep as well."

Ana recoiled. "I'm not sleeping here."

Brona stole the chance to break Charlie free from Ana's grip. She smiled. "Suit yourself. But I invite you to . . . make

189

yourself at home." And with that, she led a numb Charlie toward the staircase.

Her voice softened, and the kind, sad eyes he remembered from his dreams were locked on his, filled with love and relief. "Welcome home, Kieran. Welcome home."

ꙅ 22 ꙅ

Brona stopped on the landing of the grand staircase and peered at Charlie expectantly. He, in turn, despite having allowed her to lead him away, peered down the stairs at the staring crowd, wishing there was some way to get back down.

"Do you know the way?" she asked.

Though this building hadn't been in any of the dreams, Charlie was unnerved to find he knew that the children's bedrooms were down the hall to his left. "Um . . . over there, I think?"

Brona grinned, shook her head, and pulled him in the other direction. "Oh, no, you aren't in the dormitories, love!

Your room is next to mine now."

Charlie found it quite disconcerting to have someone to whom he'd never been properly introduced talk to him so intimately. And yet . . . he knew her already, didn't he? Her history and sorrows were as familiar to his heart and mind as his own. She called him by the wrong name, yet they had breathed the same cold air outside the burning house, crossed an ocean together, wiped tears from each other's faces.

Except he hadn't *done* any of that stuff, he had to remind himself.

She led him to the last door of the corridor with a look of eager anticipation. "I do hope you'll like it." She opened it and stood back.

Charlie crossed the threshold and couldn't help but mutter, "Whoa . . ."

"The master, for my little master." She rested her hands on Charlie's shoulders. Their weight was comforting. "This was Mr. Kettering's bedroom."

The room was huge and rich with carved mahogany, each piece—window casings, end tables, cabinetry—resplendent with intricate horns, lions, ivy, and fruit. It was how Charlie imagined a king's bedroom might look. Two high-backed embroidered chairs sat before his personal fireplace, inviting him to sit and stay awhile.

Charlie stepped forward to run his fingers along a pillar of the massive central four-poster bed but drew his hand back. "I probably shouldn't touch it, right?" He had only ever seen things like this in museums.

"Touch whatever you like," Brona said. "This is all yours now."

Not for long, he thought, checking the face of a curious child passing by out in the hallway. It wasn't Liam.

Charlie walked to a table that sat beside the bed, its surface polished to a mirrorlike sheen. A lace square hung over the edge, topped by a porcelain bowl and pitcher. Not sure what else to do, Charlie sat down and bounced slightly, the way he had seen his dad once do in a mattress store. He ran his finger along the nubby flowers of the yellowing bedspread.

"Do you like it?" she asked, hopeful.

". . . Yeah. It's really nice." *Not really my style, but nice.*

Brona came to the foot of the bed to pick up something from a stool. As she leaned over, Charlie was surprised to see a chain identical to his tucked into the neckline of her dress. It fell out of view again when she stood, holding up a folded piece of fabric.

"Is that a dress?" he asked.

She laughed at his skepticism. "No, silly. It's a nightshirt, or what you now call pajamas. I make one for each of my children. I know it is hardly the style you are used to, but I do think you will find it very comfortable. Familiar, even."

Charlie smiled awkwardly and looked at the floor. He wouldn't be here long enough to wear it. He drummed his fingers on the mattress, unnerved by Brona's intensely contented gaze. He became very aware she was between him and the door.

"You know who I am, don't you?" Brona said, her hands clasped in front of her as if praying.

He knew who she was in his mind; in his dreams. But he didn't understand how she could possibly be real. "Um, I think I do . . . ," he offered lamely. "I dreamed about you. About your life."

"Our life."

No, my life's in Kingsberg. He needed to move—to break this moment, whatever it was. He stood and took a step away from the bed but stumbled over a large bowl at his feet. A deafening clang rang through the room. He hastened to right it, but Brona was already there.

Is that a chamber pot? Charlie wondered, backing away. He resolved to find Liam and get out of here before nature called.

Brona placed the bowl at the bedside calmly and sat where Charlie had been. He retreated farther and sat on the dense cushions of a window seat. A small poof of dust tickled his nose. The lush red-velvet fabric under his fingers reminded Charlie of a Touch and Feel book his mother used to read to him. His other mother.

They can't both *be your mother, Charlie. Get a grip.*

He nervously turned toward the window—just a frame, he noted; it didn't open—and tried to clear his mind. He froze, however, at what was beyond the glass.

Snow.

The air was heavy with it, and the lawn was blanketed in white; drifts rose to impressive heights in the corners of the courtyard. The nearby oak branches were heavy and bent under its weight. Charlie couldn't tell if his bike was gone or buried as he looked at the edge of the clearing.

It was impossible for snow to pile up like this in such a short period of time.

Not to mention it was May.

He pulled himself up to his knees and gripped the window frame. Snow-covered pines stretched away from him and down the hill, abutting the edge of the road—the same road they had turned off that morning. A convertible zipped past on the sunny asphalt, top down. The field on the other side was spring green and speckled with dandelions.

"Wha—?" Charlie muttered.

"It's beautiful, isn't it?" Brona said, her voice only inches from his ear.

Charlie whipped around and bumped his head on the glass.

She was sitting beside him, hands folded in her lap. "Please, don't be frightened. Not of me or this house. You're safe now. Safe as you've ever been."

"I . . . I just don't understand what's going on. I'm sorry, but I didn't come here to see you. I came here to . . . find someone. And to bring him back. Home."

Brona took his hand and gently stroked the back of it with her thumb the same way he had done to hers on a day long, long ago. "Kieran, the pains and sorrows of that world"—she pointed out the window—"are no longer yours. All that is behind you. You are *here* now. Everything you'll ever need is right here."

He shook head slowly. *Get in, get 'em off, get out,* he tried to tell himself. *Save Liam, save Mom, save my family.*

She gently steadied his chin in her hand, and her eyes welled with joyful tears. "You're free now, my son. You can't hurt anyone, and they can't hurt you."

It was those words that wormed their way under his skin, into his veins. After a year of pain, yearning, and neglect, Brona's touch and gaze filled a gaping hole in the center of him. The adoration and caring he had ached for over the past year—that he had felt only in his dreams—was right here, in this strange place. He should have been frightened at what she was saying, but even more frightening was how he yearned for her touch, her gentle voice.

Brona would never hurt him, he knew, somehow. She loved him far too much to let anything ever hurt him again.

"I have something for you." Her voice broke the trance that was holding him.

LIAM! the back of his mind screamed at him.

"Come here, a stór." She stood to her full height and offered him her hand.

A stór. My treasure. The words felt as warm as hot chocolate after a long day shoveling snow. Charlie might not be able to make sense of much in this moment, but he knew this: She loved him. And at some time, in some place, he had loved her too.

He took her hand and stood.

"Here. Let me have this," she said.

Charlie watched with disbelief as Brona lifted his chain and key lifelessly over his head—no slithering, no shrinking, no choking. She gently turned Charlie to face away from her and lowered a quarter-sized polished stone before his eyes. *A gift passed from mother to child for as many generations as they knew.* He felt chills as her fingers deftly tied a leather cord at the nape of his neck. The intricate, symmetric pattern on the face of the medallion—a line that twisted and bent, ending where it began—was a design he already knew by heart.

He had traced it with his finger endlessly on his parents' wedding bands. His real parents. His father had explained to him that it symbolized the uninterrupted cycle of life and death, birth and rebirth, and never-ending love.

"An eternity knot," Charlie said.

Brona turned him around and appraised him at arm's length. A beautiful smile warmed her face. "It's perfect."

Charlie's head reeled with new questions. Was he still forgotten without his chain? Could he leave now? Would the leather shrink if he tried to remove it? This too had *not* been part of their escape plan.

"Thanks," Charlie said, not wanting to appear ungrateful. "It's cool."

"Yes," she laughed. "*Cool*, indeed."

The sounds of other children talking in the hallway snapped Charlie to attention. He was supposed to be finding his brother, he reminded himself again, not hanging out with Brona. Why was he complicating matters with necklace switches and bewitching conversations?

"Thank you for showing me the room, Miss Brona. It's really great." He rotated, spinning Brona in an awkward dance that put him closer to the door. "Would it be okay if I . . . found my friends again? They're probably wondering where I am."

"Of course," she said, lowering her eyes, "but please, don't call me Brona. Everyone here calls me Mother." She reached up and touched his cheek. "And there's no need to rush. We're all here, together, now. We have all the time in the world."

✺ 23 ✺

Descending the staircase, Charlie's chest felt as heavy as his head felt light. His mind was addled by his time with Brona; he felt both drawn to and frightened by her. In that room, Charlie felt like a captive. Yet when he left, he found himself longing for her words, her gaze, her embrace.

Focus, he thought. *Liam.*

Back in the grand entry, he found himself alone. He looked at the blank wall where Brona had entered the Asylum. *That* was the way out. To escape, they had to figure out how to conjure that door. However, at this mere thought, Charlie felt movement on the nape of his neck. He brushed at his skin, expecting to feel an insect, only to notice the leather rope shrinking, the stone medallion creeping a few millimeters closer to his neck. It stopped when he turned his back to the exit.

He had been warned.

The sound of voices mixed with the cacophony of forks on plates came from behind a door to his left. Then, a whiff of food. A growl rose from Charlie's stomach. Had it just been a couple hours since he'd had that bowl of cereal? It seemed days, weeks, a lifetime ago.

Charlie pushed the door open to find the dining room. A long table lined with girls was to his left, their plates filled with scrumptious-looking potatoes and greens. An identical table of boys extended to his right.

A boy elbowed the guy next to him and stared. Charlie nodded and waved meekly. He floated around the perimeter, scanning for anyone familiar, but by the time he reached the far end of the room, the only people he'd seen were strangers.

"First day can be rough." A heap of a boy dressed entirely in baggy black clothing sat alone near the end of the table, reading a book. A curtain of long black hair veiled his face.

"Sorry?" Charlie said.

"First day of anything is hard, right? You'll get used to it."

Charlie nodded, though he was pretty sure the guy behind the hair couldn't see it. He didn't need to make new friends in this brief journey, but he also didn't need to make any enemies.

"Cody," the boy said.

"What?"

"The name's Cody. How about you?"

"Oh, I'm Charlie. Nice to meet you." He extended his hand.

Cody flicked his hair out of his face. Charlie stood, frozen, as his eyes danced over Cody's stubbly, pimply, and metal-covered face. He looked about seventeen; he had a silver ring in each eyebrow, one in his lip, and another in his nose like a bull. Both ears held more rings than Charlie could quickly count, and large disks had been placed in nickel-sized holes in his earlobes. Black eyeliner intensified Cody's gaze as he grinned.

"Not used to a face like mine, huh?"

"What do you mean?" Charlie scrambled. He retracted his hand, using it to cover a pretend cough. "What's wrong with your face? I mean, nothing's wrong with your face. I don't think there's something wrong with your face. Why? Do you think there is something wrong with it?"

Cody laughed and closed his book. "Charlie, be cool. I know it's not something everyone's used to. Believe it or not, I don't bite."

Charlie smiled sheepishly. "Sorry."

"Have a seat," Cody said, pushing the chair next to him out with his foot.

Charlie gave one last glance around the room before sitting down. His stomach's demand for food was becoming as loud as his brain's demand for Liam.

"So what'd you do to end up in our cozy little home?" Cody asked.

Charlie wasn't sure how to answer this. "Um, I don't really want to talk about it," he hedged.

"Ah. You're a keeper. No problem." Cody opened his book again, seemingly content for the conversation to end there.

"A what?"

He peered out from behind the book. "A keeper. You keep your story to yourself."

"Um . . . I guess?"

"That's cool. You should know, though, that almost everyone spills their guts eventually. It's the one thing we all have in common, after all. There's only a few true keepers, like Fink over there." He tipped his head toward a thin, white-blond teen sitting alone in a chair by the window. He looked almost see-through in the sunlight. "He's never told a soul why he's here. Rumor has it he murdered his parents and he's here to avoid the death penalty. I've also heard he drowned his sister, stabbed his dog, and poisoned his grandma." Cody laughed and shook his hair out of his eyes. "That's what happens when you're a keeper—people are more than happy to create a past for you. For all we know, he just broke his dad's favorite bowling trophy."

"Sheesh. I wonder what awful crimes will be created for me," Charlie said, pretending he was going to be around long enough to find out.

Cody slid his half-eaten plate of food across the table toward Charlie. "Here. Help yourself. I'm not that hungry, and you missed the meal cart."

"Are you sure?" Charlie felt a little weird eating off a stranger's plate, but his mouth watered at the thought.

"Absolutely."

Charlie inhaled the remaining half potato and what he thought was collard greens, but the food was impossibly bland. It was as if someone had stuck a syringe into each bite and extracted every bit of flavor.

Cody watched him with interest. "Whatcha think?" he asked once Charlie was done.

In the absence of napkins, Charlie wiped the corners of his mouth with his sleeve. Not wanting to sound ungrateful, he said, "It . . . smells a bit better than it tastes."

Cody smirked but stayed silent.

"Do you have any idea where Michael is?" Charlie asked.

"You met Michael already?" Cody said, turning to look

around the room. "Nah, I haven't seen him since before lunch. He was helping some newbies get settled. Did you come in with those guys?"

"Yeah," Charlie said.

"Man, I do not know what Jonathon is up to. He's a legend for getting out of this place, and then he shows back up with new recruits in tow. What did he tell you guys, anyway?"

Charlie hesitated before deciding on "It's complicated."

Cody laughed. "Yes, little man, it sure is."

He appeared to be waiting for Charlie to say more, but instead Charlie said, "Well, thanks. I should go try to find my friends," and stood up. He had wasted far too much time already.

"I'll help you look, if you want," Cody said when it became clear Charlie didn't even know which way to go.

"No, that's okay." He didn't want an audience any bigger than necessary when he, Liam, and Ana attempted their escape. "Thanks, though."

"If you want a tour later, just find me. It's a big place."

Charlie nodded in thanks and headed out on his own.

He was halfway up the main staircase, heading for the dormitories, when he saw him. Coming from the second floor were Jonathon and Michael, followed by Ana and a boy with a face that was like looking in a mirror, but with enthusiastic green eyes.

Liam shouted a disbelieving and elated yelp and bounded down the steps. "Booper!"

Charlie shook his head in disbelief and smiled so broadly his cheeks ached. He raced up the steps, not knowing whether to hug Liam or put him in a stranglehold followed by a vigorous noogie. He ended up doing a mixture of all three.

Instead of the normal protestations and cries for help came the sound of Liam's laughter through happy tears. Then Liam buried his face in Charlie's chest, and full-on sobs racked his bony body. Charlie hugged him tightly and rested his chin atop his little brother's head, a soggy blend of tears and snot soaking through his shirt.

"It's okay, bud. . . . It's gonna be okay."

Liam looked the way Charlie remembered—toothy grin and a pile of messy hair on his head—but he was different too. His limbs were longer, his face was sharper, his arms were stronger. A year had passed.

Charlie beamed at Ana. Her eyes reflected his thoughts exactly. *We did it. We found the boy who doesn't exist.* Everything he had told his mom, his dad, Dr. Barton, everyone . . . it was true.

"You're an idiot, you know that, right?" Charlie laughed

into the crown of Liam's sweaty head, the words catching in his throat as he spoke. It was impossible to tell if Liam was laughing or crying in response.

Liam pulled back and wiped his nose on his hand. "How's Mom?"

"She's . . . fine," Charlie lied. *Or she will be.*

"Really?" Liam smiled. "And Dad?"

"He's good."

"So we finally got you two in the same place," Michael said. "We've been looking all over for you, Charlie!"

"Yeah. Sorry about that." Charlie wondered why he'd ever let Brona lead him away from them.

"Ana says you all have a surprise for us." Michael looked skeptical, but was also smiling at Ana, who was bouncing from toe to toe, an eager and impatient grin on her face. Jonathon was smiling too, but the concern etched on his features by Brona earlier was still firmly in place.

"Showtime!" Ana said. "Where to, Michael?"

"Come on. Let's go down to the game room," he said.

It was now or never. Charlie threw his arm around Liam and looked to Jonathon, needing a nod or a thumbs-up; any sign of encouragement that their plan was still on track.

Jonathon's eyes, however, remained steadfastly on the carpet.

ᔐ 24 ᔑ

What Michael called a "game room" was laughably different from the image Charlie had in his mind. No TV, no PlayStation, not even a Ping-Pong table. "Gaming" in the 1840s apparently consisted mainly of chess. There were four tables of inlaid checkerboard marble, each topped with intricately carved black and white stone queens, kings, and pawns. It all looked beautiful, if perhaps a bit boring, like it belonged in a museum.

A semicircle of chairs faced a fireplace, and some modern additions lay stacked on a wooden shelf by the wall: mostly board games, like Monopoly, Sorry, Life.

"We should have smuggled in an iPad or something,"

Charlie said. He liked board games as much as the next guy, but a screen would be nice.

Michael laughed. "By definition, electronics need electricity. Not much of that to be found around here. Brona tries, however, to keep us entertained. You should have seen this place when she brought back this game Pictionary a few years ago! We had tournaments and everything."

"Can I speak to you for a sec?" Jonathon whispered into Charlie's ear. The vehemence and concern in Jonathon's words were like a cold wind.

"Um, sure." Charlie took his arm off Liam's shoulders and asked him and Ana to give them a moment. Ana shepherded Liam to a seat by the fire.

Jonathon glared. "Why did Brona act like she knew you? What haven't you told me?"

Charlie had never made a deliberate decision to *not* tell Jonathon about his dreams. But given that neither he nor Ana had understood the connection between his nighttime visions and Liam, it had simply never occurred to him.

"And where is your chain?" Jonathon asked, his eyes locked on Charlie's neck.

"Brona took it. She gave me this eternity knot thing instead."

Jonathon shook his head rapidly, his eyes never leaving the stone. He looked green.

"What?" Charlie asked, his pulse quickening. "What does it mean? Why are you acting so weird?"

"I don't know what it means!" Jonathon rubbed his face with one hand and hugged himself with the other. "There is so much going on that I don't understand."

Charlie tucked the medallion into the neck of his shirt. "Look, let's just work on getting out of here. Okay?" He wanted to tell Jonathon to pull it together—they were so close to achieving what they'd come here to do—but he noticed something under Jonathon's fingertips. "Hey. Your scar's gone."

Jonathon touched the skin above his eyebrow where the thin white line had been. "I guess it is."

Michael's voice broke up their conversation. "Charlie, Jonathon, sit down." He sat on the edge of a chair near Liam and Ana. "So what's the big surprise?"

Charlie sat next to Liam and took one of his hands in his. "I know you came here because you made some mistake, but—"

Liam jerked his gaze away and looked down at his shoes. More than that, everyone else was avoided looking at Charlie too.

A sick feeling flooded him. Was it as bad as he'd feared? Maybe Liam had done something truly terrible. He sat paralyzed, unable to ask the simple question he needed to ask. *What did you do?*

Liam covered his face with both hands, and Charlie's chest began to hurt.

"Tell him." Ana's voice was as firm as stone.

"Charlie," Liam started in a cracking voice, "I'm so sorry." His face twisted and pinched. "I never thought you'd come here. I didn't mean to get you involved."

"Get me involved?" Charlie said, suddenly angry. "Liam, everything changed when you left. How could I *not* get involved?"

"But you weren't supposed to remember me!" He finally looked at Charlie, his eyes begging. "You were supposed to forget, like everyone else."

Charlie tried to stay calm. "I know, but it didn't work out that way. Please, tell me what you did. Why did you leave?"

In a barely audible voice, Liam said, "I . . . cheated. On a book report. I stole one of your old ones, and I copied it."

Charlie sat staring at his brother, blinking. Silence stretched uncomfortably across the room. Surely he had misheard. He looked around at everyone else; Ana just raised her eyebrows.

Charlie let out an uncomfortable laugh. "You're kidding, right? Right? Because, for a moment there, I thought you said something about a book report."

"Yeah," Liam squeaked, "that's what I said."

"That doesn't make any sense," Charlie said, his voice

growing louder. "That's so dumb it's not even possible!"

Liam nodded, his body limp.

Charlie stood up and walked toward a chess table, fully considering upending it. He turned back to Liam and then away again. He pinballed between the tables, his body bouncing as madly as his brain. He'd been back with Liam all of five minutes, and he already wanted to wring his neck. All of this . . . over a book report? Maybe life was actually better with Liam gone. At least that way Charlie could love and miss him without wanting to kill him.

"I know it was stupid now, but you gotta understand," Liam began, pleading his case. "Mom and Dad were so mad when school called and told them what I'd done. Dad went nuts. He told me I'd completely disappointed them. . . . I've never seen him like that!"

"That's what happened the night before you vanished?" Charlie barked, remembering Liam flailing around on his comic books. Charlie's ears rang so loudly he couldn't think. "All this," he said, spinning a finger in the air, "because you cheated?"

Words started spilling out of Liam. "See, I got the due date wrong and I was freaking out, so I looked in one of your old folders. I didn't think there was any way Mr. Sheldon would remember it, but he did and . . ." He trailed off into quiet tears.

No one said anything for a full minute. Charlie was almost too angry to think.

"On the bright side," Jonathon finally said, "this makes your job easy, Charlie. Liam's past is manageable. All you'll have to live with is the memory of a major fight between Liam and your parents."

The rational part of Charlie's mind knew that Jonathon was right. This was, ironically, spectacular news. Liam's regret was trivial. But that was not the part of his mind that Charlie was listening to right now. It was all so ridiculous. So much sadness and heartache, over something kids do every day! *I have more reason to be in the Asylum than Liam,* he thought, *given what I said to Mom.*

"So what did you guys do?" Liam asked into the quiet of the room.

"What?" Charlie snapped.

"I mean, what did you and Ana do that was so bad? Why are you guys here?"

"We're here to rescue you!" he said. "Ana, didn't you tell him?"

She shook her head. "We didn't really get into it before coming to find you." She sounded annoyed, but she was still taking all this better than Charlie was. She turned to Liam. "So here's the deal. Everyone moved on like you never existed, just the way Brona promised, except Charlie. He

213

never forgot you. He's been trying all year to figure out what happened. Thankfully, the clues you left last week led us to Jonathon, and Jonathon led us here to you."

"Clues?" Liam said. "What do you mean, clues?"

"The comic books, the note in Charlie's bag . . ."

Liam shook his head slowly, confused. "I don't know what you're talking about. I never left any comic books or notes."

"But . . . what?" Ana said. "That's how we found Jonathon. You left us that note telling us to talk to him."

"You guys know there's no way out of here, right?" Liam said. "The door doesn't open."

"Yeah, but Jonathon said you leave to go out on gatherings, right?" Ana said.

Liam shook his head. "There hasn't been a gathering in months. Brona still leaves every day to get flowers, but none of us have been out for a long time."

A shock shot down Charlie's spine. *Brona.* The woman who had stroked his cheek and eyed him like a rare treasure. The woman who had called him by her son's name. Charlie's heart pounded, and the ringing in his ears reached a fever pitch.

"Wait, wait, wait," Ana said slowly. "You're saying you didn't rearrange Charlie's comic books? And you never wrote a note telling us to talk to Jonathon?"

"How could I?" Liam said frantically. "Even on a gathering,

it's not like Brona lets us just wander around town."

"But the note was in your handwriting!" Ana said.

Jonathon's eyes widened.

"Oh no . . ." Charlie plowed his hands through his hair, feeling as if the leather cord around his neck was tightening. "It's *her*, Ana. Brona. She . . . wants me here. You saw her in the hall—hugging me, calling me Kieran, taking me to my own room. I don't know how she did it, but she must have set this whole thing up." He turned to Jonathon. "She knew you would bring us here, didn't she? That's what she was talking about in the entryway? You doing your 'job'?"

Ana added slowly, "Brona said she wasn't entirely truthful with you. . . ."

Brona had placed a trail of bread crumbs, leading Charlie to Jonathon, and to the truth about Liam, and finally to walking right into the Asylum on their own. Fear began to swarm Charlie's mind like ants. If Brona had set up Jonathon, what else had she lied about? None of Jonathon's information could be trusted.

Jonathon started shaking his head repeatedly. "Charlie, listen to me, you and Liam and Ana need to get out of here, now. Liam cheated off of you—you can take his key off. Do it, and we'll get that door open." Even as he spoke with authority, his face was riddled with doubt.

Charlie hurried toward Liam, only to find Michael

215

blocking his path, his hand on Charlie's chest.

"Whoa, whoa, whoa!" Michael said. "No one's taking off any chains. I don't know what wild stuff you've all been talking about, but I do know what happens when you try to take one of those off. I'm not in the mood to see anyone strangled today."

"It won't strangle him, Michael," Ana said, coming to Charlie's side. "Charlie can forgi—"

"Michael!" Jonathon said, cutting off Ana with an icy voice. "Stand aside."

"You're kidding, right?" Michael said, his hand still firmly against Charlie's torso.

Jonathon shook his head and set his jaw.

Michael backed away hesitantly. "I hope you know what you're doing, man." It wasn't clear if he was speaking to Jonathon or Charlie.

Surprised and wide-eyed, Liam shrank in his chair. "Charlie, what are you doing?"

Charlie looked down at his brother. "You are gonna have to trust me, okay?"

Liam shook his head, unsure.

"I swear, I'll let go immediately if I'm wrong, but I came here *because* I think I can safely take it off. Please."

Liam looked from Charlie to Ana to Jonathon. They all nodded. Michael answered Liam's questioning gaze with a shrug. Ultimately, Liam took a deep breath, sat up, and bowed his head. He was shaking.

Charlie was shaking too. He reached out and gently pinched the exposed chain. "Liam, I forgive you for stealing my book report."

He hadn't lifted the necklace a millimeter before the links began tightening with a hiss.

"Stop!" Liam screamed, and pulled away.

Charlie dropped the metal like a hot ember, horrified by both his failure and his brother's terrified reaction. "I'm sorry! I'm sorry!"

Ana gasped, "No . . ."

Michael exhaled and just shook his head.

Jonathon didn't move a muscle other than to mutter, "Why . . . ?"

This was their only plan. It *had* to work. But Charlie wasn't about to try to take off Liam's chain again.

Ana charged over to Charlie and said, "I forgive you for breaking my arm!" and grabbed for his necklace, but it started shrinking before she even made contact. Charlie pulled away and watched as terrible knowledge flooded her eyes.

Jonathon had been wrong. Deeply, terribly wrong. However he thought the magic of the chains worked, this wasn't how they came off.

They were trapped.

꩜ 25 ꩜

Charlie's knees buckled, and he fell into the chair beside Liam. No matter how many breaths he took, he couldn't find enough air. He barely heard Jonathon scream in frustration and pick up one of the kings from a chessboard, flinging it across the room so hard its head broke off and it left a dent in the wall. Jonathon then stormed out.

Liam receded deeper into his chair, and Michael came to him and put a consoling arm around his shoulder. "You okay, bud?"

Liam nodded and blinked back tears.

"Charlie! Try mine!" Ana said, her voice high. Charlie stared up at her as if she'd spoken to him in another language.

"Forgive me," she pleaded, grabbing Charlie's limp hand and placing it on her chain. "You have to try!"

"Ana!" he snapped, freezing her. "It didn't work! It was never going to work. . . . Brona set us up."

Something in Ana shifted, and what Charlie saw in her eyes was nothing he'd ever seen there before. It chilled him to his core.

Defeat.

As if awaiting her cue offstage, Brona drifted through the door, a teenage girl at her side. Her expression was unreadable, but Charlie wondered if she had in fact been listening the whole time. She announced, "Time for chores, everyone! Off you go, Michael, Liam."

Liam scurried from the room with an apologetic and confused glance back at Charlie, hand on his neck and fear in his eyes. Michael did as he was told and followed Liam out with a crisp nod to Brona.

"Ana, this is Julia. She will take you to the dining room to show you your tasks."

Charlie braced himself for Ana to start screaming, or breaking things, whirling and spitting like a Tasmanian devil. Instead she said, "Okay."

It was the most frightening moment of their ordeal so far.

"I'll go with you guys," Charlie said. He didn't want to

leave Ana's side again. "I can clean up too—"

"Oh, no, Kieran." Brona wrapped her arm around Charlie's shoulder and pulled him close. "You will never have to lift a finger here."

Julia held her hand out to Ana, who let herself be led away, eyes on the floor. Charlie helplessly watched her go, and as she passed, his eye caught on a certain spot on the wall. He blinked and checked again. Where there had been a dent moments ago, from Jonathon throwing the chess piece, now there was nothing but a clean wall. He looked to where the chess piece rested on the floor. It was unbroken.

"You, my dear," Brona said with a tender squeeze, "will come with me."

Brona kept Charlie close for the rest of the day, first supervising chores, then escorting him back to his room, where she read aloud to him from *New Fairy Tales*. She took frequent pauses to simply gaze at him. "It is so wonderful to have you home," she said repeatedly. "Can I get you anything? A snack? Afternoon tea?"

Charlie was too consumed by a blend of fear and failure to do anything more than shake his head.

The disappearance of the last ray of sunlight brought a knock at the door. The boy Cody had pointed out—Fink, Charlie seemed to remember—appeared, bearing dinner.

He nodded to Charlie, set down the tray, and left without a word. The sumptuous smell of pork, potatoes, and beans made Charlie's stomach growl, but again, the food tasted like nothing.

When the last bite was gone, Brona placed the book on the hearth, took his tray, and patted the linen garment at the end of the bed with a smile. "I'll step out so you can change into your nightshirt."

The door clicked closed behind her, and he stared at his antique-looking pajamas. Was Ana getting ready for bed right now too, dejected and alone? Was Jonathon somewhere filling Liam in on why they were here, and working on discovering a new way out? All while Charlie sat here helplessly, playing the part of Brona's son? His mind spun with questions, but there would be no answers tonight.

He grabbed the nightshirt. Instantly the feel of the fabric sent a shock wave from his fingertip to his brain. Smoke filled his nose, the weight of a quilt pressed against his legs, and flames crackled in his ears. Images of a hut, Nora, and a wall of fire flickered before his eyes. He gasped and grabbed at the bed beneath him to steady himself. The images vanished as quickly as they had come. His mind was playing tricks on him, but still, he knew.

This was Kieran's nightshirt.

"May I enter?" came Brona's voice from the hall.

"Um, not yet! Hold on." Charlie took a deep breath and picked up the garment; thankfully, he did not experience the same flash of memories. He changed quickly, the gown feeling both foreign and familiar at the same time, and crawled into bed.

Brona returned to the chair, book in hand, but paused when she looked at him, her forehead creased with concern. "Oh, my love, please don't be scared of me." Her voice was rich with warmth and concern, and to Charlie's surprise, he felt guilty that he was causing her to worry.

"It's just . . . ," he began, but he didn't know how to end the sentence.

Still, Brona nodded with understanding. "Goodness, I know. This can all be a bit . . . jarring at first." She smiled at him with a look of deep empathy, like a kind teacher who truly understands the wrenching fears of new students on their first day of school. The anxiety gripping Charlie's gut loosened a notch. "You and Liam had a pet turtle, yes? Tipsy?"

"Have." Charlie nodded, not wanting to know how she knew this. Did she dream about his life the same way he dreamed about hers?

"He was probably a bit scared of you at first, right?"

Charlie nodded again, remembering how Tipsy had wriggled and squirmed when he first picked him up. Now he loved hanging out on Charlie's palm or on his desk while he did homework. Charlie was sure Tipsy was happier as a pet than he had ever been in the wild.

"You are a kindhearted soul, my son. You saved Tipsy. He was hurt and in grave danger, but you took him in, helped him heal, and made him a wonderful, safe home with everything he needed. May I?" she asked, looking for permission to sit on the bed beside him.

Charlie hesitated, but nodded.

"That's precisely what I do. I take in the wounded and injured, offering a haven for those in need. We're not so different, you and I." Then she winked and said, "I just hope you can come to like me as well as Tipsy liked you."

Charlie thought of his little buddy at home and for the first time realized he hadn't planned for Tipsy before coming here. Who was taking care of him? Or was he still in the wild, injured? This worry broke some of the spell Brona had cast on him. "But . . . what if someone wanted to leave?"

There was a flicker of what he feared was anger, but it passed as quickly as it had come, changing instead to a nod of consideration. "Would you ever let Tipsy back into the world?"

"Well, no, because he'd never survive. The outside is too dangerous for him now."

"You see, we agree. The world *is* far too unsafe. In the

same manner that you would never want to put Tipsy in harm's way again, that's how I feel about my children. I will protect them forever from the uncaring world I know all too well—no more suffering, no more regret."

"So this place is like a human terrarium?" Charlie offered weakly.

Brona smiled wide and laughed. "Why, yes! I guess it is. I know this isn't quite what you expected, coming here. There are . . . reasons for why things had to happen the way they did. But the important thing is that you *are* here, finally, safely here. I promise, you have nothing to fear. The Asylum, everything in it, is for you. For all of you." She began to reach out, to touch his hair, but paused with her hand in the air, again waiting for his permission. He found himself nodding again. Despite the horror of the day and his sense of being caught in a trap, he wanted to feel a touch of comfort; to return to those moments in his dreams where her embrace made all the pain and suffering around them dissolve, if only for a moment.

Charlie closed his eyes and let himself accept her adoration. She stroked his bangs up and off his brow with a gentle hand.

He couldn't have said how long they stayed like that, and it was only as Brona finally tucked him in for the night—bringing the blanket snug against his chin and tightening it beneath the mattress, exactly the way he liked it—that Charlie finally summoned the nerve to ask the questions that he couldn't keep inside any longer.

"Who are you? And . . . who am I?"

"Surely you already know, don't you, Kieran?" Creases formed around her eyes and forehead.

"I guess. But it doesn't make any sense. You're from my *dreams*. You're not real."

"Oh, my darling. Whoever told you that dreams aren't real?" She kissed his forehead and squeezed his hand before rising to put out the lanterns.

It was only when she reached the door that Charlie said, "I'm sorry, Miss Brona, but I'm *Charlie*. Not Kieran."

She nodded once, whispered, "Good night, a stór," and closed the door.

ᴥ 26 ᴗ

Charlie tossed and turned for hours, skimming the surface of sleep like a skipping stone before, finally, sinking into its cool waters. There he found an endless loop of the four dreams, from Ireland to the *Randolph* to New York, over and over. There were new flickers as well, wispy and unformed: hallways, doors, and cabinets.

And through it all, Brona. *Mother.* His steadfast solace.

The brilliant white of the snow-covered world outside blared unwelcomely through Charlie's closed lids early the next morning. He was hardly aware he was awake before the truth—*Jonathon was wrong*—fell on him like an anvil.

What had they been thinking, just trusting everything

Jonathon had said? Why hadn't they demanded more proof that he could remove Liam's chain? Why had he let Ana talk him into letting her come along? Had he condemned her family to the same torture he had endured for the past year—all because he'd been afraid to come here alone? His stupidity was as bright and blinding as the morning light. It burned away any lingering comfort from his dreams about Brona.

I have to find a way to get out of here! Charlie ripped his nightshirt over his head and dressed so quickly, he toppled over trying to walk and pull his pants on at the same time. He opened the door and looked stealthily down the empty hallway. Creeping to the stairs, he peeked over the railing.

To his immense relief, Ana was alone in the entry hall, pacing the edges of the room like a tiger in a too-small cage. Her permanent ponytail had flyaway strands sticking out in every direction, suggesting that she had had a long and restless night. Fiery Ana was back.

Charlie descended the carpeted stairs two at a time, his footfalls announcing his arrival.

"Charlie!" Ana met him at the bottom of the stairs and wrapped him in a rare hug—one he returned enthusiastically. "I'm so glad you're okay!"

"I'm fine. How about you?"

Ana brushed the question aside. "Where did Brona take you yesterday?"

"Just to my room. She wanted to read to me." Charlie told Ana everything he could remember about his time with Brona since his arrival. He didn't know how to describe the attachment he had to her, though, or the perverse comfort he felt when he was with her, so he left those parts out. Ana stood, arms crossed, shaking her head.

"This is all so messed up," she concluded. "So she's definitely the woman from your dreams?"

"Oh, yeah, for sure. And I think we should keep my dreams just between the two of us, until we have a better idea what is going on."

Ana nodded in agreement. "And she thinks you're her son? Man, she couldn't be any creepier if she tried."

Before he could stop himself, he said, "She's . . . kinda nice, actually."

Ana stopped talking and looked at Charlie as though gravely concerned for his sanity.

"No, really," he tried again. "I mean, this whole situation's super weird, but Brona really believes she's helping everyone here."

Ana wasn't buying it. "You know what? I don't even care. It doesn't matter. All I care about is finding a new way out of here. The plan hasn't changed: Get in? Check. Get 'em off? That's the puzzle for today. Get out? Immediately to follow."

Charlie nodded, even if he wasn't as optimistic about their

chances as Ana seemed to be. The number of complicating factors that had been introduced since their arrival yesterday felt insurmountable. "Any thoughts on where to start?"

"We're going to grill every single kid in this place and find out what they know about how the keys and the doors work. Jonathon said that girl got out all those years ago, right? The answer's here somewhere—we just have to find it."

"Where are Jonathon and Liam?"

"Still asleep. Apparently dozing in a creepy dream-lady's asylum gets easier with practice."

"Morning" came a voice from the stairs. Cody was ambling toward them in the otherwise still house.

"Our first victim," Ana whispered conspiratorially.

"Hey, Cody," Charlie said. He wasn't quite as shocked by Cody's piercings this time. "This is my best friend, Ana. Cody was nice enough to keep me company at lunch yesterday when I couldn't find you guys."

Cody smiled sleepily. "Howdy."

"Whoa! What did you do to your face?" Ana asked.

Charlie slapped his hand to his forehead.

"No, seriously," Ana said, still staring at Cody with an open expression. "Why would anyone do that?"

Instead of taking offense, Cody laughed. "I like your style, Ana! I'll take real over polite any day. We could use more of that around here. To answer your first question, I have pierced my face. As to why . . ." He shrugged. "Well, it was something to do. That, and I have a cousin who works at a tattoo parlor who needed a little practice. And since we are keeping it real now," Cody said with a wink, "I can tell you that you two look awful."

"A freaky ghost woman roaming the halls of a nonexistent orphanage will do that to a girl," Ana said.

"Like I told Charlie yesterday, the first few days are tough, but then you get used to the routine."

"Yeah, about that . . . how do we get out of here?" Ana asked.

Cody, who was midyawn and stretch, froze and looked at her with both disbelief and admiration. "Leave? Kid, you just got here. Didn't you kiss your life goodbye yesterday?"

"Yup," Ana said, offering no further explanation.

"You're ahead of the curve, Ana. Most newbies take a couple of months before they start asking about bugging out—sometimes it takes years before they realize what a big fat mistake we all made. Turns out food without flavor, forever-fitting and clean clothes, and a thousand games of Sorry! don't make for much of a life."

Charlie remembered the vanishing blood from yesterday. "Clean clothes . . . ," he repeated.

"Been wearing this for three years," Cody said. "Always clean, always fits, even though I'm a foot taller."

"So you want to leave too?" Ana asked.

"I didn't say that." He walked away, cocking his head for them to follow. "Breakfast isn't served till after eight. Let's go grab a snack from the kitchen."

Cody led them to an inconspicuous door tucked under the grand staircase; it was smaller and narrower than any door Charlie had ever seen. Ana hesitated as they passed where the tree door had appeared the day before.

"Cody? Liam told us yesterday that Brona goes out for flowers every day, but I haven't seen any around the house."

"I guess I always assumed she likes fresh flowers in her bedroom, but who knows? I don't exactly spend a lot of time there." He shivered at the thought and then ducked his head and started down a small stairwell. A chill passed over Charlie as he entered the tiny, damp stone corridor.

They stepped out into the basement, and the fractured tiles of the floor crunched under their feet. The air was slightly warmer, heated by the bustling kitchen Charlie could hear and smell to his left. A series of closed doors stretched to their right. He halted and stared into the dark that stretched away from him.

He had seen this hallway before.

With the same déjà vu sensation he'd had with Brona yesterday, Charlie knew the corridor, just like he knew the house, but he didn't know how or why. Were there more

231

dreams he didn't fully remember? Were these fragments additional pieces of the story?

"Hey, Cody," a girl said, passing the three of them on her way to the kitchen. "Whatcha doing down here? You're not on breakfast duty today."

"Just showing the newbies around," Cody said, pointing his thumb at Charlie and Ana.

"Hey," Charlie said with wave.

She turned and walked into the kitchen.

"Well, she's chatty," Ana said once she was out of earshot.

"Ayla's cool. She's just kinda shy. She was a keeper longer than anyone I've met. Besides Fink, of course."

Charlie explained keepers to Ana before asking, "So you know what she did now?"

"Oh, yeah, everyone knows. Her parents were having this crazy nasty divorce, and they were fighting over everything. The furniture, cars, Christmas tree lights, a set of Mickey and Minnie Mouse coffee mugs, a dustpan, you name it. She told me she was pretty sure they cared more about who got the TiVo than who got her. So she made her wish. She figured they wished she'd never been born too." He walked toward the kitchen, waving a hand for them to follow him.

"Were you a keeper?" Ana asked.

"Oh, sure."

"Are you still?"

232

"No. I've got nothing to hide anymore. My crime is that I broke my grandmother's heart. I deserve to be here."

"What do you mean, you broke her heart?" Charlie said.

Cody turned, his friendly smirk falling slightly. "I couldn't afford anything nice for my grandma's birthday, so I went to the mall and tried to steal a bottle of perfume. I didn't even get out of the store before the security guy was all over me. I tried to run but dropped the bottle, and it shattered on the floor. A four-hundred-and-forty-dollar puddle."

Charlie let out a snort of disbelief. "Four hundred and forty dollars? What was it made of, liquid gold?"

"Rose oil, which, it turns out, costs even more. Who knew I had such expensive tastes? I just liked how it smelled. So instead of a nice gift from me on her birthday, my grandma got a call from the cops. She had to come down to the police station and go in front of the judge. I got six months' probation and she got a four-hundred-and-forty-dollar fine."

"Your parents must have freaked out," Ana said.

"I don't have parents," Cody said.

Ana shifted from foot to foot. "Sorry, I didn't—"

"Don't worry about it. But no, my mom *wouldn't* have freaked out about me being a crook. She's the one who started that family tradition. She had me pretty young, and was in and out of jail when I was little; I only have a handful of memories of her. When she did come around my grandma's place—usually drunk—it was to ask for money. She died when I was six. They found her car submerged in a roadside pond four hours after she got out of jail for drunk driving."

Charlie was stunned. What could he say? *I'm sorry? That's too bad? That sounds rough?* His parents were a mess of their own, but nothing like that.

"And, to answer your next question, I've never met my dad."

"Cody . . . ," Ana sputtered. "That's so sad."

"I guess." Cody shrugged. "To me, the sad part is how I let my grandma down. She always told me that I was different—that I had a good heart, that I was smart, that I could ride my solid grades to something better. But nope. I was just another bad egg. When she picked me up at the police station, she looked as upset as she always did when she talked about my mom. She didn't need a grandson who added to her huge pile of misery. But enough of that. Come on. I'm hungry!"

Ana and Charlie exchanged a look of shocked disbelief before following Cody down the hall and through a doorway.

The large and stuffy kitchen was dominated by a hulking black cast-iron stove against the opposite wall, its multiple doors and compartments like so many menacing eyes and mouths. Dozens of copper pots hung from hooks to its left, their surfaces shimmering in the lamplight. Wooden spoons and ladles of various sizes dangled beside them. To his right, rows of shelves held old-fashioned canisters and food tins. They looked like items from the general store in *Little House on the Prairie.*

A kitchen crew of five or six kids was preparing breakfast. The girl named Ayla was loading clean bowls and spoons into an opening in the wall. Another girl, after adding a stack of napkins, grabbed a loop of rope hanging from the opening and heaved it downward.

"What's she doing?" Charlie asked Cody.

"Sending it up."

"The cabinet? It's an elevator?"

"It's a dumbwaiter. Sends the food and plates up to the dining room, brings the used ones down. You can even take out the shelves and ride it down from the second floor for midnight sandwiches," Cody said with a mischievous grin. He then ducked through a small door behind them.

A cramped pantry awaited them, shelves packed wall to wall and floor to ceiling with mason jars of pickles, beans, tomatoes, peaches, and carrots. It looked like a history museum exhibit.

"The bread's here." Cody opened a shoe-box-sized tin, the metallic clatter reminding Charlie of the Royal Dansk cookies his grandmother always brought over at Christmas-time. Cody tore a piece for himself and extended the loaf to Charlie. "If you're ever looking for me around one a.m., you'll find me down here. A bit dry, but not bad."

"How old is all this stuff?" Ana said, wrinkling her nose. "Isn't this, like, a setup for botulism?"

"All the food is just like the house: timeless, my friends. Check it out." He put the bread away, reached up for a jar of peaches, and twisted the lid with a pop. He removed a pale, waxy plug that looked like a white hockey puck and tossed it in a trash bin before fishing out a slice of peach. Cody slipped the morsel into his mouth and offered the jar to Charlie as he chewed happily.

Charlie dunked his fingers into the cool syrup and took a slice. It looked like a peach. It smelled like a peach. It felt like a peach as it left a drip on his chin and slithered down his throat.

But it tasted like nothing.

Charlie frowned. "What is up with the food here? There's no flavor."

"Welcome to the land of no consequences, my friend."

Charlie shook his head.

"You fell when you got here, right?" Cody said.

"Yeah."

"Did it hurt?"

"No . . ."

"Right. Check it out," and before Charlie could respond or brace himself, Cody's fist crashed into his shoulder. It knocked Charlie off-balance and he had to steady himself on a shelf.

"Dude!" Charlie said, spooked by being attacked. "What the—?"

Ana raised a fist, ready to rumble.

"Be cool, guys. Just a little lesson. How's your shoulder?" He popped another peach into his mouth.

"It's . . . fine." It didn't hurt. Not even a little.

"Like I said, no consequences! No pain, no pleasure, no hurt feelings, no apologies. The food tastes like paste, but it also can't make you sick. I can't hurt you and you can't hurt me. We are all in Brona's magical Bubble Wrap. Everything we do vanishes, like it never happened. Just like what I did to my grandma." Cody tipped the peach jar toward Charlie.

Charlie shook his head, too busy thinking to eat.

Cody closed the jar and held it out to Ana. "Now try putting it back on the shelf."

"Shouldn't we put it in the fridge?" she asked.

"Well, for one thing, there is no fridge. You'd need electricity for that." He shook the jar. "Try it."

She took the jar and turned to the shelf. Each row was

exactly as it had been when they'd entered. No gap where a jar was missing.

"How did you do that?" Charlie asked.

Cody smiled and took the jar back. "*I* didn't do anything. That's how the kitchen works. Never empty, never in need. Everything we want, right where it always is." He opened the bread box again to show them the loaf he'd torn a bite from. It was whole. "You may get hungry, but you'll never go without. As Brona says, we have everything we could ever need." He tossed the jar into the trash. "Come on—let's head back upstairs."

Charlie looked into the trash can as they passed by. Despite his having just heard the jar thunk against the wood, there was nothing there now.

"This is all very interesting," Ana said once they were back upstairs, "but you never answered my question."

"Which one?"

"The *only* one. How do we get out of here?" More kids were filing down for breakfast, and Ana was looking impatient.

Cody hushed her and looked up the stairs and around the entry. "You might want to keep your voice down. Brona doesn't take too kindly to talk of leaving."

"Then answer quietly."

Charlie couldn't tell which of them was more frustrated with the other.

"Ana," Cody said, "there's no answer to give. There's no way out."

"What about Jonathon?" Ana pressed on. "He found a way out of the Asylum, even though everyone thought it was impossible. And Jonathon said there were stories of one person who figured out how to take off her chain."

Cody let out an exasperated exhale and nodded for them to follow him. He led them through a doorway and into a vast chamber. "Whoa." Charlie sighed, looking upward.

Paintings hung on every inch of the four walls, stretching all the way to the vaulted ceiling. The frames varied from grand to tiny and were put together like a jigsaw puzzle; barely a postage-stamp-sized piece of the wall was visible. Charlie felt dizzy as he looked up and spun around, taking in what appeared to be an entire museum packed into one room. Half of the frames held vast landscapes—trees, mountains, rivers, and skies with sunlight that radiated out of the canvas as if lit from behind. The rest were portraits—ivory-skinned women in velvet and men in Napoleon-like getups, all staring directly at them. Charlie felt watched.

"What is this place?"

"The Kettering Gallery. All these paintings were supposedly worth millions before the place burned down. Mrs.

Kettering left them to the orphanage when she died. She believed the poor orphaned children of New York would 'benefit from the civilizing influence of the arts to become model citizens of the future,'" he said in a prim, high-pitched impersonation. "Kinda ironic now, since the only kids who see them are ones with no futures at all."

Cody's words hit Charlie like a fist. *No futures.*

"Okay," Cody continued, "escape attempts aren't as common a thing as you seem to think they are. Still, some of us have spent a little time wondering if there's any way to get out of the Asylum. Let's set aside the question of getting the chains off for the moment, because the theories on that are . . . complicated."

Charlie felt the rope of hope he was dangling from begin to fray. He nervously chewed a fingernail that was already painfully short.

"As for simply leaving the building, there are only two exits, as far as anyone knows."

"Two?" Ana stood up a little straighter, and Charlie stopped midbite.

"Yup. The first is obvious, of course: the tree portal. Brona goes in and out of it all the time, gathering children, gathering flowers. There might be a way to sneak out while she opens it for one of her daily trips."

"That's the way Jonathon escaped, right?" Charlie said.

Cody paused and regarded Charlie like a curiosity—a rare creature in a zoo display. His tongue played with his lower lip piercing and he nodded slowly. "Is that what Jonathon told you?"

"Yes," Ana and Charlie answered together.

The gears of Cody's brain were practically visible as he read their expressions, carefully considering his next words.

Charlie's breath quickened. It was one thing for Jonathon to have been wrong about how to get the chains off. But it was quite another thing if Jonathon had lied to them about how he'd left the Asylum. The first could be a tragic mistake. Together, they felt like active deception.

"Well, then, yes." Cody laced his fingers together and let them hang in front of him. "I guess that's how Jonathon got out. I didn't personally see him go."

Charlie and Ana exchanged a nervous glance. "Okay, what's the second exit?" she asked.

"The other way to get out of here is to turn eighteen."

Ana let out an exasperated sigh. "Well, that's not exactly helpful. That's six years from now!"

"But not for Jonathon . . . ," Charlie recalled. "Ana, didn't he tell us it wouldn't be long before he could stop lying to Mr. Cutter about his age?"

"Correct," Cody said. "Your buddy came back just in time to leave. He's out of here in three days."

Charlie's mind burbled with the beginnings of a new plan. "Okay, so if we know the door will be opening for Jonathon, maybe we can come up with a way to get out at the same time he does." Ana nodded with a look of serious consideration.

But Cody laughed in a way that made Charlie's heart sink. "Slow down, bud. That's not how it works. Truth is, we don't know what happens when someone turns eighteen. Brona gathers everyone together for dinner the night before a birthday, tells us all that the kid in question is moving to 'the next chapter'—whatever that means—and has everyone say goodbye. By morning? Poof." He spread his fingers like two fireworks explosions.

Ana flinched. "Poof? What do you mean, poof?"

"Gone."

"Like, she kills them?" Ana said, eyes wide.

"Ana! Don't be ridiculous." Charlie didn't completely trust Brona, but it wasn't like she was a murderer. She'd lost so many people in her life, and he knew she'd do anything to protect her children, to protect any children. That was what this whole place was about: a safe place for kids, no matter what they'd done.

"Well, then where do the eighteen-year-olds go?" Ana asked.

"Nobody knows," Cody said. "In the past, kids have

snuck out of their rooms on birthday nights to stake out the door and the portal. No one's ever seen a thing. But come daylight, our number's down by one."

"Well, Jonathon clearly doesn't believe Brona's secretly murdering anyone," Charlie said. He had brought them here just days before he faced this unknown fate.

Ana set her jaw and shook her head. "That's a good point. Why didn't Jonathon tell us any of this?"

"He probably thought we'd all be long gone by then," Charlie said. "We were supposed to be home already."

"What else hasn't Jonathon told us?" Ana said, voicing the thought Charlie had pushed away earlier. He still had no answer.

"Sorry to be the one to drop that bomb on you," Cody said. "I assumed he told you. Man, the real world must have been pretty bad for Jonathon to sign back up for this."

Charlie felt more defeated than ever. Ana, however, spoke with a new lilt of hope in her voice. "Well, then there must be some other way out of the building, right? If the kids who turn eighteen don't leave by portal, there's another door somewhere. All we have to do is find it."

Cody bobbed his head side to side, a doubtful look on his face. "I like your enthusiasm, Ana. Maybe you're right."

His words ushered a somber silence into the room,

broken only by light footfalls of the late risers coming down to breakfast.

Cody shook his head. "For what it's worth, most kids around here assume that this place works like a real orphanage—that when kids turn eighteen, Brona lets them return to the world, forgotten but real, to start a new life as adults."

"What do the rest of the kids think?" Charlie asked.

Cody ran a finger across his throat. "Ana already answered that question."

ꙮ 27 ꙮ

They needed to talk to Jonathon. Charlie and Ana had started the day knowing they had to find a way out of the Asylum somehow, and soon. But *soon* had rocketed to *now*. They had only three days before Jonathon's birthday and the uncertain fate that came with it.

It had also become increasingly clear Jonathon hadn't been entirely honest with them. It was time to find out why.

Charlie and Ana stormed up the stairs two at time. Liam was starting his descent to breakfast but let out a small squeak as Charlie and Ana spun him around like a top, slipped their arms into the crooks of his elbows, and escorted him back toward the bedrooms.

"Hi! Where are we going?"

"We need to find Jonathon," Charlie said. "Which room is his?"

"I think he's second door on the right." Liam looked at them, curious for answers.

"We need to talk to him," Ana said, reaching for the knob.

"Ana! You can't go in there. It's a boys' dorm!"

"Whatever," Ana said, but instead of opening the door, she moved her hand up and rapped on it urgently. There was no answer.

Charlie gently took his brother by the shoulders and crouched down, eye to eye with him. "Do you have any idea where Jonathon is?"

"No." Liam looked worried. "Is he in trouble?"

Weren't they all? It struck Charlie how much Liam had gotten used to this place over the last year. "No, but we need to find him."

"Well, I know he was pretty upset yesterday after you tried to take off my chain," Liam said, offering what little information he had. "He whipped through his chores, then went to the library and started ripping books off the shelves. I don't know what he was looking for, but he was in there all through dinner. I don't think he even came to bed."

"Well then," Ana said, turning around, "lead the way."

Liam nodded and smiled. "Sure! The library's downstairs—I can show you." He may have been a year older, but he still had the same spring in his step that Charlie remembered.

Moments later, they found themselves next to the dining hall in a small room that would more aptly be called an office. "This is a library?" Ana asked.

A grand mahogany desk anchored the center of the room, its work surface a rich burgundy leather. There were no windows, as bookshelves filled every wall, floor to ceiling. A pleasant smell of old paper filled the air. Behind the desk, a lantern flickered dimly on the floor beside a pile of books and a lump of fabric.

The lump moved.

Charlie took a step back, but then leaned forward. "Jonathon? Is that you?"

The lump suddenly jerked to life, causing everyone to jump. Jonathon's head shot up, narrowly missing a shelf, and he drew a huge breath in through his nose. His hair was wild, and a horizontal line of drool glistened on his cheek.

"What . . . ?" he said, hastily wiping his mouth with his sleeve. "What time is it?"

"It's breakfast time," Liam said.

Jonathon shook his head. "Oh no . . . how long have I

been asleep?" He started flipping through the pages of the nearest book.

Ana cut right to the point. "Why didn't you tell us what happens when you turn eighteen?"

Jonathon's frantic searching continued uninterrupted. "Good morning to you too, Ana. And I don't really know what happens when you turn eighteen. No one does, as I'm sure you are now aware. So I guess it didn't occur to me to mention it."

"Didn't occur to you?" Ana said loudly. "Jonathon, you're three days away from . . . whatever Brona does, and you didn't think to mention it?"

Jonathon's hands became still. "What happens in three days doesn't matter, because we're going to find a way out before then. You'll be long gone." He picked up another book and resumed his search.

Ana plowed on, peppering Jonathon with questions: what he *did* know about turning eighteen, what he was searching for, how he'd escaped last time.

Charlie, however, was hung up on Jonathon's last words. "*You'll* be long gone?" he repeated.

Jonathon continued to ignore them.

"Hey!" Charlie said more loudly, "You mean '*We'll* be long gone,' right? *We'll* be leaving, together. Like you promised."

"Right," Jonathon said without looking up.

Charlie pushed on. "Jonathon, what else haven't you told us? How exactly did you get out through the tree door?"

"I didn't . . ." Jonathon stalled. "Look, how I left won't work again, okay?"

"But if you tell us exactly what happened, maybe it will help us figure something out," Ana said.

"Ana!" Jonathon said with a ferocity that startled Charlie and pushed Ana back on her heels. "I don't know how to get us out of here. Okay? Isn't that obvious? My plan was Charlie! Charlie was supposed to be able to take off the chains and get us out, but he can't." Jonathon returned to his task. "I don't have any answers—apparently I never did."

"So is that what you're looking for?" Liam asked softly from behind Charlie. "What's with the books?"

"He's searching for information about the mines" came the answer from behind them. Michael entered the room and nodded to them. "Jonathon, come on, man. I told you, I read them all. You're not finding anything in there."

"Maybe you missed something."

Michael sighed and shook his head. "Suit yourself."

Information about mines? Charlie tilted his head to read the cracked leather spines of the books Jonathon had discarded: a book of poems by Edgar Allan Poe, essays by Ralph Waldo Emerson, Charles Darwin's *Voyage of the Beagle*.

A ripping sound came from the direction of Jonathon's rapidly flipping hands.

"Careful!" Michael said.

"Like it matters," Jonathon mumbled, and continued undeterred.

A piece of paper with a ragged edge floated to the floor near Charlie's foot. In the margins of the page, tiny handwriting wrapped around the edges of the type. He squinted to read the cursive scrawl.

Château de Goulaine, 1822 Muscadet, three cases
Barone Rissaioli, 1831 Castello di Brolio, eight cases
Schloss Johannisberg, 1833 Riesling, two cases

Charlie peered over Jonathon's shoulder. More names. More dates. Page after page had similar listings around the printed words, all in the same handwriting. The only word he recognized was *cases*. "What is this?"

Jonathon didn't answer but instead pointed at Michael for him to explain.

"Jonathon has taken an acute interest in an old theory of mine. A theory of what that handwriting represents. I believe these books were a kind of ledger for the Ketterings' secret line of work."

"Ketterings? You mean the people who built this place?" Charlie asked.

Ana came to Charlie's side. "Who keeps a ledger inside a book?"

"Someone who has secrets to keep," Michael said, "and knows a traditional ledger could be used against them. I think the Ketterings were smugglers."

"Guys, guys," Liam said, making a time-out sign with his hands. "What are you talking about?"

Michael held up a hand for everyone to stop for a moment while he caught up his lost little friend. "A ledger is like a journal where you write down things you buy and sell—it helps you keep track of your money when you run a business. Or in the case of a smuggler, when you run an *illegal* business."

Liam's eyes went wide, changing from lost to deeply interested at the intrigue of it all. "And what did the Ketterings smuggle?"

"Wine."

"Oh." Liam's expression of interest dropped as quickly as it had come. "Borrrr-ing."

"Riesling, Muscadet—those are types of wine," Michael said. "I think the other words in there are the vineyards, all of them in Europe. Taxes on alcohol were crazy high back in the 1800s. People smuggled wine into the country so they wouldn't have to pay, but they needed someplace to hide it all. What better place than underground? The Ketterings got rich by owning and operating the salt mines here in town, but I think they *stayed* rich hiding and selling wine through the tunnels."

"I don't get it," Charlie said. "What does any of this have to do with us?"

Ana, whose slow nodding had become faster and faster, darted to the shelf and grabbed a book in each hand. She plopped down next to Jonathon. "If there was a way for illegal wine to get in and out of this house, that means there's a well-hidden secret entrance somewhere. One that, if we can find it, might be our ticket out of here!"

Michael appeared impressed that Ana had connected the dots so quickly. He shelved a few of the stray books and said, "Well, if my many assumptions are correct, then yes, I think the salt shafts connect to this house. That's my theory, at least. I've been spending my free time searching the Kettering notes in these books for years, looking for more information as to where the entrance might be. I've never found it, but it seems Jonathon has found a reason to pick up the hunt for the secret door."

"It's behind a wooden wine cabinet," Charlie blurted, the words out of his mouth before he knew they were in his mind.

Every head in the room turned to Charlie. Even Jonathon stopped his incessant page flipping.

"What?" Michael took a step closer.

"The opening to the salt mines. It's behind a wine cabinet, a wooden one, but there aren't any bottles in it anymore." Flickers and flashes lit up his mind, shadows of a dream that was still somewhere in his subconscious.

Jonathon stood and stared at Charlie in a manner that seemed almost menacing. "How do you even know there is a wine cellar?"

"I just . . . Maybe I'm wrong." But even as he said this, he knew he wasn't. It was down the dark corridor in the basement. Last door on the right.

Michael nodded and looked at Charlie like he was one of the most curious and interesting things he'd ever seen. "No, you're right, there is a wine cellar in the basement. But Brona keeps a combination lock on the door."

Ana's jaw dropped. "There's a locked door in the basement and you're all wondering where the entrance to the mines might be? Spoiler alert: I think it might be in there!"

"Thank you, Ana," Michael said with a smile. "Believe it or not, we've explored that idea, but the one time Brona let me follow her into the cellar, I saw that it was just that—a cellar. Wall-to-wall shelving. No doors."

Charlie didn't need this description, however, to see the room in his mind's eye, the individual cubbies of all the cabinets, each awaiting a bottle like little wine mailboxes. The image blossomed into a full-fledged memory—he smelled flowers, tasted salt, and felt a gritty resin on his skin. "The third rack on the left, near the back corner of the cellar. It swings out. The salt-mine entrance is behind it."

"How do you know that?" Jonathon demanded.

"I . . . I just know."

Liam stared at him in disbelief. "How are you doing this, Charlie? If you're right, maybe you *can* take me home after all!"

Michael put a calming hand on Liam's shoulder. "Charlie, do you also 'just know' the combination to the lock?"

Charlie blinked and stayed silent. He waited for another bolt of mental lighting, a flash of additional information— but nothing came. "No."

Liam's excitement was not so easily quashed. "Let's go down there tonight! You'll know how to open it, Charlie, I know you will. We'll wait until Brona goes to bed, then break into the wine cellar and break out of the Asylum." He flung his arms around Charlie's middle and squeezed so hard it made Charlie grunt.

Ana announced to the room the new plan. "Get in, get out, get 'em off later." Taking off their necklaces would have to wait until after they'd gotten out of the Asylum. Until *all of them*—Charlie quickly glanced at Jonathon—had escaped.

"Good morning, children." The soft voice came from the doorway. They turned to see Brona, clad in her all-black garb, leaning comfortably on the doorframe.

"Hi," Charlie replied, trying to make it seem like nothing suspicious was going on, despite the dozens of books lying open around them. But if the condition of the room or their activities bothered Brona, she gave no sign. She nodded good morning to each of them and held out her hand to Charlie. "You must have been up early. Did you sleep well?"

"Uh, yeah," he lied. He was rewarded with a stunning smile. It felt good to make her face brighten. It appeared to be a power he, and he alone, possessed.

"If I may borrow you for a little while?" Brona said, seeking permission from the others. "I have something I think you'll like."

Charlie girded himself for Ana's protests, but instead she popped up and said louder than necessary, "See you later then!" She hugged Charlie and used the opportunity to put her mouth to his ear. "Find out about the combination lock," she whispered. She then backed up and said, even louder, "See you at lunch!"

Charlie grimaced. Ana would never win an Oscar.

Brona guided Charlie leisurely down the hallway to the drawing room. The room had clearly been luxuriously appointed once. Heavy red-velvet curtains bordered windows that stretched from floor to ceiling. A gold-framed mirror, its surface foggy and stippled, hung above a marble fireplace.

The room was sparsely furnished now, housing only a small coffee table and a couch. On the table, a pastry sat atop a delicate china plate. Charlie recognized the scrumptious aroma of cinnamon, butter, and caramelized brown sugar immediately. This was, unmistakably, one of his mother's "baby's butt" sweet rolls. Charlie stepped closer, circling the table with the plate but not yet touching it. How did Brona know about O'Reilly rolls? The clean and distinct line between Kieran and Charlie felt uncomfortably blurred.

"Go ahead!" Brona laughed. "It's for you. It is your favorite, after all." The carved creases around her eyes seemed less sharp today, the pale line of her lips pinker.

Charlie's fingers sank into the gooey caramel, and the soft dough collapsed just the right amount as he lifted it. "Where did you get this?"

"I can't go telling you all my secrets," she said with a wink.

The scent of the yeast and sugar was intoxicating. He took a bite and the roll melted in his mouth, warm and . . .

flavorless. Charlie sank onto the couch.

Brona lowered herself beside him to the sound of innumerable layers of rustling fabric. The noise was harsh but comforting, like his parents' coffee grinder waking him each morning. "I'm sorry it can't be exactly the same, but I hope you still like it." She flattened the surface of her lap with hands that shook ever so slightly.

Only an hour ago he had been talking with Cody about whether Brona secretly tormented kids, and now here she sat, humbly offering him the best version of his favorite food this place had to offer.

"Yeah," he said, "I do." And he meant it. She had made this just for him, even if it wasn't the same. At least she was trying. "My mom hasn't made these in, like, two years."

The smile that had brightened Brona's face faded at the mention of his mother. "I'm sorry," he said quickly. "It's just . . . I have a lot of questions. . . ."

"To be honest with you, Kieran, so do I!"

The jarring sound of that name hit him like a punch. He wasn't Kieran. He didn't want to disrespect her kindness and caring, but he couldn't pretend to be someone he wasn't. "Can you . . . call me Charlie? Please?"

She didn't answer at first, but finally she nodded. Without anger in her voice, she said, "I can try."

Charlie wrestled with the dozens of questions that were

in his mind. The one that made it out of his mouth was "Why do you know me?"

She shifted, rustling, to better face him. "I know you because you are my son. That may not make any sense, but I've known it in my heart since the moment I saw you."

"But yesterday," he said, recalling his arrival, "it was like you were already expecting me, like you knew I was coming."

"Oh, yesterday was not the first time I saw you, Kier— Charlie." The name sounded awkward in her mouth. "I heard your brother's wish and came to gather him, like I had done for so many children before him. But when I arrived, I saw my beautiful boy beside him." Brona stopped. The memory seemed to pain her.

"You were in our house?"

She shook her head, and seemed ready to correct him, but stopped herself. Instead she said, "Seeing your face brought me the only pure joy I've felt since . . . since I lost you."

Lost you. Charlie felt the tug of two strong men on his arms, his feet dragging down the steps and into the dirt. The squeal of a pig echoed in his ears. He felt the wrenching pain of being torn from that tenement long ago—from his mother. From Brona.

She placed a warm, soft hand on Charlie's cheek. "A stór . . ."

Her touch was like medicine. Charlie couldn't help but lean into her hand and close his eyes. Tears leaked from them as a calm settled in his body.

Her voice drifted over him. "For more than a hundred years I've hovered between the end of my life and the peace of death. Every day, I've eased the suffering of children to make up for what I did, hoping that one day I could finally be allowed to rest by your side. But when I saw you, I knew that my work would soon be rewarded. It's all been leading up to this. Now I can finally save *you*." She lowered her hand to her lap.

With the spell of her touch lifted, Charlie said, "But . . . I don't need *saving*."

Brona cocked her head. "Don't you? Don't you need saving from a mother who hardly speaks? A father who's never home? A house so empty that a baby blanket is your greatest comfort? Don't you deserve better, Charlie? Don't you deserve this?" she said, echoing the wish in his heart.

She knew his family, his house, and his secrets. She knew everything he'd been thinking, feeling, ever since Liam was taken. She knew . . .

"Wait." Charlie abruptly stood up, and the table shifted, the plate clattering. "Did you . . . let me remember Liam so that I would try to find him? So that I would discover the Asylum and find my way in here?"

She gazed calmly up at him, but there was a coolness in her eyes. "Family is all that matters, Kieran."

"Don't call me that. . . ."

"You and I are alike, aren't we? Willing to do anything for family, yes?"

Charlie's heart raced. He had played his role in this little play exactly as Brona had scripted it—seek out Liam, play the hero, and walk willingly into the Asylum like a mouse to the cheese. *Snap.*

He shook his head, trying to rid his mind of her voice. He scrubbed the residual warmth of her hand from his cheek. He wasn't like her. They weren't the same. Liam wanted to come home. She was holding him here against his will. She'd manipulated him, the way she'd manipulated Charlie into coming here.

For how many other kids had it been the same?

"Tell me what happens when they turn eighteen," Charlie demanded.

Brona's features turned to stone, and she rose, smoothed her dress around her hips, and crossed to the door. Before leaving, she turned back to him and in an airy, distant voice that sent a chill down Charlie's spine, she said, "I set them all free."

ꙮ 28 ꙮ

Charlie sat alone, gripping the edge of the couch cushion, replaying what Brona had said. She had compared herself to him—had said they were the same, would do anything to save their families. But he wasn't her family; she could say he was Kieran—it didn't make it true.

If Brona had been trying to convince him to stay with her by telling him what she had done to get him here, it had backfired. How could someone who professed to care for children in need above all else be the same person who had taken Liam away and left Charlie with his memories and no answers, wondering if he was crazy? How could someone who professed to love him also hurt him so badly? As these confusing thoughts swirled in his mind, Charlie realized it wasn't the first time he'd felt this sort of sting. His real mother had loved him dearly his entire life, and that hadn't kept her from disappearing for the last two years, as if he didn't even matter. Her words from that stretcher had burned him like a brand, and he had turned his own fiery words back on her, wounding her too.

Maybe he and Brona weren't so different after all.

His thoughts were interrupted by Michael, who knocked on the drawing room's open doorframe. "Can I bother you for a moment?"

Charlie practically ran to the door. He desperately wanted to be bothered, if only to get out of his own head. "Did you guys find out anything more about the wine cellar?"

Michael tipped his head for Charlie to follow him into the entry, where Ana stood waiting for them.

Ana held up an imaginary cup and saucer, pinky finger raised. "Did you learn anything useful from your mid-morning tea with Brona?"

"Only that we have to find a way out of here," Charlie said.

"Duh," she said with a dry laugh.

"We didn't find out anything more," Michael said, "but Jonathon's going to keep looking through the books, and he made me promise to help you guys out here."

"How?"

"Well, if you're right about what's behind that wine cabinet, you may be the best source of information we have. Do you think there's more where that came from?"

"Maybe?" Charlie said very noncommittally. He had no idea what else might be lurking in the inky shadows and corners of his mind.

"If you're okay with it," Michael said, "I'd like to mine your brain a little." When Charlie hesitated, Michael said with a mischievous grin and a wink, "I promise it won't hurt."

Charlie could see why Michael was the leader here. Despite their awkward first moments, Michael had a kind manner and gentle demeanor. Charlie trusted him. He returned the smile. "I don't really know what you mean, but I'm game."

"Good! Come on." Michael led them up the stairs. "All you have to do is listen. Whenever we get some new arrivals, we have a sort of meeting, to get to know each other, tell whatever bits of our stories we want to share, that sort of thing—to make your landing as soft as possible. Liam's gathering some people, and I figure once they start talking, maybe it will trigger something for you, like it did when I talked about the wine smuggling."

Now Charlie understood. A detail about someone's time here that meant little to them might open up a memory for him that would help them crack the lock or get their chains off. The idea of chatting with a larger group, however, gave him pause. "Did you tell all these people about the wine cellar?"

"Oh, no. They don't know what we're up to. They're just being friendly. But *if* you figure out how to get out of here, I think there might be some kids who would want to know about it."

"Why only some?" Ana said.

"Well, of the thirty-some kids who live here, only about half would want to leave."

"Half?" Ana balked. "That's crazy! Why would anyone want to stay here?"

Michael reached the landing and turned. "Ana, there are as many opinions about this place as there are people. In general, however, I would say we fall into two groups: those who are relieved to have erased themselves and are content to be here until they turn eighteen, and those who don't love the Asylum, and would maybe want to leave, but not if it means their mistakes return. The kids who would want to take their chains off and go right back into whatever mess they'd gotten away from, though? There aren't many of those. Brona makes it pretty clear what's happening during your gathering. It's not something anyone agrees to lightly."

"Who could be content to stay here?" asked Ana. "In a

creepy old house with a noose around your neck all day?"

"Fink?" Charlie guessed. Surely someone who wouldn't even talk about what he'd done would want to stay.

"Who knows?" Michael replied.

"But this isn't a life!" Ana said. "Sure, you can't hurt yourself or anyone else while you're here. But there's no pleasure either! The food tastes like paste, I haven't heard a single person laugh, and there's nothing to do but read the same books and play the same games all day long."

Cody, who had been climbing the stairs behind them, working a Rubik's Cube, stopped next to Ana, holding up a completely red side. "I did this," he offered.

Ana growled in frustration, and Cody giggled.

"There are a few of us"—Michael pointed to Cody—"who would like to try the path Jonathon took. Escape. Before turning eighteen, chain on, and see what kind of life they can pull together without a past or a family. Ultimately, however, none of this matters, since none of us know how to get out. You, Charlie, may hold the answer."

The twinkle in Michael's eye gave Charlie an uneasy stomach. "Or not. . . ."

Michael put his arm around Charlie's shoulder. "There is clearly something different about you. I know this is a long shot. All you have to do is listen, okay?"

Charlie nodded.

Michael led them to a door on their far left that once again seemed like a distant echo in the recesses of Charlie's mind. The strange memories were getting stronger. He had not yet been in this part of the house, and yet he knew. *The classroom.*

Two boys and a girl were chatting at the front of the large room, and four more girls sat farther back, clustered in antique wooden chairs with built-in writing surfaces. All the desks faced a huge blackboard hanging on the wall. Charlie blinked; he knew that board. He could feel chalk between his fingers, hear the scratching of talc against slate, and smell the dusty cloud made by pounding erasers.

But Charlie's school used whiteboards. He'd never touched a chalk eraser in his life.

"Hey, Booper!" Liam said playfully, standing up from one of the front-row desks, which Cody immediately stole while continuing to work his Rubik's Cube. Liam came to Charlie's side, punched him playfully, and whispered, "I know you're going to figure everything out." If he was attempting to instill Charlie with confidence, it did the exact opposite. Charlie startled as Liam announced loudly, "Hey everyone! This is my brother, Charlie. And this is his best friend, Ana."

"Wow . . . so it's true," one of the boys said, taking a step closer.

"Charlie, that's Kellen." Liam introduced them. "And that's Sasha and Amir."

Charlie guessed the blond, redhead, and black-haired one were in their midteens. He nodded to each in turn before asking, "So what's true?"

Kellen pointed at Charlie's eternity-stone necklace. "Brona's got some weird thing for you, right?"

Charlie wanted to deny it but knew there was no point. "Yeah, I guess so. But it's only because she thinks I'm somebody I'm not."

"Who does she think you are?" Amir asked.

"Her son."

"Whoa," Cody said, looking up.

Kellen let out a long, low whistle, and the other two boys stared at him with disbelief.

"Her son?" Amir looked at Charlie with a mix of fascination and fear. "I didn't know she had a kid."

"I haven't heard any stories about Brona's family," said Sasha.

"I don't think she likes to talk about it," Charlie said. Images of the burning thatch home and the *Randolph* flashed in his mind.

"I'm not surprised," Kellen said. "Brona's the biggest keeper of all of us."

Ana's ears perked up immediately. "What do you mean?"

"Well, Brona's got a key and a chain," Sasha said, "just like everyone here. She keeps it tucked into that old dress thing she wears, but she's always got it on. At least I think she does."

"Wait. Why would Brona have one?" Ana said.

Sasha just shrugged.

"Maybe she just needs a key to open the door." The group of girls from the back of the room had come up to join the conversation, and a brown-skinned teenager with long, dark hair who was leading the three younger girls was speaking. "She's the one who makes the keys, isn't she? She might just need one for the lock."

Ana was like a foxhound on a scent. "Hi, I'm Ana," she said.

"Neha," the older girl replied.

"Nice to meet you, Neha. So whatever the deal with her key is, it must have been made a long time ago, right? Back when her clothes and the Asylum and all this stuff in it was new?"

Neha crossed her arms thoughtfully. There was a calm, deliberate manner to her movements, which stood in sharp contrast to Ana, who looked like she was about to climb the walls. "Well, that's the big mystery, now isn't it? Brona doesn't exactly tell anyone much about herself, and I guess it doesn't really matter. We're one big, damaged family here—

mistakes and all, whether we like it or not. Brona might be a bit odd sometimes, even creepy, but if there's one thing I know, it's how much she cares about every kid in this place."

"So why are you here?" Ana asked.

Charlie knew Ana's question was more out of curiosity than rudeness, but it still made him cringe. They had just met this person, and here was Ana, asking her to tell them the most painful decision of her life. "Neha, you don't have to tell us if you don't want to."

"I don't, but I will," Neha said, her velvety voice soothing Charlie's anxiety. "It all seems rather . . . pointless now, but I left my life because I couldn't bear how much of a disappointment I was to my parents."

"What did you do?" Ana said.

"It was more about what I *didn't* do. I didn't live up to 'my potential,' as my dad would probably say."

"Grades?"

"No, I was fine in school. It was all about sports for my parents. My parents were both world-class athletes: my mom was a sprinter, my dad was a distance runner. They met at the Olympic trials. I, on the other hand, have the coordination of a baked potato. I embarrassed myself at every sport I tried: soccer, basketball, baseball, golf. I'm slow; I can't hit, catch, or kick a ball; I hated everything about the practices and the games. No matter how clear it was that sports just weren't my thing, they always told me to just try harder, that I would find my way sooner or later. They would get frustrated when I told them I didn't like what I was doing; they would get angry when they felt like I wasn't trying my best. The pressure of making them happy got to be too much. When I didn't even make the high school track team, I decided I didn't want to deal with seeing their disappointment anymore. I came here instead."

Charlie could feel Michael's eyes on him, watching eagerly to see if anything she was saying had mined any sort of thought or memory from his brain.

Nothing.

"Do you regret it now?" Ana said. "Would you go back home, if you could?"

Neha tipped her head and quietly stared at Ana before saying, "Those are actually two very different questions." She turned with an arm outstretched and introduced the three other girls to Charlie and Ana: Amanda, the girl who thought she had killed her grandfather; Shayla, a very young girl who clutched Neha's pant leg; and Madison, who Charlie guessed was his age.

"I'm the one with the grade problem you asked Neha about," Madison said with sarcastic pride, reaching forward to shake their hands.

"Is that why you're here?" Charlie said.

"Basically. I was all Ds and Fs in school, and hated every minute of it. My mom and stepdad were jerks about it. I just wanted out. It wasn't until I got here that Neha figured out I was dyslexic." She threw her arm around Neha and squeezed.

"Just like my cousin," Neha said, hugging her back with a smile.

Ana shook her head. "I can't believe Brona would take you away for *that*. Your life, for a learning disorder that was never diagnosed? You didn't even *do* anything!"

Michael held out a hand and pulled some desks around to form a circle. He signaled for everyone to sit before answering. "That's not how Brona thinks about it. She's thrilled when someone makes the wish without the burden of a huge mistake. They get the gift of life here without the regrets. In her mind, *no matter what*, the Asylum is *better* than the outside world. Always. Out there is just too painful."

"But a stolen book report?" Ana said. "A couple of Ds? How many other kids are here for—no offense, Madison—such dumb reasons?"

"Ana, you're missing my point. There is no 'dumb reason' to make the wish in Brona's eyes. She offered us a ticket out of a world with pain and into a place of understanding. She never gets angry or frustrated with us. She would never

271

tell us we were wrong to feel the way we felt. Shame, embarrassment, regret, whatever."

"But . . . don't you eventually get over all that? I mean, surely everyone realizes making the wish was a mistake, right?"

"No, it wasn't." The words came from the little girl who had clung to Neha's leg. She had nervous fingers that twisted the hem of her shirt and a gaze that flitted from face to face. As she spoke, tears welled up in her eyes. "I'll never leave, because I killed Piper." She leaned against Neha's side, hiding her face in shame.

Neha stroked the girl's hair. "Piper was Shayla's dog. She wandered into the road after the front door was accidentally left open." The tremors of Shayla's shoulders left no doubt who had been the last one to use the door. The older kids all watched the tiny girl, looking like they might cry right along with her.

For the next hour, Ana and Charlie listened to each tale of landing in the Asylum: how Amir could never live up to the example his amazing older sister set; how Kellen had moved to Kingsberg and promptly become the target of a bully, and had no friends to rely on; how Sasha had embarrassed her best friend in front of the whole school and knew their friendship would never be the same; and more. They also told Charlie and Ana everything they knew about the Asylum, but nothing they said triggered any flashes of knowledge for Charlie.

They weren't any closer to getting out, but Charlie at least felt less alone.

They all hung out again after lunch, getting to know each other and playing some of the old board games in the game room. Just before it was time to break for dinner, Charlie went in search of Jonathon, who had been notably absent, but he hadn't made it halfway down the hallway before Brona intercepted him.

"Charlie, forgive me." She came to him, head bowed and hands held out for his. He couldn't do anything but stare at them. "I understand you might feel frustrated and angry with me. Of course you'd feel hurt to know that I hadn't been truthful with you about how you came to be here. I'm sorry."

Charlie *was* angry with her, but as she stood apologetically before him, he softened. If she truly believed he was her son, wouldn't he *expect* her to do anything to be with her child? Wasn't that what a good mother would do? Still, he didn't know what to say, and so he said nothing.

"Please, come with me to dinner. I want to show you something that might help you understand this place a bit better."

She led him to the dining hall, where a fair number of kids had already lined up and appeared to be waiting for her. Brona had Charlie stand beside her at the entrance to the dining hall as she greeted every child with a hug, kneeling if necessary. Charlie wondered if there was something magical in Brona's embrace, as many of them seemed to feel the same way he did when she touched them. "I'm so glad you are here," she said every time.

Before each child could pass, though, Brona helped each of them peer through their key's clover-shaped handle. She would stand by as they relived whatever experience had made them wish they'd never been born. It was almost like a prayer—somber and thoughtful. At the end of each memory, Brona would kiss the child on the forehead, smile, and let them pass.

Charlie wasn't aware he was grimacing at this spectacle until Brona looked at him and with sad eyes said, "I know this might seem cruel, but everyone must remember why they chose the Asylum. It's this choice that holds our family together. No one should ever forget."

At this, Charlie glanced down at Brona's neck, where a few links of her own chain were barely visible over the high collar of her dress, just as Sasha had said. His desire to ask her about it was outweighed by his fear of what her key might hold.

Ana was the last one in line, and when she came to the front, she refused the entire affair, recoiling from Brona's touch, arms crossed defiantly over her key. If this bothered Brona, she didn't show it; rather, it seemed like she expected it. "Remembering why we are here is most painful for new arrivals. You don't need to do anything you're not ready to do, Ana."

Ana flashed Brona a sarcastic smile and walked past them into the dining hall.

Charlie worried for a moment that Brona would make him look into his own key, but then he recalled that his was upstairs. There was no hole in his pendant to peer through.

When all the children were seated, Brona let Charlie eat with his friends, but she came to his side as he was leaving, to escort him to his room after dinner.

She left him alone briefly to tuck in the younger children. Though the wind howled distantly around the Asylum at all hours of the day, the sounds came alive in the quiet of evening. Gusts whistled through the tree limbs, and Charlie's windows rattled in their panes. A branch of the nearby oak rubbed back and forth against the glass like a fingernail.

Brona returned with a serene expression and floated into one of the high-back chairs by the fire, book in hand. She pointedly avoided revisiting their conversations from earlier in the day, instead reading more fairy tales to Charlie. But he heard none of it, his mind too full of everything he'd learned and all the mysteries they had yet to solve. He tried to focus on the only thing that mattered—finding a way out before Jonathon's birthday—but he struggled. His head swam with questions about Brona, the Asylum, and the other kids. Was Brona a savior or a captor? Had the children here been rescued or imprisoned? Was life here better or worse than the real world? The answer always seemed to be C: all of the above, which didn't make sense at all.

It was well past eleven on the grandfather clock in the corner of the room when Brona finally rose, tucked Charlie's blanket under his chin, and kissed him on the cheek. "Good night, a stór."

The door clicked shut, leaving Charlie to wonder how it was possible to feel so cherished and so alone at the same time.

᷈ 29 ᷈

Charlie stared into the glowing embers of his fire, wondering how much time he should wait before making his move. When all seemed quiet, he sat up and reached for his pants, but he flopped back down and pulled up the blanket at the sound of footsteps pacing outside his door. She was coming back.

The latch clicked open and the hinges creaked. He clamped his eyes shut and slowed his breathing to appear asleep. She came close, looming over him. Had she done this last night while he slept?

Suddenly her hand clamped painfully down on his mouth and nose. Charlie struggled for a breath that wouldn't come, and his eyes shot open. He scrambled up the headboard and clawed at her hand, struggling and failing to cry for help.

"Would you shut up?" came Ana's voice beside his ear.

"Shhhh!" Liam said behind her.

Charlie collapsed back onto his pillow, his fear melting. Ana loosened her grip enough for him to yank her hand away.

"What are you doing?" he whispered. "Are you trying to scare me to death?"

"Um, no. We're trying to get out of here, dummy. We came up with a plan after Brona took you away for your adorable mother-son time. Come on, get dressed."

"Turn around," he told Ana, and pulled off his nightshirt. "Did you guys already go down to the wine cellar?"

Liam put a finger to his lips, and his other hand flew up to silence them. Charlie froze middressing. Liam tiptoed to the door and put his ear to the wood. After a long minute, he let out a breath and beckoned them over. "I think she's gone. Come on."

With a scratch and a hiss, Liam lit a lantern. The scent of the match tip prickled Charlie's nose.

Moonlight through the tree branches dappled the carpet of the grand stairway. It didn't seem possible to Charlie that this same moon beamed down on his home a few miles away. Were his mom and dad, the couple with no kids, sleeping peacefully at this very moment?

"So we checked out the basement after dinner." Ana's voice echoed in the empty and vast entry hall, despite her efforts to keep quiet.

"We tried every lock combination we could think of," Liam said even lower, "but it didn't budge. Then Ana told us about your dreams." He looked up, and the sparkle of his eyes in the moonlight told Charlie how hopeful he was that Charlie would save the day.

"You told them?" Charlie asked Ana.

"I had to, Charlie—everyone wanted to know why Brona's been so weird about you. Jonathon and Michael were a little freaked out; they don't think it's a good sign."

"Oh, really?" Charlie said sarcastically.

Liam put his hand up, like he was in class. Charlie nodded for him to go ahead. "So Brona thinks you're her son? Because that doesn't make any sense, right? I mean, I'm your brother, and she doesn't think I'm anything special."

"Brona said she's sure of it. She said she knew I was Kieran from the minute she saw me the night she gathered you."

Liam's forehead crinkled. "But she—"

A lantern at the top of the stairs stole their attention. The absence of rustling fabric meant it wasn't Brona, but it wasn't until the light was a few feet away that he made out Jonathon's face. In the glow of the flame, he seemed years

279

older. His cheeks were hollow, and his easy smile from two days ago was hard to imagine.

"Let's go." Jonathon didn't pause as he passed them and entered the doorway under the stairs. They followed.

"Where's Michael?" Charlie asked Ana.

"He's hanging back. If we aren't back in our beds in one hour, he's going to bring anyone else who wants to try to leave."

With a lilt of optimism, Liam asked Charlie, "Do you think you know the combination?"

"I have no idea," he answered, shrugging. "Brona didn't exactly whisper, 'Thirty-four . . . two . . . fourteen' before kissing me good night."

"Oh, it's not numbers, it's letters, like that old bike lock Dad used to have. It spells something."

"Six letters long," Ana said from the rear, her voice and footfalls echoing against the stone. "I thought for sure the code would be Kieran, but it didn't work."

Charlie was disappointed by this, as that would have been his first guess too. He stepped off the last stair and turned right. At the end of the corridor, Jonathon held up his lamp for Charlie. "Time to work your magic."

Glinting in the light, hanging from a door latch, was the most unusual lock Charlie had ever seen. The top of the contraption was like any lock at school, an upside-down U of metal. It was fastened, however, into a large brass cylinder that held six rotating rings, each decorated with the letters of the alphabet.

Charlie stepped closer. He spun one of the rings and felt a soft *clunk* with each letter change. Nothing about it was familiar.

"Can you think of anything from your dreams?" Jonathon asked in a low voice.

"Nothing specific that would fit a six-letter lock . . . ," Charlie said.

"Walk us through each one. I'll tell you when to stop."

"Okay, um, in the first one I wake up in a small cottage, super hungry—"

"Stop," Jonathon interrupted. "Put it in."

"What?"

"Spell out 'hungry.' On the lock."

Charlie did as he was told, but the lock didn't open.

Over the next hour, Charlie meticulously recounted each dream, stopping every few sentences to dial in any key six-letter words. They worked together, mining dozens of possibilities within the stories: thatch, mother, frozen, graves, blight, famine, typhus, loiter, orphan, asylum, and many, many more.

The lock stayed closed.

"That's it," Charlie said, his fingertips raw from the edges of the rings. "That's the last dream."

Jonathon sighed and his head fell forward.

"Here, let's go through it again!" Charlie said, rubbing his hands on his pants. "I probably just forgot something." He grabbed the lock and started to spin the letters, waiting for something familiar to pop into his head, but Jonathon put a hand over it.

"What has Brona told you since you got here?" Jonathon asked.

Charlie hesitated. "She said she'd have done anything to get me back. She said that she and I, and even everyone else in the Asylum, are a family. And family is all that matters. . . ."

Jonathon nodded with slow solemnity and took his hand away.

Was it that simple? Charlie dialed in F-A-M-I-L-Y. Maybe he did have the power to get them out after all. He took a breath and pulled the barrel downward.

It didn't budge.

"No!" Charlie yelled. He pulled the brass cylinder downward repeatedly before slamming it against the door.

Jonathon laced his fingers together atop his head and turned to pace the small hallway. Liam sat down in the corner.

Ana pushed past Charlie to yank at the lock herself.

She fine-tuned the letters into perfect position. It changed nothing.

"Where are you going?" Liam asked Jonathon, who was walking back toward the stairwell. "Aren't we going to keep trying?"

Jonathon stopped but didn't turn. "Brona wins. She got what she wanted. Her family's back together, and our families never will be. At least you and Liam have each other."

"Together . . . ," Charlie repeated slowly. He seized the lock from Ana's continued efforts. "Brona's family was never just her and me . . . I mean Kieran. Her family, her *whole* family, was six people."

"What?" Liam said, standing.

"My dad's name in the dreams was John, and there were four kids. Siobhan was the eldest, and then Kaitlyn, Kieran, and Nora." Charlie spun the first letter to J for John, then B for Brona, and the rest. "The reason no word works is 'cause it's not a word!"

J-B-S-K-K-N

Without even a pull, the lock fell open.

Jonathon was at Charlie's side before the lock was off the latch.

"You did it, Charlie!" Liam said, almost tackling him from behind.

"Now let's see if you're right about a passage out of here," Jonathon said. He swung the latch open and pushed. Air escaped around every edge of the door, blowing back the dust at their feet. The taste of salt filled his mouth, and a scent permeated the air, something sweet and fragrant.

Ana held her lantern aloft and stepped forward into a cavernous cellar. Rows of wine racks stood empty except for a thick layer of white dust.

I've been here before, Charlie thought. *I know this room.* He could hear his pulse in his ears. Despite the room being twice the size of the hallway, the idea of entering it felt more stifling than crawling face-first into a sleeping bag.

Jonathon and Liam entered the cellar. When Charlie didn't budge from the threshold, Liam turned back. "You okay?"

"Yeah, I'm good," he lied. Charlie forced himself to take baby steps forward onto the dirt-floored chamber. The effort it required was almost more than he possessed. "I feel really weird."

"So which one is it?" Jonathon asked, scanning the racks.

Charlie pointed to the back left corner.

"Come on!" Ana took his hand and tried to pull Charlie with her, but he was like an unwilling puppy on a leash.

"It's the last one," Charlie croaked, breathing now almost impossible.

Jonathon and Liam set down their lanterns and searched the wine cabinet like bloodhounds, fingers running along the edges, eyes darting around each side. "How does it open, Charlie?" Jonathon said.

"You just need to pull it—there should be a track in the floor." Again, the information that came from him was as much a surprise to Charlie as it was to the others.

Jonathon got down on his hands and knees. "Found it." He swept his foot like he was clearing home plate. There was a glint of metal. Liam dropped down beside him, and within seconds they had exposed a curved silvery track, extending from the front corner of the wood. They scooped dirt out of the groove with their fingertips, making way for the shelf's edge to slide within it.

Jonathon stood and pulled the cabinet toward him. It didn't budge. Ana and Liam joined him, each trying to make the wood budge. "Come on!" Jonathon begged— then, finally, there was a creak. The cabinet shifted, and one side pivoted forward an inch. Jonathon wrapped his fingers around the exposed edge, scraping the cabinet open along the track. Charlie could breathe easier with each inch it opened.

Liam held a lantern forward. The flickering wick was reflected in the glistening walls of a salt-mine shaft, like there were diamonds embedded in it.

Then he let out a scream. His lantern clattered to the ground but remained lit.

The rest of them looked past him, deeper into the shaft. Extending as far as they could see in the lantern light, rows and rows of low cots lined the shaft.

And lying atop each cot was a body.

ᴥ 30 ᴖ

Liam buried his face in Charlie's flank, whimpering.

"Oh . . . ," Jonathon sighed, as if he'd just heard the answer to an unasked question.

Charlie clutched Liam and tried to take in what he was seeing. The long, narrow mine shaft extended beyond the reach of their light; so did the cots. He could count seven on either side before darkness took over.

Fresh flowers overflowed from vases beside every cot—roses, lilies, and daisies—their beauty contradicting the macabre scene. The floral aroma Charlie had sensed when entering the wine cellar was now thick and cloying.

"Are they dead?" Liam asked, his question hot against Charlie's skin.

Charlie didn't dare answer. He moved into the corridor and peered down at the nearest cot. A young woman lay on her back with her hands crossed peacefully over her stomach. Her clothes were eerily familiar: leather boots; a gingham cotton dress cinched at the waist and ballooned at the sleeve, a matching pink bonnet tied beneath her chin, covering ringlet curls. She looked like she had just stepped off the *Randolph* and had lain down to take a nap. A century-and-a-half-long nap.

If her clothes told the story, this girl had been here an impossibly long time.

Ana was at the side of a young man wearing knickers and a vest over a linen shirt. With a courage Charlie didn't possess, she reached out to touch the cloth of his vest. She gasped and moved away so fast, she almost fell over backward. Charlie felt Liam's fingers dig deeper into his side.

"This one is breathing!" Ana said. "He's alive!"

Jonathon knelt down by the young woman with the pink bonnet and touched her cheek. "Ana's right. She's warm."

"That's not even possible!" Ana said. "They're like a hundred years old."

"Guys . . . ," Charlie said hesitantly, fighting the urge to run. "It doesn't matter. If there's an escape route down this tunnel, we have to find it. Ana, grab the lantern. Let's go."

Jonathon joined Ana in the lead. Charlie walked behind them, whispering into the top of Liam's head, "It's going to be okay, bud, don't worry." He tried not to look at the beds and the lives they held, but it was impossible to ignore when the handful of bodies they could see when they opened the door became dozens. Bonnets changed to pillbox hats, then cloches, before headwear disappeared altogether; knickers changed to pants, which changed to shorts. Skirts shortened, then lengthened, shortened again, and then mostly disappeared, replaced by shorts as well. Each person rested comfortably in the same casketlike position.

And they all appeared to be the same age. Eighteen.

There were no forks in the path, only twists and turns for what seemed like an eternity.

"How much farther?" Liam asked after fifteen minutes.

Charlie wasn't sure if Liam was referring to the bodies or the tunnel. He didn't have an answer to either. Then Jonathon slowed.

"What?" Charlie asked, straining to see down the shaft.

But Jonathon wasn't looking ahead. He was staring at the last two cots—the final bodies. A young woman wearing an Alicia Keys T-shirt lay on one; a heavyset young man in a plaid shirt and jeans on the other. Jonathon's lantern arm dropped to his side. "Brooke and Luke," he said weakly. "They're my friends."

In the silence, Charlie thought he heard a faint noise behind them. He had terrifying visions of the kids all waking up and following them.

"Jonathon," he said, "we need to keep moving."

"Right . . . ," Jonathon said, resigned. He started to move forward but then froze. One last cot stood in the tunnel. It was empty. Waiting.

"Jonathon, we need to go!" Charlie said, sure he could still hear the sound behind them.

They all sped up, and Charlie wondered how much farther the shaft could possibly go. Within a few minutes, the sounds of their feet echoed differently, like the tunnel was getting smaller. The ceiling lowered with each step.

Ana saw it before Charlie.

"No . . . ," she said. "No!"

Ana ran forward, her hands searching for a gap or hole in the rubble that blocked their path, but Charlie could see all he needed from where he stood. The tunnel had caved in, and there was no way past it.

The familiar scratch and sizzle of a match strike filled the air. Charlie and his friends spun around.

"Jonathon," Brona said softly, her head tilted. "Surely you didn't think I would let you take my son away from me, did you?"

31

Ana was immediately at Charlie's side. She grabbed his wrist and squared her footing, but she need not have bothered. Brona's attention was, instead, on Jonathon. She moved within inches of him and touched his key with a finger. "I expected so much better of you."

Jonathon closed his eyes and turned his head away, as if enduring physical pain.

"This is how you repay me? I erased your pain and you try to steal my child?" She spoke only barely above a steely whisper. "And what was your plan? Bring these three to live in your garage apartment with you and mow lawns for the rest of your forgotten lives?"

"At least they'd have lives," Jonathon said quietly, unable to look into Brona's face.

"Your lives are *here*! Have you forgotten that you *asked* to be taken away? I didn't steal your life, Jonathon—I granted your wish." Her cheeks reddened and her jaw tightened.

Jonathon winced with each word.

"What about me?" Ana demanded.

Brona took in a large breath to steady herself before turning, calmed, to Ana. "What about you, my dear?"

"Why won't you let me go? I didn't cause anyone pain. I just came here to get Liam!"

"Ana," Brona said, her voice even. "You think you know what is best, but you don't. You have no idea what life has in store for you."

"Oh, and you do?"

"Yes, I do!" Brona's fragile composure began to crack. "Ana, the world you left behind when you came here is nothing but agony. It is a torture chamber. Look at this poor child," she said, pointing toward Jonathon, who continued to stare motionless at the floor. "What do you think his future would be if I released him? A life of regret and solitude. *That* is the real world, my child. Life will knock you down, and when you get up again, it will kick you down again even harder. You might be lucky enough to feel love so immense that you burst with happiness, only to have it ripped away!"

Brona's eyes blazed in the reflected lantern light.

"You don't know that!" Ana yelled.

"Outside these walls," Brona roared back, "sorrow and loss lurk at every corner! They are sharpening their claws, always ready, waiting to pounce. *This place*, the Asylum, is the greatest gift you will ever receive. This is where the pain stops. You are simply too young and reckless to understand it."

Images from Charlie's dreams flickered through his mind as Brona spoke. Three daughters, taken from her one by one. A loving husband in terrible pain. A home lost, and a son stolen.

"Look," Ana said, "I'm sorry your life was a huge bummer, but mine isn't, thank you very much! And neither is Charlie's."

Ana looked at Charlie like she was hoping he would back her up, but he just nodded weakly. His life was hard to characterize as "pretty good" these days. Having Liam back would certainly help, but between his wisp of a mom and his rarely there dad, his days were more realistically somewhere between "fairly depressing" and "downright sad."

"Yes, child. My life was a *bummer*," Brona said, spitting the last word. "You cannot know."

"So, what? You want us to stay here until we're eighteen and become one of those . . . *things* back there? *That's* the glorious future you have for us? They might as well be dead!"

Brona's eyes pierced Ana as she spoke, each word sharp. "They are at peace." With a slight shake of her head, Brona took another breath and smoothed the fabric of her skirt. She stood up a bit straighter and tucked her hair behind her ears. "Jonathon. You haven't told them, have you?"

He gave no response, cast in stone.

"I know you haven't. I know so much more than any of you understand. They need to know."

Jonathon's eyes were closed, but that didn't stop a tear from escaping, falling from the tip of his nose. "Please. Don't."

"I don't see how you are in any position to ask for favors," she said, gently wiping the next tear from his cheek. "Do you want to tell them, or shall I?"

Charlie felt sick watching her soothe Jonathon while so clearly hurting him with her words.

"Sneaking around in the middle of the night," Brona said, "trying to take my children from me. Come now. It's time they knew. They need to know what they are truly asking for."

"I'll stay!" Jonathon said, looking up for the first time, his eyes imploring. "This isn't about me. Please, just let them all leave. None of them should even be here."

Brona made a small *tsk* sound as she shook her head. "Absolutely not."

"Jonathon," Ana said, "we don't care what she tells us. It changes nothing." Charlie nodded.

"Please," Jonathon said to Brona, "I was going to tell him. I'm just not ready yet."

Brona took a step aside, giving Jonathon the floor. She crossed her arms and assumed a relaxed posture, her face unchanged. "Take all the time you need."

Charlie stepped forward, into the path of Jonathon's stare, and said, "Hey, man, it's okay, whatever it is. Just tell us."

Jonathon's steely anger melted away. Sorrow replaced it, stirring a flurry of butterflies in Charlie's gut.

"Charlie . . . I need you to look into my key."

"What?"

"Please, just do it. I don't think I can say it again." He stepped in front of Charlie and held his key in the air, the chain sagging.

"But you told us no one can see the memory in a key except the person wearing it."

Jonathon shook his head. "No. I said only people *within* the memory can see it. You'll be able to see just fine."

Closing one eye, Charlie peered through the clover-shaped space in the key. At first he saw Jonathon before him, eyes closed, two tears making their way down his cheeks. But then Jonathon's face blurred and faded away completely, leaving nothing but white light.

Colors emerged like a ship coming through dense fog. First came grass, increasingly green across a wide-open field. Next, a row of trees appeared in the distance, perfectly spaced, marking a property line.

Charlie felt water seep between his toes. He looked down and found his feet bare and his body clad in shorts and a T-shirt he hadn't worn in years. The smell of pine and campfires surrounded him.

"Ana!" he shouted. "Jonathon!"

No response.

A powder-blue pickup truck with a white hood passed by on a dirt road, kicking up a plume of dust. It looked exactly like the beat-up old Ford that Grandpa's neighbor, Mr. Trummel, used to drive. It couldn't be Mr. Trummel, of course—he'd had a stroke last summer—but Charlie had never seen another truck quite like it.

As the dust settled back down, Charlie was able to see across the street. The sight stole his breath.

Through another row of trees sat his grandparents' cabin. The sign at the head of the driveway, O'REILLY'S FISHING HOLE, was unmistakable. Beyond the house, he could see the glint of Knife Lake in the midmorning sun.

Charlie had never seen a more welcome sight in his life.

He had no idea how he had gotten to Minnesota, but he knew his family was near. Would they remember him? He sprinted across the field toward the cabin. Surely if he made contact with someone here, it would anchor him back in the real world.

He slowed, however, when he saw someone walking toward him: a boy carrying a large bag. Charlie stopped and waited, only recognizing Jonathon when he was a few yards away. He looked different. Rounder. Softer. He was six inches too short and wore a tank top that revealed skinny arms, not so different from his own.

"What are you staring at?" Jonathon said. He sounded like he'd like to punch Charlie in the shoulder if his hands weren't full. Sunlight shimmered off his dewy peach-fuzz mustache.

"Jonathon?" Charlie whispered.

"Yeah?"

"What is going on?"

"What do you mean? Why are you acting like an idiot?" Jonathon passed him and set the bundle on the grass. "Check it out. I grabbed the lighter when Grandma wasn't looking."

Charlie turned. Sparklers, bottle rockets, and Roman candles. He felt his breathing get ragged.

"Jonathon . . . who am I?"

Jonathon looked up, annoyed. "What the hell are you talking about? I go inside for five minutes and you get amnesia?"

Charlie tried to settle the lump in his throat.

"Okay, I'll play along," Jonathon said. "Let me guess. You are . . . a dork? Oooh, oooh, oooh," he said, now putting his hand in the air like an overeager student. "I got it! You're the stupid little brother I'm stuck with for all eternity!" Jonathon's face fell flat, and he rolled his eyes before turning back to the fireworks.

Charlie counted down as they each burned though three sparklers. He hoped for more, but Jonathon was ready to move on.

The Roman candles were next. Charlie watched the first one streak into the sky, its four balls of fire exploding loudly. *Dad heard that one,* Charlie realized, suddenly remembering the exact words of Jonathon's story. *He started looking for us the minute he heard the first explosion.*

Charlie watched Jonathon whoop and holler as the second candle sprayed across the sky, this one launched from his hand like a gun. Charlie's head spun as the horror of his situation finally found purchase. He knew how this story ended for the little brother.

And he was the little brother.

He wanted off this ride. Now. "Here! Let me hold that

one!" Charlie said, clawing at his brother's arm, terror electrifying his every nerve.

"Stop it!" Jonathon said, swatting Charlie's hands away as the third Roman candle shot into the sky. "You're not old enough!"

Jonathon took the last one from the bag.

"Dude! Please!" Charlie said, jumping up to try to grab it. "Let me do this one. You have to give it to me!" He was furious at the fifteen-year-old Jonathon for being such a pompous fool, but he was also livid at the seventeen-year-old Jonathon for allowing him to relive this; relive being set on fire.

Jonathon held it high, out of Charlie's reach. "Charlie, step off!" He shoved him back. "You'll hurt yourself."

He held the lighter to the wick.

"Jonathon! Please!" Charlie said, backing away, hoping one of the two Jonathons would listen.

"JONATHON O'REILLY!"

Charlie spun around. His dad, sporting a beard Charlie hadn't seen in years, was marching across the field. His eyes were slits and his fists pumped at his sides. Charlie heard the thunk of the Roman candle hitting the earth ten feet away.

And that's when it went off. Four golden balls, all rocketing directly toward my brother.

"NO!" Charlie cried. He threw his arms over his head

and dropped to the ground. He held his breath and braced for the unimaginable.

He waited.

After ten ragged breaths, Charlie slowly lowered his arms and peeked out. In the dim lantern light, Brona stood behind Jonathon, one hand on his shoulder.

Jonathon's eyes were empty. "I'm so sorry, little brother."

ꙮ 32 ꙮ

If anyone spoke after that, Charlie didn't remember what they said. Brona marched them back past the eternal eighteen-year-olds, back into the Asylum. She delivered them, one by one, to their bedrooms.

Charlie couldn't feel his legs as they carried him. He didn't even care when Brona helped undress him for bed, pulling his arms from his sleeves like a toddler.

Brona guided him to bed, lifted his legs, and took a seat beside him. "I'm sorry. I lost my temper."

Charlie stared at her, dumbfounded. Her temper was the last thing on his mind at the moment.

"But now you understand. You know why I do what I

do. Don't you?" She rubbed his arm over and over. "I am sick when I think of the pain the world caused you. All I have ever wanted was to keep all of you safe. Even Jonathon. I still do." Brona reached into the folds of her dress, into a hidden pocket, and produced a key ring. It held dozens of keys of varying sizes. All had a cloverleaf opening in the handle. "But I think it is time you knew the whole truth about your brother." She removed a smaller key from the ring and held it in the air between them. "These keys aren't like the others. They're my memories, to share with whomever I choose. Let's start with this one."

A key ring full of memories. Dozens of pieces of history, all in her hand. Charlie stared at them with both fear and intense curiosity. What else did he not know? Slowly he pushed himself up onto elbows that felt shaky. He wanted the truth; he needed it.

Brona lowered the key to his eye.

Once again, he wasn't in his bed anymore. He was standing in the entry of the Asylum, Brona beside him. Was he Kieran or Charlie? He opened his mouth to speak but stopped when he saw Jonathon storming down the stairs toward them. This time he looked like the Jonathon Charlie knew.

"How could you bring him here?" Jonathon demanded of Brona. "Why?"

"He made his wish," Brona replied.

"He's only nine years old!"

"Liam is lucky, child. He discovered the truth so young. Now he doesn't have to suffer the way you have. Isn't that what you would want for your little brother?"

"I came here because I had to!" Jonathon trembled with anger. "He's going to live a meaningless life here because of a *book report*? How could you?"

"Jonathon, I would advise you to keep your voice low." Brona glanced up the staircase, to where Liam was likely meeting some of the other kids. "Now, you know I would bring every child in the world here if I could, but I must wait until they ask. Would you rather I wait until Liam does something he regrets even more? Something like what you did?"

Jonathon moaned in frustration. "Send him home. Please, I'm begging you."

"This is his home now."

"No!" he said, shaking his head. "You think you are some sort of savior, but you're not. You're the grim reaper!"

"Silence," Brona said, still quiet, but with the same glint in her eye Charlie had seen in the salt mines. "I saved you. I took you from your sad little life and brought you to a home full of warmth and calm. I gave you an escape from your shame, your guilt. I gave you peace."

"No, you didn't. You put me in a state of suspended animation. It's not the same!"

"You *ruined* Charlie—you ruined your whole family— and I took you in, erasing what you did, forever. What more would you have me do?"

Jonathon stood silent, his face so sharp Charlie could see the muscles at his temple knot. His knuckles blanched white.

Brona dropped her voice and advanced on Jonathon. "My dear, I know how you feel right now, I promise. But you don't get to play the hero now, trying to save Liam, to save your family. You don't have what it takes."

Jonathon said nothing.

"You played your part to help them." Brona circled him. "You left. Only Liam's family can bring him home now. Charlie, perhaps. Someone who didn't leave him behind. That was the choice you made."

Through gritted teeth, Jonathon said, "Please. Let Liam go."

"No. I think I will do quite the opposite." Brona moved to the portal and passed her hand over it. The oak door materialized beneath her fingers, and she pulled it open with a full-body tug. "If you truly have no more value for the life I offer here, if I am the monster you make me out to be, I will not keep you here." Jonathon didn't move; a look of horror transformed his face. Brona moved over and ushered him toward the door with surprising strength. "If you realize the mistake you're making, you know where we will be. Until then, I wish you luck."

Inches from the doorway, Jonathon began to struggle, pushing and prying her fingers off his upper arm. "No! Not without Liam."

Brona's fluid movement stood in stark contrast to Jonathon's flailing. "Liam is where he needs to be. You, it seems, are not."

"Stop!" Jonathon yelled as she heaved him over the threshold of the door. "Don't do this. Liam!" he called out. But Jonathon's voice was silenced as Brona swung the door shut, the echo of its closure drowning out the last trace of his pleas.

At the sound of the slamming door, Charlie found himself back in his room, in his bed, with Brona sitting placidly beside him.

"You kicked Jonathon out? He told us he escaped."

"I would surmise he felt that if he told you the truth about his leaving, it would require he tell you he was Liam's brother. And yours."

His brother. Once upon a time, there had been three O'Reilly boys.

"But why don't I remember him?" Charlie asked. When he thought of Jonathon, there was only the young man who coached his baseball team, who led them into the Asylum. Jonathon was a black hole in his memory, just as Liam had been to his parents.

"Because I made it that way," Brona said with a pleading smile. She reached out to take Charlie's hand, but he snatched it away.

"I don't get it," Charlie said. "Why?"

She looked at him sideways, appearing to weigh what to share. "After I first saw you, I wanted nothing more than to bring you home. But I would never take in a child who hasn't made the choice freely, and you are tenacious; you don't give up on anything, least of all your own life. So I helped you along."

"I . . . don't understand. . . ."

Brona took a deep breath. "After I saw you, it became everything to me for us to be together again. So I watched Liam like a hawk, and when he made the wish, I was ready. I let you remember him, knowing you would come after him."

"But," Charlie said, "you told me the first time you *ever* saw me was the night you came for Liam."

"No, my love. I said I first saw you when I came for your brother. I did not mean Liam. I first saw you when I came for Jonathon."

Charlie gripped the sheets, feeling like the bed was shifting underneath him.

Brona became more somber, though he couldn't tell if it was because of his reaction or the memory she was about to share. "I first came for Jonathon when he made his wish. I found him beside a hospital bed, sobbing next to the young brother he had burned. Filled with guilt and regret. That night became the most important night of my life. Bandages and tubes riddled your small body—" The pain of this memory danced across her features, and she covered her mouth with her hand. "You were unconscious, and a machine was breathing for you. The burns had spared your face, but you were so swollen. Even though you were covered in bandages and wounds, your beauty ran me through like a sword. My Kieran. You were so sick, but you were *alive*." She had a faraway look in her eyes and a distant smile on her lips, but then she pierced him with her gaze. "I had to bring you home."

Charlie swallowed so as not to scream. With a trembling voice, he said, "But if I was the one you wanted, why didn't you just take me? Why Jonathon, or Liam?"

Her brow furrowed. "Don't you understand yet, Charlie? I do not *snatch* children. I grant wishes. I take only those who ask."

Slowly the pieces started to fall into place in Charlie's

mind. "And I never asked . . . I never wished I had never been born until Jonathon told me to. Until Jonathon told me I could bring Liam back." He recalled her words from the key memory, right before she exiled him. "Jonathon truly believed I could save Liam. Because you told him I could."

She nodded.

"But it was all a lie. I can't."

"No," she said with a gentle shake of the head. "You can't."

"You tricked him into bringing me here!"

Brona shook this wording off as distasteful. "I *waited*. So patiently. But without Jonathon, you were happy."

Charlie's face flushed. "So you took Liam and watched as I tried to find anyone who remembered him. You watched as my mom . . ." He swallowed a sob. "You ruined our lives."

"Ruined is such a harsh word, a stór." She scooted closer to him on the bed, but Charlie sat up and moved away, gathering the blankets around him. "I tried to give you hope! I knew Jonathon was getting closer to you, scheming to bring you here, and so I gave you dreams of our life before. That way, you'd know me when you saw me. So it would be easier for you, when you arrived."

"But you took Liam as bait. His whole life, wiped away, just to bring me here!"

"Please, Kieran—Charlie. His life here is better—

308

everyone's is. And now we are together, again, finally. You and I . . ." Her eyes implored him to see it her way, to understand her truth.

And he did know her truth. Death, illness, heartbreak, and never-ending loss. He had no doubt that the eternally numb cocoon of the Asylum was preferable for her, after all she had endured.

But her truth wasn't his truth. Her pain wasn't his pain. Charlie carried plenty of regret with him, but no matter how earnestly she begged, this wasn't his choice. Not his, and not his brothers'. Not anymore.

"We want to go home!"

Brona's features shifted. Her warmth cooled and her eyes hardened. She sat up painfully straight and lifted his blanket in an attempt to tuck him in. He averted his face with his eyes closed.

"Stop it! You are not my mom! I want to go home!"

She stood, and with a soft "Good night, a stór," she was gone, the door locking behind her.

↜ 33 ↝

Liam sat silently beside Charlie at lunch the next day, their food long cold. Ana silently picked at a piece of bread across from them. They had exhausted all words, having talked for hours about Jonathon being Charlie and Liam's big brother, about Jonathon's lies, and about what would happen when Jonathon turned eighteen. Without an escape plan to offer, they agreed it was best to stay silent about the salt mines. The last thing they needed to add to the Asylum was mass panic.

Ana had spent the early morning searching for Jonathon, but he was nowhere to be found. Charlie was partly relieved;

he had no idea what he would even want to say to Jonathon right now.

"How is everyone doing?" came a voice from behind them. It was Michael. He sat down next to Ana heavily, dark bags beneath his eyes.

"Michael! We never saw you last night. What happened?" Ana asked.

"I walked into the hallway an hour after Jonathon had left, just like we planned, and Brona was standing there, arms crossed. She shooed me back into my room, and all I could do was stare at the ceiling, terrified for you guys. There was no way to warn you she was coming."

Charlie, however, had no interest in hearing about how Michael had or hadn't spent his last twelve hours, terrified or not. "You knew, didn't you?"

Michael didn't move for a moment, then nodded. "Yes. I knew Jonathon was your brother."

"From the moment we walked in, right?" Charlie said, recalling Jonathon's bizarre behavior when they'd arrived. "You knew I was the reason for his wish."

Michael nodded slowly again. "I've known about you for years—even you, Ana, Charlie's know-it-all bestie." He playfully nudged Ana, but she didn't respond. "I couldn't imagine why he'd bring you here, until he filled me in."

311

"Why didn't you say anything?" Charlie was more disappointed than curious.

"It wasn't my place to tell you, Charlie. If Jonathon had his way, you still wouldn't know. All he's ever wanted in this whole thing was to get you two home," he said, pointing at Charlie and Liam. "He never wanted to reveal the truth. He'd erased it for a reason. Everything he's done has simply been about getting Liam home, getting you two and your parents back together. He's been trying to do what's best for everyone. The same thing that made him make his original wish, I guess."

Charlie hung his head. He thought he'd been able to remember Liam because he was such a good brother—that he was stronger than whatever magic made everyone else forget. But there was nothing special about him. He was no better than his parents, not when it came to Jonathon. "I don't remember him at all. I remembered exactly what Brona wanted me to."

Ana reached across the table and put her hand on top of his. "I don't remember Jonathon either, Charlie."

"Yeah, but Ana, you're not part of our family."

Ana's face hardened. She pulled her hand away and sat back in her chair.

"You should have told me," Charlie said to Michael. "Or

Jonathon should have. Someone should have."

Michael tipped his head in thought. "I think he couldn't bring himself to tell you because he likes the *new* Charlie and Jonathon. You guys didn't really get along before. And there's no handbook for, like, *Interacting with Family Members Who Have Forgotten You Exist.*"

Charlie rubbed his face with his hands before dragging them slowly downward, pulling his cheeks and lowering his lids as he let out a moan of frustration.

"Dude, gross," Ana said. "I can practically see your brain when you do that."

Charlie let his hands drop to his lap. "You don't know where he is, do you?"

"Actually, I do," Michael said. "He's in the courtyard. Come on."

Michael pointed to an outer door Charlie had walked past but had never thought to open. For one, the driving snow was not particularly inviting, and two, it offered no chance of escape. The courtyard was completely surrounded by the walls of the house—sheer stone extending three stories up. Looking through the small window in the door, Charlie could see a curved bench encircling the largest tree, and seated, leaning against the bark, was a lump of a person partially covered by mounds of powdery white. Jonathon looked like a seated snowman.

"How long has he been out there?"

"Since before I got up," Michael said. "Maybe all night."

"All night? He must be frozen by now!"

"He's okay," Michael assured Charlie. "Remember, this is the Asylum. He's fine—at least his body is."

The door creaked loudly as Charlie pulled it inward, and flakes streamed through the opening. As he stepped outside, snow fell into his shoes, chilling his ankles. The wind whipped at his face and snow pelted against his ears. It should have been uncomfortable, but, in the magic of the Asylum, it was almost pleasant.

Jonathon didn't move, even after Charlie came to stand directly in front of him. There were dark circles beneath his eyes.

"I guess we have a lot of catching up to do," Charlie yelled over the wind, with an attempt at a smile.

Jonathon's face remained blank, making Charlie worry that maybe he was frozen after all.

"Jonathon?"

"You weren't supposed to find out."

"Like, ever?" Charlie's voice cracked. Everything he had done for the last year had been fueled by his desire to put his family back together. Jonathon was part of that family, whether he chose to be or not.

"I always wanted a big brother, you know," Charlie said.

"Yeah, well, I'm not the kind of brother you were probably thinking of."

"But you are."

"No, Charlie, I'm not," Jonathon said, finally meeting Charlie's eyes. "I wasn't this great guy who would grow up to coach the baseball team and buy kids breakfast. I was the kid who cut class and smoked with my friends. The one who was ignoring you during the times he wasn't giving you a hard time. That's the real me. You don't like me."

"What are you talking about? I totally like you."

"No, Charlie. You don't! You hate me. And after what I did to you—not just the fireworks, but everything about the way I treated you growing up—you have every right." Jonathon turned back to the snow. His words burned far worse than the driving flakes.

Charlie's mind flashed to the memory in Jonathon's key; to the person he had met in that field. *Stupid. Idiot. Dork.* That guy was a real jerk. But that wasn't the Jonathon he'd gotten to know in the last year.

"You were supposed to follow me here, save Liam, say goodbye to your trapped buddy Jonathon, and get back to your life."

315

"But I can't get Liam out. Forgiving him for stealing my book report wasn't enough."

Jonathon let out a sad little laugh. "Dude. Don't you get it yet?"

"What?"

"The whole catch-22 'forgiveness is the way out' thing? The fact that Liam had talked about Booper? I made all that up. None of it's real. I just said what I had to say to get you here."

So many lies. Charlie had never been punched in the stomach, but he was certain he knew exactly how it felt. "But if Liam never said that, how'd you know my nickname?"

"I'm your *brother*, Charlie! Who do you think came up with booping? I'm the original Booper! We shared a room for ten years, took baths together, played and fought together, slept right next to each other."

With each word, Charlie began to realize the extent of what was missing from his mind. Jonathon had a lifetime of memories—vacations, inside jokes, arguments—and so many of them included him. He thought of the Yellowstone picture. *Was Jonathon on that trip too?*

"Brona told me you could get Liam out. She said you were the brother who hadn't abandoned him, that you had a power I didn't, but it was a lie. She just wanted to trick me into bringing you here. And guess what? It worked. Game over."

Charlie had to sit down. In this intricate chess match, he was the captured king. Liam, Ana, and Jonathon were just pawns. Almost without thinking, he murmured, "How long do you knead dough for cinnamon rolls?"

Jonathon's stoic exterior temporarily cracked, and with a sad smile he said, "Until it feels like a baby's butt."

Charlie's heart broke. For Jonathon. For himself. For Liam and his parents. They had been shattered into a thousand pieces without even knowing it. And Jonathon had carried the burden of the truth—the entire truth, alone—this whole time. They sat quietly for a while before Charlie, still trying to make sense of all that had happened, said, "How did you know that Brona was going to leave me that note, telling me to talk to you?"

Jonathon looked at Charlie though heavy lids. "Come on, little brother. Think about it for a second."

And there it was. Brona had never written that note or rearranged his comics. She didn't have to. Jonathon had believed Charlie was the key to saving his baby brother—their baby brother.

"It was you," Charlie said slowly. "You left that note. You rearranged my comics."

"We have a winner."

"But how?" Charlie felt like he was stumbling around in a hall of mirrors, finding his way one moment, only to knock face-first into a glass wall at the next. "How'd you get in my house?"

"Nothing to it. Dad still leaves a key to our back door under the grill—"

Dad. Not "your dad," just *Dad.* Not "your back door," *our.*

"—and you can apparently drive a freight train past Mom these days without her noticing. She just said, 'Hi, Charlie,' as I walked through the house, never even turning around."

Their mom.

"Liam always messed with your comics, so I knew you'd think it was a sign from him. Then I snuck the note into your baseball bag at practice."

Jonathon's words peppered him like buckshot. Charlie struggled to make all the puzzle pieces fit. "But the note was in Liam's handwriting."

"It was in *our* handwriting."

Of course. Jonathon was an O'Reilly. Each bit of proof that he really was Charlie's lost big brother felt like a body blow to Charlie's guilty conscience.

"So what do we do now?" Charlie said. "Brona lied to you, you lied to me. I can't get anybody's chain off, and the mine shaft has collapsed. How do we get home?"

Jonathon shook chunks of snow from his head and brushed off his thighs. "Charlie, let me ask you something.

Do you remember me now?" There was an edge to his voice.

Charlie remembered the fireworks nightmare the same way he could recall an intense movie—it was a memory, but it wasn't *his* memory. He'd simply watched it. There was still no Jonathon in his mind prior to Coach Jonathon. His face burned and he wanted to say, "I'm sorry," but the words wouldn't come.

"I know who you are now," he finally sputtered, "and that's all that matters. We're in this together until we all get home."

That's when Jonathon looked at him with an expression he didn't expect: pity.

"Charlie, don't you get it? *We* aren't in this together. There is no we. There's you, Liam, and Ana. You three need to get home. That's the goal. That has always been the goal. I'm not going anywhere."

"That's ridiculous! We're not leaving without you." Charlie felt like he was trying to launch a lifeboat off this sinking ship, only to look up and see Jonathon still aboard, sawing away at the rope.

"I know you and Ana assumed there was some way to fix me. Fix my family—*our* family. But it's unfixable."

"Don't make that decision for me! All I've ever wanted in this whole messed-up situation was to get my brother back.

That includes you now." Charlie's eyes begin to sting, but not from the wind.

"Charlie, think about it. If I get this chain off and go home, everything comes back with me. The accident, your burns, Mom's tears, Dad's anger. All of it. Don't you get it? Why do you think Mom's a mess? What do you think made her so depressed? It was *me*, Charlie. It's my fault."

Charlie shook his head, but he thought again about the last couple years, even before Liam had disappeared. Mom had been well until that day years ago when he and Liam had come home to find her crying inconsolably in the kitchen. She couldn't tell them why—she said she didn't really know herself.

Two years since Jonathon had gravely injured him.

Jonathon hadn't simply burned Charlie; he had set their whole family on fire.

Charlie thought he was going to be sick. He stood up and raked his hands through his hair. Jonathon was right: there wasn't a fix. No matter what came to pass, his family would be broken. If Jonathon stayed here, they would never be whole, and if he came home, the damage of his mistake would come with him—Charlie's wounded body and his mother's wounded heart.

"I came here for a reason," Jonathon said calmly. "I'm not going back."

"At least come back unremembered, like you were before. You can mow yards and live above your boss's place and be my coach again. You promised you would come back!"

"I said a lot of things that weren't true."

"But you can't stay here and turn into one of those living corpses down there!"

"Charlie," he said, "maybe that's for the best."

His words landed like a bowling ball on Charlie's hot-air balloon of hope. "You can't be serious."

"I can't do this anymore, Charlie. Two years of looking into my key every night, reliving that nightmare, and now, knowing Brona used me to get to you . . . it's like I couldn't stop at ruining your life just once, and now Liam, and Ana, are all wrapped up in this mess. It's unbearable." Then a calm came over Jonathon's face as he said, "Charlie, in two days, I can finally be free."

৶ 34 ৶

A na and Liam found Charlie alone in the game room later that afternoon, mindlessly pushing chess pieces around the board. "So what did Jonathon say?" Ana asked.

Charlie didn't even know where to start. "He . . . he's quitting. He basically wished us luck and said he's done."

"What? He can't mean that," Liam said, taking a seat across from Charlie. A group of four younger kids entered the game room, talking loudly. Ana gave them a withering stare that stopped them in their tracks, turned them on their heels, and pushed them back out the door.

Charlie recounted how Brona had led Jonathon to believe Charlie alone could save Liam; how Jonathon had left the clues for him to find; how Jonathon had made up the whole thing about how forgiveness could remove the necklaces. He concluded with the truth about his mother. "He thinks it's his fault Mom's the way she is. He believes he deserves whatever happens here."

Ana shook her head. "I'm pretty sure that's not how depression works, Charlie. And besides, if the accident was the reason why your mom's the way she is, then she should be fine. Jonathon left. The accident left with him." Ana pointed at Charlie's unburned skin as proof. "She can't be hung up on something that's never happened."

"But Ana," Charlie said, "the timing lines up. If it isn't Jonathon's fault, then why is she like that?"

"I don't know, but it's not because of the accident," Ana said.

Charlie and Liam shared a look. Liam shrugged.

"Something else could have happened two years ago," she offered. "Something we don't know about."

"Yeah. You know what we didn't know about?" Charlie said with a sad laugh. "We didn't know we had a big brother."

Ana cocked her head and sat up. "Charlie! That's it."

"What's *it*?"

"That makes so much more sense!" she said, the pitch of her voice raising.

"What does?" Liam said.

323

"*That's* what happened two years ago! If the way your mom feels was caused by anything, it wasn't the accident. The accident was erased, but the thing that *did* happen two years ago was that *Jonathon left.*"

"What do you mean?"

"I mean, deep down, I think she knows there's something missing. A piece of her family."

Charlie and Liam shared a look again. Liam didn't appear to understand, but Charlie couldn't help but see the connections. He'd seen firsthand how his mom had fallen even deeper into depression last year. After Liam disappeared . . .

"Guys!" Ana woke them up from their thoughts. "Think about it! Some part of her has known all along."

"But she hasn't," Charlie said, remembering his mom's exasperation whenever he spoke about Liam. "She thought I was as crazy as my dad did."

"I'm telling you, she's sick because her boys are missing. She never fully forgot them. Maybe her head did, but not her heart. Her heart's broken because pieces of it are gone!" Ana smacked her hand down on the table.

It made sense. And Charlie's next thought stole his breath. *She remembered more than I did.* He closed his eyes as guilt slapped him across the face. He had been so angry at her for forgetting Liam. But if Ana was right, some unconscious part of her *did* remember her boys—*both* of them.

Not only *could* Jonathon come home, he had to.

"Come on, let's find Michael," Charlie said. "If anyone can help us change Jonathon's mind, it's him."

Charlie and Liam were halfway to the door before realizing Ana wasn't by their side. Charlie turned back to see Ana uncharacteristically hesitant.

"What?" Charlie asked.

"You know this is a package deal, right?"

"What do you mean?"

"Bringing Jonathon home might help your mom, but . . ."

"Yeah." The Roman candle streaked through Charlie's mind. "I know."

Ana nodded and rose, joining them at the door. She put an arm around each of them, and together they headed into the hallway, in search of a way out.

Michael was not difficult to find. He looked up from his seat in the library at the sound of their approaching feet.

"You've got to help us," Charlie said. The three of them stood, side by side, like a red rover team.

He glanced at them with a curious smile. "I'll do what I can, but it probably isn't as much as you want."

"We have to find a way out of here, and you have to help

us convince Jonathon to leave with us!" Ana said.

Michael turned a page in his book. "That sounds suspiciously similar to our last plan, and that one didn't work out so well."

"So Jonathon told you about the bodies in the mines?" Charlie said.

"He did."

"Then you know we have to get him out of here!"

"Guys, I don't think anything could change Jonathon's mind at this point."

Charlie fell into an overstuffed chair in frustration. A huge plume of dust engulfed him. The way Michael spoke reminded Charlie of Jonathon—accepting and resigned. "How can you be so calm about what we found down there?"

Michael closed his book and folded his hands atop it. "Honestly, it's no worse than what I feared. I've never held out great hopes for what my eighteenth birthday would bring."

"But it's like you are okay with it!" Charlie said.

"No. I'm not. Not at all. I've got a few months left, and I'm completely not okay with it. That's why I'm in here." He gestured to the books around him. "Maybe I'll find some new idea, some new plan. But I also have to accept that I'm no closer to finding answers than I was the day I got here. In fact, after last night, I feel further away than ever."

"Michael," Ana asked with a lilt of trepidation, "what did you do to end up here?"

"My case is a little different. I didn't 'do' anything."

"But everyone *did* something. Isn't that the whole reason you're here? To erase a mistake?"

"We're all here because we wished we'd never been born. Most people, like Jonathon, did it because they regret something they did or said. I did it because of who I am."

"What do you mean?" Charlie said. If anyone in this place seemed to have it all put together, it was Michael.

"I wished myself out of my life when I didn't feel like I could tell my parents a big secret. I don't like girls."

"I am right there with you," Charlie said. "I mean, other than Ana," he added when she punched him in the shoulder.

Michael laughed. "No, Charlie. Not like that. I mean I don't *like* girls. I don't want to date girls, or marry a girl. I've known for a long time that I want to do those things with a boy."

"You're gay?" Ana said.

"That's right," he said.

Liam looked between Charlie and Ana. "You guys didn't know that?"

Charlie thought about how close Michael and Jonathon were, about how happy Michael had been to see Jonathon when he returned, and how happy Jonathon was to see him as well. "So, wait. Are you and Jonathon . . . ?"

Michael mirrored Charlie's questioning glance and said "So, wait. Are you and Ana . . . ?"

"No!" Charlie and Ana said in unison.

"Ana's my best friend," Charlie said. "It's not like that!"

Michael laughed and nodded at them both with a raised eyebrow.

"So you and Jonathon are just friends," Ana said.

"Just because I'm gay doesn't mean I don't have friends who are boys, just like you, Ana. I don't want to kiss Jonathon any more than you two want to kiss each other."

"Dude! Gross," Charlie said, and then, scrambled, adding, "I mean, me and Ana kissing is gross. Not you and Jonathon. I mean . . ." This was not the conversation Charlie had anticipated when they had come to talk to Michael. Charlie had never talked to any other kids who were gay before. At least, not that he knew of. Though he had known Michael before, just not this part.

"Charlie, I'm cool with you and Ana just the way you are." Michael winked. "I hope you can be cool with me the same way."

"Well, yeah, of course. So you didn't do anything bad to bring you here?"

Michael shook his head. "Simply *existing* was bad enough in my family. When I look in my key, all I see is my first crush smiling at me. When I got here, just seeing his face was excruciating—it seemed worse than anything anyone else had done."

Charlie looked at all the books and papers around Michael, the same ones Jonathon had been searching for information about the salt mines. Ana asked the question he was thinking. "But now you want to find a way out of here?"

"I do. I was happy to be here with no one but Brona knowing my secret for a long time, happy to live in a place where I didn't have to worry about telling anyone, where I could maybe 'fix' this part of me. But I didn't get any straighter here than I had at home, or in church or at military school. Then, a little over a year ago, I finally got up the courage to tell Jonathon why I was here. What did I have to lose, right?" The corners of Michael's mouth lifted as he shook his head; his eyes sparkled. "And it was *fine*. I couldn't believe it. I was finally me, the true me, to someone I knew. It gave me the courage, slowly, to tell more people. I'm not a walking secret anymore."

"So what will you tell your parents if you find a way home?" Ana said.

"The only thing I have to offer: the truth. Coming out to my family would not be like coming out here—I'm still scared that telling my father would be like lighting a stick of dynamite—but I'd like the chance to try. I've been able to be myself here, and it turns out I like myself."

"We're going to figure it out," Liam said earnestly. "We're going to get you home too."

Michael thanked him for his enthusiasm with a smile, but his eyes said, "Best of luck."

❧ 35 ❧

Brona was conspicuously absent all day, as if allowing Charlie, Ana, and Liam some space after the upsetting things that had happened last night. Ana spent the evening grilling half the kids in the Asylum about every story about someone trying to take their key off. She returned with numerous tales of failure, each ending with a painfully short chain. Charlie and Liam heard various versions of the same from the kids they talked to, except Fink. He was the only person who had nothing to say, answering all their interview questions with silence or a simple "Don't know."

Finding an escape wasn't the only thing that proved elusive—Jonathon was nowhere to be found either.

Liam gave in to fatigue around ten o'clock, but Charlie and Ana stayed up to brainstorm further. They played chess as they sat and talked, but by midnight, they had run out of words. The only sound in the room was the click of the marble pieces against the board. With only a day left until Jonathon's eighteenth birthday, they were losing hope.

"It's your move," Charlie said.

Ana sat with her chin in her hand, staring out at the snow. She said, "Right," but didn't budge.

"You okay?"

She shook her head and looked back at the board. "Yeah."

"What's up?"

"It's nothing." At Charlie's insistent stare, she added, "I just . . . I miss home."

Charlie closed his eyes and lowered his head.

"See. That's why I didn't want to say. It's not your fault. You couldn't have stopped me from coming here if you'd tried."

But he hadn't.

"I just hope everyone's forgotten me, you know?" Ana reached out and moved her bishop. "Checkmate," she said unenthusiastically. In the land of no pain, no pleasure, winning was as thrilling as emptying the dishwasher. Charlie actually missed the lavish and self-congratulatory celebrations

Ana used to perform whenever she beat him. Her revelry was incredibly annoying, but he somehow always ended up laughing.

"So, what, no backflips off the side of the garage, like when you beat me in horse?"

"Well, if it's backflips you want, then it is backflips you'll get. I bet no one's ever tried one off the wall in this dusty old place." Ana stood, eyed a spot on the wall—and seconds later she kicked off and performed a perfect backflip. With a broad smile on her face, she straightened the bottom of her shirt and said, "Now, *that* feels more like home."

Charlie stared at her, wide-eyed. "Ana."

"What? Did I scuff the paint? Don't freak out, it'll fix itself."

Charlie pointed at the floor by her feet. Lying there, like a giant amoeba, was Ana's necklace and key.

"How did you do that?" Charlie repeated.

"I don't know!" Ana said, grabbing at her neck and chest to confirm it was no longer there. "You saw what happened! I didn't do anything. It just fell off!"

Charlie rifled through his necklace memories: Jonathon's chain had shortened when Ana had tried to remove it at the mill; Liam's had slithered under his fingers the day they had arrived; his own leather cord had shrunk when he even thought about leaving. But Ana?

"What happened when you tried to take yours off before?"

"I never tried! We've all seen what happens."

"What was in your key? When you looked through the handle?"

"I never did that either. I didn't want to see my arm get broken again. Once was plenty."

Charlie moved to where Ana's chain lay and touched it with the toe of his shoe, as if checking to see if it was alive or dead. They stared at it, dumbfounded. Then Ana spun toward Charlie, her eyes on his eternity stone. "Maybe it's because Brona didn't give us our chains? Try taking yours off."

"Yeah, that might have been true of my chain, but this thing I have now is different. It shortened the one time I even thought about taking it off, and I doubt anything's changed."

"One way to find out."

"Ana, I really don't—"

"Charlie! Just try!"

He stared at her and took a deep breath. He wiggled his fingers by his side and barely began lifting his arms when the eternity stone cinched violently against his neck, the leather cord tightening like a trap.

"No!" Ana grabbed at the stone, her fingers getting

pinched between the cord and Charlie's neck. "Stop, Charlie! Don't move!"

"Okay!" Charlie struggled to say through the pressure on his throat, but he wasn't talking to Ana. "Okay! I didn't . . . mean it!"

The necklace loosened slightly, as if to say, "Go on . . ."

"I didn't mean it," Charlie repeated. "I'll stay!" With these words, the pendant lowered down onto his chest.

Ana stood stricken, with her fingers still wrapped around the leather. Any elation she might have felt from her own necklace falling off was gone. "I'm not leaving here without you," she whispered. "In case you were going to tell me I should."

Charlie felt a small wave of guilt. He was thinking nothing of the sort, but maybe he should have been. He reached up and extricated her hands before rubbing his neck and checking for blood.

Then Ana gasped. As if a fly was buzzing around her head, she looked frantically side to side, and her face looked pained. To Charlie's surprise, she bent down, scooped up her chain, and threw it around her neck. Only when the key and chain were back in place did Ana exhale in relief. She looked, however, close to tears.

"What just happened?" Charlie asked hesitantly.

"I could hear my mom, saying my name." Ana wiped one

eye with the back of her hand. "She sounded . . . terrified. Heartbroken. This thing may not stay around my neck, but it works."

"Ana, look in your key handle. I want to know what you see."

She held the key to her eye but stared directly at Charlie. He knew the answer before she said it.

"I don't see anything."

Ana and Charlie stayed up for hours trying to decipher what it all meant. The best theory they could come up with was that Ana's chain didn't hold her here because the wish that she'd never been born hadn't been in earnest. Ana lamented that Charlie didn't have his original chain for comparison, but he was quietly glad Brona had taken it. He wasn't as innocent as Ana. If his key held the things he had said to his mother, he never wanted to see that again.

By three a.m., exhaustion won. Charlie walked with Ana to the girls' dorm, then lay atop his own covers for hours. His body screamed for sleep, but his mind refused. Surely Ana's discovery revealed something essential about the chains, but what was it? Could others remove their memories from the key, eliminating its magical choke hold? He tried to remember the mistake that each key held: Liam saw their dad, enraged, on the phone with the principal;

Jonathon watched the fireworks strike Charlie over and over again; Cody stared at his grandmother's broken face at the police station; Amanda saw her grandfather collapse from his heart attack.

Maybe Ana just didn't do anything bad enough? Charlie thought, but then his thoughts turned to Michael. His key held the image of a boy smiling. He had simply believed that there was something wrong with him for being gay, something he couldn't admit to his family, even if he had since learned to accept himself.

A jolt of realization shot through Charlie. *Could it be . . . ?* He bolted to the door and walked quickly but quietly toward the boys' dorms.

Charlie opened Michael's door with a low creak and found him on the third bunk. "Michael," Charlie whispered. He shook him. Finally, after he pushed and pulled Michael's shoulder back and forth with almost comical force, the older boy sprang to life.

"Wha—!" Michael said, flipping over, his hands at the ready, his eyes squinting.

"It's okay. It's just me, Charlie."

Michael's body relaxed; his head fell back to the pillow. He flopped a forearm over his eyes, shielding them against the dim light starting to creep through the windows. "Charlie? What time is it?"

"I need to talk to you. I may have figured something out about the chains."

"That's great," Michael said sleepily. He rolled away and pulled his blanket over his head. "I can't wait to hear about it tomorrow."

"It *is* tomorrow! I need to talk to you now!"

With a sigh, Michael gave up and pulled the blanket down to peer at Charlie. He shook his head. "This better be good."

Charlie almost needed to put a hand over his own mouth in order to stay quiet all the way down the grand staircase and into the library. Michael dropped into the desk chair, looking ridiculous in his nightshirt. He rubbed his face and squinted at Charlie, but a touch of curiosity twinkled within his bleary eyes. "Okay, what the heck is so important?"

"Take your necklace off."

"Beg your pardon?" Michael said, crossing his arms over his key.

"I said, take your necklace off."

"You woke me up so you could watch me choke myself?"

"Not if I'm right."

Michael lifted an eyebrow.

"I'm serious!" Charlie said, almost bouncing with excitement. "When was the last time you even tried?"

"I don't know. A while ago. I got tired of feeling like it

was going to squeeze my head off."

"Have you tried since you told Jonathon that you're gay?"

"What do you mean . . . ?'"

"You told us yesterday that you aren't the same kid who asked to come here. You said you weren't afraid of who you are, that you'd even be willing to tell your parents. Have you tried taking it off since then?"

"I . . . I don't know." Michael shifted from skeptical to reflective. He leaned back in the chair in thought.

"Ana can take her chain off. I thought maybe it was because the memory she claimed to regret didn't involve her doing anything wrong. But that's not it. *You* never did anything wrong either, but I bet your necklace still shrank, right? When you first got here?"

"Even if I barely touched it, it would shrink a couple of inches."

"And did you mean what you said yesterday? That you wish you could go home *as you are*? Not ashamed, not guilty?"

"Absolutely."

"Then please, try it now."

Slowly, with a dawning understanding of Charlie's theory, Michael reached up with both hands and gripped his chain. Charlie's heart lurched as Michael extended his arms up and over his head. The chain came with them, hovering over his head like a halo, clear of his body. Michael stared at the key, now dangling a few inches in front of him, with bright eyes. His mouth hung open with disbelief.

"Oh my god, Charlie. I did it!"

Charlie let out a breath it felt like he'd been holding for days. Guilt was the fuel that fed each chain; guilt, shame, and fear of mistakes and consequences. Fear of the lives they had left behind. Ana had none. And neither did Michael.

They had both forgiven *themselves* long ago.

Charlie grinned widely. "Brona doesn't hold the power keeping us here—*we do*. She makes everyone look in their keys every night to remind us of what waits for us outside, but all that does is refresh the fear and guilt that holds us here."

"I can go home . . . ," Michael said quietly, the sides of his eyes crinkling.

"Anyone can. You can't change what brought you here, but if you can live with it, you can *live* with it."

Michael slowly lowered his arms to his sides. He stared at the stone that hung from Charlie's neck. "What about you, Charlie? That thing comes off too, right?"

The balloon of excitement that had been rising between them popped. Charlie softly shook his head. "No. It doesn't."

The eternity knot symbolized life and death, birth and

rebirth, never-ending love. This, he suspected, was much stronger magic than fear or forgiveness. A plan, however, was forming in Charlie's mind, and his resolve made any distress he might have felt at being trapped seep away.

He would stay. It was all Brona wanted, anyway. It seemed like a reasonable price to pay for everyone's freedom.

Everyone's, including Jonathon's.

The sounds of breakfast began to drift into the library as Michael and Charlie finalized their plan. After Brona floated past the doorway without noticing them, Michael grabbed Charlie's hand and muttered, "Follow me."

Jonathon didn't seem surprised when they burst into his bedroom. He just continued pulling on his socks. Charlie was glad to see Jonathon wasn't still buried under a pile of snow.

"Man, you're going to want to see this." Michael reached up, removed his chain, and dangled it by one fingertip.

Jonathon stared at Michael. "Holy . . . how did you . . . ?"

"Tell him," Michael encouraged Charlie.

"You were almost right, without even knowing it," Charlie said. "Forgiveness *is* the answer, but you have to be able to accept who you are and what you did before you can ask for understanding from anyone else. If you can do that, you can leave."

Jonathon stood up with a whoop and gave Michael a bear hug. He pulled back and held Michael by the shoulders. "Dude, you can get out of here! You can go home!"

Michael nodded enthusiastically. "I know. And so can you!"

The joy slid off Jonathon's face, and he turned to Charlie as if he were the one who had spoken. "I've already told you. I'm not going back."

"Listen! We think you're wrong about Mom. The accident never happened, right?" Charlie pointed to his arms. "But she's still sick. We think she might be the way she is because you *vanished*, not because of the accident. She knows there's something missing. *You.*"

Jonathon shook his head.

"Mom says she doesn't remember Liam," Charlie went on, "but some part of her must—him *and* you. It's the only explanation that makes sense. The only way she'll get better is if you *both* go home."

"Charlie! You don't get it! I'm not hurting you again!" Jonathon stood and tried to push past them, his face contorted.

Charlie caught him by the arm. "You won't hurt me again."

Jonathon ripped free of Charlie's grasp. "Even if I try to come to terms with what I did, and you forgive me, you still get torched! You have no idea what you are asking for."

"Jonathon. You won't hurt me because I won't be there."

Jonathon froze. He stared at Charlie with a deep groove between his eyes before looking to Michael. "You think I'm just going to walk out of here without you? How many times do you think I want to ruin your life?"

"Jonathon," Charlie said, "this isn't up to you. And it's not up to me. Mine doesn't come off." He nodded at his pendant.

Jonathon stared at the eternity knot and sat down hard on the nearest bunk. He held his head in his hands.

"I'm stuck," Charlie said. "So go home and put our family back together. Even if you're right—that Mom's sick because you hurt me with the fireworks—the accident won't exist, because I won't. You can't burn a brother you don't have."

"But won't Mom still sense you're gone?" Jonathon asked, a look of shame on his face that he was even considering Charlie's plan. "If you're right, she'll still be missing one of her kids."

Charlie finally had to say aloud what he had been afraid of for over a year. "I can't make Mom better. I've been there the whole time, and it hasn't mattered. I'm not the missing piece." A lump in his throat nearly strangled his final words. His face burned like he had been in the sun for hours. He thought about his dreams; about Brona. He was everything to her. Charlie hadn't been enough for anyone at home—not his dad, his mom, or Liam. But he was enough for Brona.

That would have to be enough for him too.

"Go home. Take Liam with you. The only person I can help is here."

Michael spoke for the first time. "Jonathon, everything you've done for the past year was to get Liam home. Now you can take him there yourself."

"I wasn't trying to save one brother just to lose the other one," he spat.

Michael was unfazed; he spelled it out simply. "Saving Charlie is off the table—only Brona can let him go, and that's not happening. You turn eighteen at midnight. If you stay, you're sacrificing not only yourself but the rest of your family as well. Fix what you can."

"And you have to do it today," Charlie said. "You're out of time."

Jonathon cupped his face in his hands, shaking his head slightly. His shoulders slumped; Charlie knew he was coming to the same conclusion they were.

"I need you to do one other thing," Charlie said. His family wasn't the only one that needed fixing. "No matter what Ana says or does, you have to take her with you."

Jonathon looked up. "What?"

"She'll say she won't leave without me, but she has to go home. Her family needs her. Get her out of here."

Jonathon's features were riddled with doubt. He started to argue, but Charlie cut him off. "Promise me!"

He finally exhaled and nodded. "Yeah. I promise."

ꕥ 36 ꕥ

Michael and Charlie sat at the breakfast table across from Ana and Liam, heads low. They shared how Charlie had cracked the code of the necklaces, and how they were going to escape that night, before midnight struck.

Ana pointed her spoon at Charlie's markedly different neckwear and whispered, "What about that thing, Charlie? It tried to choke you just last night."

"I got it off this morning with Michael," Charlie said, looking intently at his oatmeal. "I'll be able to do it when I need to."

Michael confirmed this with a nod. Ana looked suspicious, but she fell silent when Cody came over.

"Hey, guys," he said, sitting down. He slowly scanned each of their faces. "Um, what's going on?"

Michael calmly signaled for him to keep his voice down. "Charlie figured it out."

"Figured *it* out? What do you mean?"

"I mean *it*. Escape route, chains, all of it. We can go home for good."

Cody listened as Charlie told him everything, but instead of getting excited he seemed less and less interested. When Charlie was done, Cody said, "That's awesome for you guys. Good luck."

"Aren't you coming?" Ana said.

Cody gave his full attention to his breakfast. "Nah. My grandma doesn't need all that again." Charlie, Ana, and Liam made a few meager attempts to change his mind, but he ate quickly and excused himself before they could, tossing his dirty dishes into the dumbwaiter on his way out.

"I don't get it," Ana said, watching him walk away. "Why would he stay?"

"I don't think he'll be the only one," Michael said. "Half the kids here aren't anywhere close to accepting what they did."

After breakfast, they waited for Brona to leave to gather flowers before going to the portal wall for a quick trial run. Michael removed his necklace, and the doorknob began to sprout from the stone almost immediately. "I can hear my dad," he said with a nervous smile. He put his chain back on, and the knob vanished.

"This is really going to work!" Ana said, beaming at Charlie.

Charlie smiled back but said nothing.

The rest of the day took forever. Charlie tried to reflect Ana's excitement like a mirror, choosing his words carefully, playing the part he needed to play. Ana even complimented him that evening at Jonathon's birthday goodbye dinner, on how sad he was pretending to be about Jonathon's impending departure.

By the time Brona tucked Charlie into bed, he felt years older. He lay awake, waiting for Brona's bedroom door to shut and the grandfather clock to strike eleven, before bolting out of bed and down the stairs.

Ana, Liam, Michael, and Jonathon were already standing in the entryway. Ana was actually bouncing up and down, as if warming up for an inning to start. She smiled at Charlie and he returned the grin, praying it looked genuine.

They had one hour to get Jonathon out.

Ana placed one hand each on Charlie's and Jonathon's arms. "Are you sure you're both okay with the accident? The burns?"

"Yup," Charlie said.

Jonathon added weakly, "Yeah, we're good."

Liam stood by the small table in the corner, staring at the blank wall. "I can't wait to laugh, you know? Really laugh. The kind that makes it hard to breathe." He looked like he was thinking of some pleasant, faraway memory.

Ana walked to his side and threw one arm around his shoulder. "I want a chocolate-chip cookie."

Liam sighed and leaned in to her. "Chocolate! I haven't tasted chocolate in so long."

"Well," Charlie said, "I can't wait to crush Ana in a game of chess and rub it in properly."

"Yeah, good luck with that," Ana said with a smile so wide Charlie felt his heart start to crack in two. He swallowed hard to quash the lump in his throat and checked his watch.

11:09 p.m.

Ana eyed Jonathon, then came to Charlie and whispered, "Are you sure Jonathon's going to be able to do this? He looks too scared about hurting you again."

"He's fine," Charlie said. "He's worried about me, but he'll be able to get his necklace off. I'm sure of it." He wiped his sweaty hands on his pants.

Ana didn't look convinced.

"Liam, you're first," Michael said, herding them to the wall. Michael and Charlie had planned the order—Liam, followed by Ana and Jonathon. Michael would stay with

Charlie until the end, assuring all were gone. By the time the others realized Charlie wasn't coming, they'd be helpless to change it.

Or—Charlie hoped beyond hope—once they had their chains off and were clear of these walls, they wouldn't remember him at all. That would be best.

Liam shifted from foot to foot. "Let's do this!"

His grin was so goofy and bright. This was the last time Charlie would see that face—the one he had come to save. His eyes stung, and he turned away. Ana was staring at him, head tilted and eyes narrowed.

Play it cool. She can read you like a book.

"Liam, whenever you're ready, give it a try," Michael guided. "Remember. No guilt, no fear. You can apologize for copying the book report, and your dad will understand."

Liam gripped his chain with no hesitation and lifted it with a triumphant smile. "I can hear Mom!" he said as the knob blossomed and the tree sprouted. His face crinkled and his eyes started to fill. Pointing to the portal as proof, his voice cracked. "Charlie, I can hear her, thinking about me. She's saying my name."

"Go" was all Charlie could manage.

Liam stepped timidly toward the door as it grew, but then scurried back to Charlie and gave him a hug. "See you on the other side!"

Charlie couldn't breathe.

Liam went back to the door, twisted the knob, and heaved it open. He hovered at the threshold for a moment. There was snow falling beyond every window, but Charlie suspected all Liam saw was green grass. With a whoop of joy, he stepped out, and the door swung shut behind him.

As one, Ana, Charlie, Jonathon, and Michael hurried to the nearest window. They watched as Liam glanced around like someone who had just awakened from a dream. He turned and looked at the house before walking away, down the snowy hill. He left no footprints.

"Ana, you're up," Michael said.

"Can I go next?" came a voice from behind them.

They swung around to find Cody standing at the bottom of the stairs.

"If I don't do it right now, I think I'll chicken out," he said.

"Of course," Michael said. "I'd hoped you'd come."

Charlie was thrilled Cody had decided to go home but, checking his watch, wished he'd shown up a little later. It was 11:21.

Cody crossed slowly to the blank portal wall, his key rising and sinking on his chest with three deep breaths. He nodded repeatedly, like he was listening to a voice in his head. He reached up and twisted a loop of chain around his index finger. He lifted it an inch.

It immediately began to shorten.

"Stop!" Ana yelled, much too loudly. She grabbed Cody's hand and yanked it down.

Cody's head tipped forward. After a long silence, he said, "I guess it doesn't work for everyone." He looked small, folded into himself. Terrified.

Charlie came to his side. "Cody, you can do this."

"I don't know how," he said, shaking his head. "I can't disappoint her again."

"Listen to me. You made a stupid, careless, and idiotic choice with that bottle of perfume, and you hurt your grandmother real bad. . . ."

Cody shrank even further.

"I don't think you're helping," Ana muttered.

Charlie touched his shoulder. "You told me that you were everything to your grandma, right? That she had faith in you? Well, now it's your turn. Have faith in yourself. Have faith in her. You will get through this together. Focus on that, and the fear will take care of itself."

Cody stood up a little straighter and nodded. He chewed on his lip ring and said, "That makes—"

"*Stop!*" came a shriek from the top of the stairs.

"Go! Now!" Michael said to Cody.

Hair down and in her dressing gown, Brona raced

toward him. The image was so familiar from Charlie's first dream that he half expected his dream dad, fist bloodied, to appear behind her.

Charlie moved toward the stairs, hoping to absorb Brona's attention and allow Cody time to escape.

"Why?" Brona wailed, pulling Charlie to her chest. Though he couldn't see it, the sounds of the door emerging from the stone told Charlie that Cody's necklace was off. "Why are you doing this?" she demanded. "You are safe here!"

Her words were cut off by the door slamming shut. Cody was gone.

Michael spoke for them all. "We're leaving. This is not a life."

"Life is suffering!" she spat, clutching Charlie to the point of pain.

"Maybe for you." Michael's words were calm, almost meditative. "Ana, why don't you and Jonathon go together?" Michael already knew what they were all coming to understand: Brona was powerless to stop them.

"I'm not going without Charlie," Ana said. She glared at Brona, her eyes full of hatred.

"Well, then I guess you will be staying," Brona said, regaining her stony composure. "You may know how to remove your chains, but Charlie's not wearing a chain, is he?"

A flicker of worry crossed Ana's features. "Well, joke's on you," she said hesitantly, "because Charlie already took it off once."

"Oh, is that right?" Brona said sweetly.

"Jonathon, now," Michael said.

Jonathon didn't move.

"You promised!" Charlie added, twisting in Brona's arms to face his older brother.

Ana looked suspiciously at all three of them in rapid succession. "Promised what?"

Jonathon lifted his chain. He dropped it to the floor with a clatter as the bulge of the doorknob and the sprouting of the tree again brought the portal door to life.

"Jonathon!" Ana yelled. "You can't leave us here!"

Michael put an arm of comfort around Ana's shoulders.

"Stop it!" she said to Michael, trying to shake him off. "You can't let Jonathon leave without Charlie!"

Michael's hand grazed the back of her neck, and he looped a finger under her chain. When Ana recoiled from him, it only served to make his job easier. With a quick lift and pull, Ana's necklace was off.

She stared in shock, then dove for her key. Michael took a simple step back to avoid her grasp at the same moment Jonathon grabbed Ana's wrist.

"Let go of me!" Ana tried to wrench her arm loose from

Jonathon's grip, but it was useless. Ana was strong for a twelve-year-old, but she was no match for a young man about to turn eighteen.

"I'm sorry, Ana!" Jonathon said in a tormented voice as he inched both of them closer to the door.

Brona let go of Charlie and rushed toward the portal. "Stop, both of you!" She reached for Ana's outstretched hand, but Brona's fingers passed right through her flesh. Brona tried again and again, sweeping her hands, but it was as if her limbs were made of smoke.

"Charlie!" Ana screamed.

Jonathon tugged her, straining toward the door. "I'm sorry!"

"Go home, Ana," Charlie said, though he couldn't know if she would hear. "Forget me." He steadied himself on the staircase railing; he was sure the impossible weight of Ana's anguish would crush him.

With a final scream of protest and a grunting tug by Jonathon, Ana crossed the threshold. The door swung shut, and the commotion screeched to a halt.

It was done.

Charlie couldn't tell if Ana's wails were truly still echoing around the room or simply ricocheting around in his head. *We had to. Ana's family needs her. She had to go home.*

Then why did it hurt so much?

Again, Charlie found himself certain that Ana would forget him, now that she existed chain-free and he didn't; Jonathon and Liam too. This thought should have brought solace, but instead it tore Charlie apart. If only forgetting went both ways.

Michael walked over to Charlie, his dark brown eyes reading his doubts. "You did the right thing," he said softly.

Charlie sat down hard on the steps behind him. The "right thing" felt unbearable.

Brona stood at the wall, hands and forehead on the stone. Charlie and Michael watched her shoulders shake, grief racking her body. Charlie understood—as misguided and lost as Brona was, she truly believed in what she did here.

"You have sentenced them to a far worse fate," she said, her voice steeped in sorrow.

The sorrow of standing by three small gravestones. Of leaving those graves, and her life, and crossing the ocean. Of enduring her husband's death. Of watching as her last remaining child was stolen from her.

Charlie understood her pain in a way no one else could. He had lived it with her. To her mind, numbing those who had suffered was the one gift she had to give. And yet, it was the one thing she would never attain. She would never die. She would never rest in the salt mines, forgetting and forgotten.

"I could stay for a while," Michael offered Charlie.

"No. You've missed enough of your life already. Staying here doesn't change anything."

"Are you sure?"

"Yeah, I'm sure. Go."

Michael stood straight and thrust his chin up and saluted Charlie. "You are braver than I'll ever be, little man. I'm going to miss you."

I hope not, Charlie thought. He stood and wrapped his arms around Michael, the only true goodbye their plan had allowed for. "Check in on them, okay? If you can, if you remember them, make sure they're okay."

"You know I will." Then, with a final squeeze, Michael turned to go. He lifted his chain from his neck and let it fall to the floor, joining the other four lifeless necklaces on the hardwood. Brona stood in his way, but it didn't matter. He reached through her—her body no more an impediment than a cloud—twisted the knob, and opened the door. He walked out of the Asylum and didn't look back.

ᴥ 37 ᴥ

Word of the escapes swept through the house like fire.

Brona took to her room, inconsolable at the loss of her children—her inability to save them, as she would likely say, from the choice they were making. Charlie, for his part, served as a sort of coach to all who wanted to leave. People swarmed him at breakfast for information, and by dinnertime, more than half of the children were gone. For others, it took days to come to terms with what escape meant: accepting the lives and mistakes each had deliberately left behind.

Forgiving oneself takes time.

Charlie watched boy after girl open the oak door and

walk out onto the grass and down the hill. He hugged Neha and Shayla goodbye, the young one still clutching the older girl's pant leg as they left together. Sasha, Amir, and Madison left hand in hand, each with a mix of fear, excitement, and conviction in their eyes.

After a week, Fink was the only one left. He and Charlie ended up hanging out together for days, talking about everything *but* the chains and the door—Fink had heard all he needed to hear, and he wasn't sharing anything with Charlie. Charlie figured Fink would go, or he wouldn't, whenever he was ready. It was another full week before Charlie stood with him at the portal wall for an hour in silence before the boy finally reached up, lifted his chain, and walked out.

Now Charlie was the only one left. Just him and Brona. Here, forever. The weight of his isolation made climbing the stairs nearly impossible.

As Charlie passed by Brona's bedroom door, he hesitated. She was all he had now. Despite all she had done—to Jonathon and Ana and Liam, to all the kids over the years—he had to try to live with her. It was that or lose his own sanity. He thought of the dreams and wished he could just fall asleep and live inside them forever; live in the world where his love for Brona was genuine and easy. If he could close his eyes and be with her in Ireland, or on the *Randolph*, or in New York City, this would be so much easier. But the dreams had stopped the day Ana and the others had left.

He stared at the door for a full minute before deciding to knock. The life of Charlie O'Reilly was over, but maybe another was just beginning.

"Come in."

Brona sat by the window, looking almost translucent in the white-blue light of the snow. She stared out the window even as he entered. "Good afternoon, Charlie."

Her room was far smaller and simpler than his— firewood stacked on the floor instead of in a cradle, bed linens that were thin and white. A simple bench sat in front of the fire. Charlie entered and perched on the edge of her bed, fighting the urge to say, "Hey." Instead he said, "Good afternoon," the words clunky in his mouth. That was how Kieran had talked, right? "How are you doing today, Mother?" he offered.

She cracked a sad smile, acknowledging Charlie's gift, but still gazed forlornly over the snow. "I loved each of them as my own, you know. I really did. I would have protected every one of them forever."

Charlie knew she was telling the truth. Or at least the truth as she saw it.

"And how are you, Charlie?" she asked.

"You can call me Kieran, if you want."

The sorrow on her features lightened slightly, and she wiped her eyes with the tip of a finger. "You are as remarkable as I remember. I will call you whatever you prefer."

Charlie honestly wasn't sure what he preferred. Instead he said, "I don't know if you can do this, but can you give me those dreams again?"

She cocked her head like he didn't understand something very simple. "Of course. I can give you any of our memories at any time."

"Any?" Charlie asked. "You mean there's more?"

"Oh, a stór," she sighed happily, pulling the heavy key chain and its dozens of keys from her pocket again. "I have all thirteen years of your life ready to share with you."

This sentence hung in the air between them. Brona's smile melted, and she suddenly looked away, staring intently out the window again. Her every muscle was tensed.

The truth began to dawn on Charlie. "All thirteen years?" Charlie repeated. "Like, you mean, *only* thirteen years?" His knowledge of Kieran's story was like a book with its final chapters ripped from the spine. He knew Kieran had been taken from Brona, but not what came next.

"I'm sorry." Brona cleared her throat and pushed the keys back into her pocket. "I shouldn't have said that."

Charlie shook his head, his forehead knotted. "But you did!"

361

"There's no need for you to have that memory!" Charlie couldn't tell if the anger in her voice was aimed toward him or herself. "I've relived it enough for both of us."

Charlie was tired of so many things, but nothing more than being lied to by people who said they loved him. "Tell me. Now."

"It will only bring you pain. . . ." Brona clenched her mouth shut as if trying to trap any further words from escaping.

Charlie let a silence rest between them as he gathered the courage to press on. "Mother," he said as kindly as he could, "there's so much pain here already. Please, just tell me the truth."

The severe edges of Brona's cheeks and jaw softened, and a mask of guilt settled on her features. Brona folded in half, her face in her hands. Charlie watched as she crumpled; he drew a deep breath and went to where she sat by the window. He knelt down before her and took her hands in his. "Please."

At his word, her muscles relaxed. All of her fight was gone. She pulled one hand free from his, but instead of reaching into her pocket again, she moved her hand up and curled a finger around the chain around her neck. She pulled, fishing out the key from beneath her bodice. "I can tell you or I can show you."

He was in her key. Or Kieran was. The idea of experiencing whatever memory bound her here filled Charlie with dread, but he needed to know how the story ended. Not just in his mind, but in his heart, just like the rest of Kieran's life.

"Show me."

Brona lifted her hand and held the key inches from his face. He could feel warmth emanating from it, and when he pressed it to his eye, it felt like a brand.

He gasped, and he heard Brona say, "I'm sorry, a stór," as everything went white.

The sound of chalk on a blackboard was the first thing he heard. Charlie opened his eyes to find himself sitting at a desk in the Asylum classroom. Twenty children sat similarly around him, clad as if costumed for a middle school production of the musical *Oliver!* Each of them also looked half starved. He looked down at his own shabby clothes and noticed his hands; as he remembered from his dreams, the skin sagged between his bones, and his nails were cracked and filthy.

Outside the window, snow fell from a dark evening sky. Charlie shivered and felt a stab of pain in his gut. He was cold and profoundly hungry.

A boy stood at the chalkboard, struggling to figure out the answer to a multiplication problem. A pinched-faced woman stood at the front of the room, arms crossed, ruler in hand. The boy scrawled an answer, and the woman barked, "Incorrect!"

The boy put down the chalk and held out his hand, upon which the woman brought down the ruler with all of her might. Charlie was the only one to gasp as the boy grimaced, then picked up the chalk again.

His next attempt at the problem, however, never happened. There were shouts in the hallway, and every head turned toward them. The yelling became frantic, and the teacher went to the door to investigate.

"You can't keep him here!" were the first words they heard. The students murmured, wondering who dared disrupt the strict discipline the New York Asylum for Orphaned Children.

A deep voice commanded, "You must leave, madam!"

"Not without my son! You have no right to keep him from me."

The voice was unmistakable.

Relief and happiness flooded Charlie's body. He'd been kept from his mother for many, many months. Half a year of cold and hunger. *She's here to save me!* It was an idea more filling and satisfying than any meal.

Then came the sounds of more voices. "He is a ward of the state, ma'am," a stern woman said.

"You must leave!" said another. The sound of scuffling blended with the voices.

"Madam, if you are looking to claim one of these children, you must file a request with the proper authorities," the first man insisted.

By this point, the students were standing up at their desks, trying to see what was going on. The teacher had moved out of the room to the railing of the grand staircase to observe the scene below. Charlie left his desk, crept out the door, and tucked into a recess of the hallway.

"You will leave, or you will be removed!" the man's voice echoed through the house.

"Kieran!" Brona's agony filled the building. The sounds of a physical struggle became louder.

Charlie's teacher returned to her classroom, her eyes wide. She wiped her hands on the front of her dress as if they had been sullied by watching such an undignified scene. Once the door closed, Charlie tiptoed to the top of the stairs and peered over the rail.

Three men were trying to remove a flailing, redheaded whirlwind. They dragged Brona to the doorway, muscling her past a table near the front door. Everything slowed as Charlie saw Kieran's history unfolding with painful clarity. Brona reached for the table to anchor herself, but her fingers only found a delicate lace table square that sat atop it. On the fabric rested a lantern.

The flame guttered as the lantern fell to the floor, but it did not extinguish. Shattered glass and lamp oil exploded in every direction, causing the men and women to freeze for one instant before the room erupted in chaos.

A fiery pool engulfed the floor, igniting the nearby curtains with a heat and speed so intense, it was as if they were constructed of match tips. The men and women released Brona, needing their hands to shield their faces.

Brona scrambled away from them. She let out a cry of surprise at seeing Charlie run down the stairs toward her, unimpeded by the staff—who were now shouting, "Fetch water!" and "Get the children out!"

Charlie threw his arms around his mother's waist, and she enveloped him in an embrace that made his heart feel like it would burst. *I'm safe now,* he thought, despite the fire around him. The walls, coated in varnish, crackled with a sheet of flame within seconds.

"Take me home! Please, take me to Mrs. Clery's again," Charlie begged, tugging at his mother's hand to lead her toward the front door.

But the front door was now a wall of fire.

The commands of the Asylum staff devolved into screams. The teacher from upstairs was herding her terrified and crying children down the stairs. She was carrying the youngest, ushering them all to safe passage through the terrace door.

"Is there another way out?" Brona asked, urging Charlie in the opposite direction of the flow of bodies.

"I don't think so. . . ."

"We can't go with them. I am not going to let them take you from me again." She grabbed his hand and pulled him down the hall toward the dining room. She ran to the farthest window and heaved at the casement. She tugged at one, then another. And another. A bead of sweat ran down her forehead.

"They won't open!"

"None of them do," Charlie said. He wasn't sure if this was knowledge from being Kieran the Orphan or Charlie the Trapped.

"There must be another way out!" she said, the fear in her voice reaching new heights. She grabbed his hand and headed back to the entry.

Charlie screamed at what he saw. Any hope they had of following the others out onto the terrace exit was gone. The rug was a lake of flame. The grand staircase was an inferno. An overwhelming wave of heat forced them back into the dining room.

Brona slammed the door, her eyes wild. She picked up a chair and flung it at a window. It bounced off with a dull thud. Charlie tried another chair with the same result.

"There must be a way!" Brona screamed, looking in all directions.

Charlie could hardly think with the hissing of the fire and the groaning of the wood and stone. It was a deafening symphony. The temperature was rising by the second.

Then he saw a spoon on the floor, under the table. Someone had missed it during cleanup, failing to send it downstairs with the rest of the dirty dishes.

Down in the dumbwaiter.

Charlie grabbed his mother's hand. "This way!" He coughed through the smoke-clogged air and searched for the right spot in the recessed paneling. The section in the corner depressed slightly with his touch, and as he let go, the panel popped forward. Charlie grasped the edge and pulled. The box awaited.

He threw the shelves to the floor. "Get in!"

"You first!" There was no time to argue. Charlie stepped over the gap and curled into the small square space. Brona grabbed the rope, and the dumbwaiter started down.

Charlie's shoulder rubbed against the shaft wall; Brona's cough and the creaks of the pulley system echoed in his ears. The box finally bumped to a halt at the bottom, and Charlie tumbled out into the kitchen. He tugged the rope to send the box back up, sucking in a breath of clean air. He peered up the shaft and saw Brona struggling to pack herself into the cube.

"Now!" she yelled frantically. She spilled out of the box next to him moments later.

The sense of hope at finding a way out of the dining room was short-lived. They had escaped one room of a burning building only to enter another. Charlie squinted into the near pitch-black of the hallway.

There's a door down there. . . . Brona kept that door locked, right? Why did she do that, again? Dream Charlie strained to remember what real Charlie knew.

He took Brona by the shoulders. "That door, at the end of the hallway? Why do you keep it locked?"

She looked at him with utter bewilderment. She had no idea what was behind that door. She'd never been here before.

Charlie's mind ached. He felt nauseated from the panic, confusion, and smoke. His throat was painfully dry, and the air was only getting thicker.

"This way!" He pulled Brona to the door.

But there was no lock.

Charlie opened it, and air escaped around its edges, blowing the dust at their feet backward. The taste of salt filled Charlie's mouth.

I've been here before. . . .

Rows of empty wine racks filled the room and lined the walls. They felt their way down the rows in the darkness, searching for a door, or an exit, anything that would offer them safety.

"There's nothing here!" Brona coughed. Her breaths too sounded raspy.

There is something here! Charlie's mind insisted.

A deafening crash and a blast of light from the hallway sent them both cowering to the farthest corner of the cellar. They huddled on the floor, gripping each other as heat rolled over them. The main floor had collapsed.

There was nowhere left to go. Brona cried as she held on to Charlie.

This was the end of the dreams; the end of Kieran. But for Brona, whose mistake had started the fire that would take her last child, it was only the beginning. She was the overseer of those who had made terrible mistakes, because she was the first.

Charlie sat in the wine cellar and held his sobbing mother. He didn't know if he was Charlie or Kieran. He could remember playing with Nora *and* Liam. He could recall harvesting a field of fetid potatoes with his father *and* helping his dad program the DVR. He could see Brona warming her face in the sun on the *Randolph* as well as the loving eyes of his mom before heartbreak stole them away.

Charlie knew what it was like to have a mother who loved him so fiercely that she would sacrifice herself to try to save him. Both of them had.

He turned to tell his mother that he didn't blame her; to tell her he loved her and it wasn't her fault. But his breath caught as something silver glinted in the earth beneath him. In the bright light of the encroaching fire, he saw a curved metal track in the floor, arcing from the corner of the cabinet they were leaning against.

His mind finally screamed through the fog. *The salt mine!*

Charlie scrambled up and started clawing at the edge of the cabinet. "This opens!" he tried to say. "We can get out!"

But the words were lost forever, as the roof caved in on them both.

↩ 38 ↪

"It's over now."

Charlie opened his eyes and tried to swallow, his mouth still salty and parched. He was back in Brona's bedroom, kneeling before her. She looked empty. Charlie, it seemed, hadn't gone through that memory alone.

"You died too," Charlie said, his lungs still burning from the smoke. "Both of us."

"You did. Quickly. The newspapers reported that I died as well—'Crazed Mother and Doomed Son Perish in Blaze.' And I suppose I did, but not in that way. They never found my remains."

"You didn't die?" Charlie recalled the unbearable heat of

Kieran's last moments. There was no way she had survived.

Her face softened at Charlie's confusion. She put a kind hand on his shoulder. "No, a stór, I didn't die. Not in the way so many others do. Death has been my solitary wish since that day, but my existence is the opposite of eternal rest. My curse is to live. A mother who kills her child does not deserve to rest in peace by his side."

"You didn't *kill* him . . . or me. . . . I mean, I died, but it was an accident. I saw those people pushing you around by the front door. It was their fault!"

"No, Charlie. It was my fault. I alone caused that fire, and even if I had carried you away that day, it would have been to a life of poverty and starvation. You deserved so much better. You deserved a better mother."

Her words hit Charlie like a bucket of ice water. A stretcher, an IV, and paramedics flashed through Charlie's mind. He felt a clutch in his throat and a feeling of panic bubbling in his chest. "Don't say that!" he said without thinking.

Tears flowed down her face, catching on her chin momentarily before dropping down into two expanding darkened spots on her collar. "All I ever wanted was to be a good mother to you," she said, "but I failed you."

Charlie reeled. Those words. Those tears. He had been through it all before.

The last piece of the puzzle fell into place. After all this time, it finally made sense.

She wasn't here to save them. She was waiting for someone to save *her*; to relieve her suffering. To forgive her. To allow her to finally forgive herself. It was the same for Brona as it had been for Michael, Jonathon, Liam, all of them. Together, they could end this.

Charlie stood up, and in the white landscape out the window behind Brona, he could see a small headstone, the one he had tripped on so long ago, peeking out from beneath the snow.

Son.

Kieran.

He took Brona's hands in his and waited for her to tip her head up. "Mother"—the word finally felt honest—"you *were* a good mother to me and my sisters. Everything you did was for us."

Brona's shoulders trembled and her lower lip shook. Charlie formed the words he had never been able to say at home, to his own mom.

"Mother, you did not fail me. I forgive you."

As he said the words, the sound of rushing air filled Charlie's ears. The flame from the fireplace leaped up the flue as if sucked by an invisible cyclone. Similar sounds echoed throughout the house.

"It's over, Mother," he said. "It's truly and finally over. I forgive you. Please, forgive yourself."

An aura of profound calm overcame Brona; the sorrow that had shaped her features for so long melted away. A mesmerizing, shimmering red glow began to emanate from her skin and dress, illuminating every inch of her from within.

A crackling noise overhead tore Charlie's gaze upward. Just like Brona, the ceiling was luminous. It was a light he had seen before—when that same ring of fire formed these walls and unveiled the Asylum to him.

Beginning where the ceiling met the chimney, the building began to peel away and vanish, revealing an expansive crystal-blue sky. The blazing halo spread outward like a ripple on a lake, leaving nothing but open air in its wake. Charlie checked the window behind Brona; it was still white with falling snow, but above his head, sunlight streamed in. He let out a cry of disbelief as a distant airplane flew overhead.

The glowing ring turned downward, descending each of the four walls. The stones remained, but every plank of wood, every piece of furniture, and every pane of glass dissolved like a sugar cube in a cup of hot tea.

As the ring approached the level at which they knelt, Charlie knew Brona had been wrong. Their story—Kieran and Brona's—didn't end in the basement; it didn't end in pain and suffering. It ended here. The swirling light of Brona's shimmering hands licked his palms in warm waves. She looked at him for the last time and placed a finger on Charlie's pendant. The eternity knot glowed with a light so bright it filled the room.

She stood and pulled him into her arms. As if electrified, a current of joy flowed from her iridescent skin into Charlie. "I love you, a stór," he heard her voice in his mind.

"I love you too," Charlie said, hugging her back fiercely.

An intense squeezing stole his breath, and he wasn't sure if it was Brona's embrace or the passage of the ring of fire around both of them. In an instant, the feeling passed, and Charlie opened his eyes.

His arms were empty.

They also didn't look like his arms. A pinkish-white, waxy substance covered his skin, beginning on his forearms and becoming more prominent up past his elbows. He lifted his short sleeves to find the pearly, thickened skin on his shoulders as well.

With brutal force, memories began to flood Charlie's mind. Painful, real memories.

A burn unit. IVs and surgeries. Bandage changes. Physical therapy.

Charlie pulled his shirt collar outward with both hands, revealing a patchwork of crisscrossed skin on his chest.

Skin grafts.

The surge of recollections was overpowering. Charlie tried to steady himself against the onslaught. The memories hurt in a way none of Jonathon's descriptions could capture. It stole his breath. But then, on the tail of all the horror, came the rest of the story.

Healing. Returning home. Laughter.

Forgiveness.

These were the parts Jonathon had missed. A life with pain *and* joy. Charlie's real life—the one with two brothers and a complicated history—was back.

Charlie turned to look around. He was standing on the ground level, directly below where Brona's room had once been. The caved-in floor of the grand staircase lay behind him. Thick green ivy and tree branches entered through the window frames, reclaiming their residence on the moss-covered scorched stones. The dirty green sleeping bag and broken barbecue grill lay at Charlie's feet, and the smell of garbage filled his nose. The wind whistled slightly on its way through the cavernous shell.

Charlie started to laugh. His mind and heart were filled with such a rush of intense and conflicting feelings. When his laughter mixed with tears, it only made him laugh harder.

"It's time to go home," Charlie said aloud. He didn't know what awaited him, but he knew he was ready to find out. The eternity stone hung around his neck, its knot still glowing slightly. It was Brona's final gift, a reminder of life and death, birth and rebirth, and never-ending love.

Charlie walked toward the gaping hole of a front door. He had only taken three steps when something caught his eye. Beneath the oak tree, in the shade offered by branches full of spring leaves, stood two gravestones—one large, one small, both weathered and blunted. They tipped inward, supporting each other. Charlie didn't need to get any closer to know the inscriptions.

Mother and *Son*.

Together, at last.

~ 39 ~

" I knew it! I knew it!"

Ana ran down the block toward Charlie, jumping for joy every few steps like a hurdler over invisible obstacles. She nearly tackled him with her final leap. "I knew you were coming home!"

Charlie didn't know if he was happier to see Ana, or his house just over her shoulder as she hugged him. The garden was a vibrant, beautiful canvas of color: purple lilacs hung heavy over the yellow, red, and white tulip beds; a pink explosion of bleeding hearts sat before a perfectly trimmed hedgerow.

His mom was back.

Ana pulled back and stared at him like he was a dream. "I knew you'd found a way out! Look," she said, pointing at the surgical scar on her forearm. "This was gone when I came home, but it came back this morning! We missed you so bad!" She glowed, smiling at him like a fool. Then, with no warning, she wound up and punched him in the shoulder. Hard.

"Ow!" Charlie yelped.

"*That's* for forcing me out of the Asylum without you, you massive jerk." As she said it, the corners of her mouth curled up.

Her punch really hurt. Charlie rubbed his arm, never so happy to feel pain.

Ana sucked in a quick breath of surprise. "Oh my g— Charlie, your skin." She touched his arms gently, and Charlie watched her face register an onslaught of new memories. It was as though the past was flowing through his scars, up her fingertips, and into her mind, flooding it like a tsunami.

"Oh!" she gasped.

"Yeah. It was bad," Charlie said quietly. Her touch cemented Ana more firmly in Charlie's memory as well. She had sat by his bed in the hospital, hand on his shin because it was one of the few places that didn't hurt. They stood in silence, sharing memories they hadn't remembered until just now.

Charlie rubbed his aching shoulder again. "So wait. You remembered me? You guys didn't forget it all when you escaped?"

Ana shook her head. "No. We remember the Asylum and our lives here too, like we were there and never left home at the same time. It's so weird. Like right now, I know that I'm still furious with Jonathon for burning you, but at the same time, I remember how kind he was as our baseball coach." Ana's gaze fell to Charlie's necklace. "How did you get out? How did you convince Brona to let you go?"

"She's gone, Ana. The whole thing's gone. The Asylum is finally closed."

They began walking slowly, and Charlie told Ana about all the kids leaving. He told her about Kieran's final dream and his death. He told her how Brona was finally at peace. "She was the one who needed saving, not us."

Ana listened, her mouth open, slowly shaking her head.

They arrived at the curb in front of Charlie's house. He slowed, wondering what exactly awaited him inside.

"They aren't here," Ana said. "I've been waiting outside for an hour, knowing you must have made it out. First my scar, then your mom's garden . . ." She pulled a lilac branch to her nose and inhaled deeply. "It's amazing."

Charlie did the same, but accidentally snapped the bloom from the stem as he realized what Ana had said.

"Wait. The flowers just changed *today*? They weren't like this before?"

"No! Just last night your yard was the same weed-covered mess it's been for two years. Charlie, your mom was no different when we got back. She only came home from the hospital a few days ago."

"What?"

"Jonathon told me your theory, that he and Liam were all your mother needed to heal. But," she said, looking slightly superior, taking pleasure in Charlie being wrong, "she needs you too."

The sound of a car approaching behind them spun Charlie on his heels. A shiny SUV that Charlie didn't recognize pulled into the driveway. Instantly, he knew it was his dad's.

Liam tumbled out the back door before the car had even come to a stop. "Charlie!" He wrapped his arms around Charlie's waist.

Jonathon emerged from the far side of the back seat and peered over the roof of the car. His face was a complicated mix of relief and guilt, happiness and regret, as he stared at Charlie's skin.

The passenger door opened, and he could hear the sounds of two people laughing. His dad's deep baritone was one, but Charlie didn't recognize the other. A woman in cargo pants and a tank top stepped out, a grocery bag in her tan, muscular arms. Her loose ponytail swung as she turned and looked over the brown paper at Charlie.

"Hey, honey! How was the sleepover?"

Had Liam not steadied Charlie, he would have fallen over. He managed to gasp, "Mom?"

"Was it fun?"

"You . . . you look . . ."

"You look amazing!" Ana added.

Charlie's mom cocked her head and eyed them with a suspicious but kind smile. "What are you all scheming? These two were just buttering me up in the car," she said, tipping her head toward Jonathon and Liam. When all she got was slack-mouthed stares, she shrugged and headed inside. "Help bring in the groceries, okay?"

Liam laughed beside Charlie, hugging him even tighter as if making sure he was real. Jonathon was staring at the yard and the house, a disbelieving smile on his face.

"Grab a bag, everyone," Charlie's dad said from the trunk. "I need you boys to put everything away, okay? Your mom's heading to work for a few hours, and I am going to go for a run."

"Work?" Charlie said.

"Yes, work." His dad pushed two grocery bags into Charlie's arms. "You know how busy the garden center gets this time of year. But we'll both be home in time for your game."

"Game?"

His dad stopped and slowly turned toward Charlie. "You didn't get much sleep last night, did you?" He grabbed two more bags and followed Mom into the house.

All four of them stared at the door as it swung shut. After a moment of stunned silence, Ana and Liam erupted in a tangled mess of questions, laughter, and high fives. Jonathon, however, stared at Charlie from the far side of the car, glued to his spot.

Charlie offered his brother a huge smile. "It's okay, Jonathon. We're all home."

"I'm so sorry. . . ."

"I know you are. That's why it's okay. We've never been more okay."

Jonathon slowly returned Charlie's smile. He came around the car and engulfed him in a hug. When they pulled apart, Jonathon dabbed his eyes and Charlie looked up at the house. It was more fresh and green than he ever remembered.

"All this changed just this morning?" Charlie asked.

"It didn't even look like this when we left for the grocery store!" Liam said. "And Mom didn't go with us. She was still in bed!"

"But . . . ?" Charlie began, pointing at the door where his mother just passed.

"I know! We were at the grocery store, and Dad sent me off to get the toilet paper, and when I came back, there she was, pushing our cart. Like she'd been there the whole time. I'm glad I didn't have pickles or something in my hands, 'cause I dropped the toilet paper right there in the aisle." Liam laughed.

"Everything changed in an instant," Jonathon said. "Dad started telling jokes, and Mom was standing there drinking a latte, talking about work. Liam and I both pretended we had to go to the bathroom so we could talk, and we figured you must have made it out. We came back and started throwing everything on the list into the cart as fast as we could. Then we got to checkout, and there's Brooke in her Alicia Keys T-shirt, scanning our milk. She winked at us! We knew it was over—the Asylum was gone, everyone in the tunnels was saved too."

"What about Michael?" Charlie said. "And Cody? Do you know anything about them?"

"Cody's great. He lives about twenty minutes from here, and it turns out his probation record will be cleared when he turns eighteen. He's going to be so stoked to see you." Jonathon elbowed Liam. "Maybe we can talk his grandma into making us her strawberry shortcake again."

Liam smiled and nodded with hungry eyes.

"And Michael?"

"Yeah, that's been harder. He came out to his parents about a year ago, and as he expected, they had a tough time with it. He's got an aunt, though, who's been awesome. He actually moved in with her for a while, to give his parents some space. But, he's back home now, and he's . . . he's actually good. I talked to him on the phone last night. He has no regrets."

"Boys!" came their dad's voice out the window. "You're letting the ice cream melt out there!"

"Ice cream," Charlie said with relish. His mouth was already watering at the thought of strawberry shortcake.

"I know," Ana said. "I'm going to turn green from all the guacamole I've eaten since I got back!"

Charlie noticed the fine white line on Jonathon's forehead. "Hey, your scar's back too."

A guilty smile crept onto Jonathon face. "You don't remember yet?"

Jonathon placed Charlie's finger on the scar, and a memory burst into his mind. He was seven or eight, and Jonathon was tickling him to the point he couldn't breathe. It wasn't fun tickling; it was torture tickling. They were both on the ground and Charlie was gasping for air, begging Jonathon to stop. Ana was yelling for Jonathon to stop too.

When he didn't, Ana clocked Jonathon across the forehead with a hockey stick.

Charlie let out a yelp at the recollection. "Dude, Ana!"

Jonathon cackled and Ana gave him a sheepish smile. She grabbed two grocery bags, and said, "I *told* him to stop. . . ."

"You have no idea how weird it was when you thought you had a crush on me," Jonathon said, getting his two bags.

"Yeah, well, I'm over that now," Ana said, blushing slightly. "Now I know how much of a jerk you really were."

Liam grabbed the last bag, and they all walked inside. The smell of bacon hung in the air, and the soft lilt of music came from the kitchen radio. Charlie's parents passed on the stairs and shared a quick kiss. The lights seemed brighter; the air felt warmer.

Charlie almost dropped his grocery bag when he saw what was hanging on the wall in the entryway. Enlarged and framed, with a field of bison behind them, smiled his family on their Yellowstone vacation. All five of them.

"Jonathon," their mom said, "if you want to work with your dear mother at the garden center this summer, you could come with me and talk to Mrs. Murphy. Or you could mow lawns with Mr. Cutter."

"What?" Jonathon said. They all froze.

"It's time you had a job, my dear. You're eighteen; your

dad and I aren't going to let you just lie around on the couch all day, doing nothing."

"Yeah, lying around doing nothing sounds terrible," Jonathon finally managed to say. "I'll talk to Mr. Cutter."

Their mom came around the room, kissing each of her boys and Ana on the cheek. "When did you start wearing that?" she asked Charlie, touching his pendant.

Charlie sifted through his mind, searching for any memory from this life that could answer her question. Anything that would make more sense than the truth.

"We found it in the attic yesterday," Jonathon said.

Charlie instantly remembered going upstairs with Jonathon to look for a sleeping bag for the sleepover. There had been an old jewelry box tucked behind the camping gear.

"Is it okay if I wear it?" Charlie asked.

His mom smiled. "You can, but you need to promise me you will be extra careful with it. It belonged to your grandmother, and her mother before that. It's one of the few things we still have from Ireland."

Ana rescued the groceries that started to slide out of Charlie's hands.

"See you all at your game. Go, Mustangs!" his mom said with a fist pump.

"Mom?" Charlie said with a step after her.

"Yes?"

"I'm just curious. Have you ever been in the hospital?"

Mom slung her bag across her body and turned to face him. "I was in the hospital when you guys were born. And I slept plenty of nights in the hospital when you were in the burn unit."

"No, I mean, for any other reason." His eyes flickered to her unmarred forehead, then to the back of her hand holding the strap across her chest. Did IVs even leave scars?

"Nope. Why?"

"No reason."

She turned to leave again, and Charlie blurted, "Mom, if I've ever said anything that hurt you, I didn't mean it."

She tilted her head and walked to where Charlie stood. Her hazel eyes looked quizzical and loving, without a trace of sadness.

"We all make mistakes, Charlie." She kissed his forehead. "Maybe you should take a nap today. Recharge your batteries a bit?"

"Yeah . . . that sounds great."

"We missed you last night," his mom said, her adoring gaze dizzying. "Things just aren't the same around here when one of you is gone."

He sank into her embrace and closed his eyes. "I love you, Mom."

"I love you too, a stór."

389

ACKNOWLEDGMENTS

I have read acknowledgments in books my whole life, always asking "How could this many people be part of making a book?" Well, now I know! Acknowledgments aren't just a list of people who helped put a book together; they are, for me at least, a record of the people who helped make me who I am and let me stay true to that for the years it took *The Missing Piece of Charlie O'Reilly* to transform from a tiny little idea to the book you now hold in your hands.

I walked into the Loft Literary Center in Minneapolis six years ago having signed up for Introduction to Young Adult Writing, where I learned that I was so green a writer that I didn't even know what I didn't know. But Megan

Atwood, and later Kurtis Scaletta, held my hand, helped me learn how to crawl, then walk, then run. The Society of Children's Book Writers and Illustrators was essential to my writing development, filling my mind at conferences and later awarding me a year-long mentorship with author Eileen Beha, who taught me how to edit and tweak and sculpt *Charlie* even further.

I owe so many thanks to my friends and wonderful writing partners: Janna Krawczyk & Jen Moore, Kurt Hartwig & Brigid Gaffikin, and Jen Mazi & Alysa Wishingrad (and the whole Highlights Foundation crew!). They've spent time, energy, and emotion on *Charlie*, telling me where things were working and where he needed a whole lot more care. Their feedback came in formal critiques, gentle suggestions, and long-winded nonspecific gab sessions that may or may not have involved a few bottles of wine.

And then there is the lovely and talented Anne Ursu, who came into my life at the Highlights Foundation "Writing the Unreal" Whole Novel Workshop. If there are guardian angels in publishing, she's mine. Anne convinced me that *Charlie* was ready—it was time to send him out into the world. Like always, she was right.

So many thanks go to my magnificent editor, Jordan Brown, who saw exactly what needed to stay untouched and what needed to be remolded and formed. Thank you from the very bottom of my heart. You made this book better than I ever hoped. The entire, wonderful staff at Walden Pond Press has made this debut process ridiculously fun. You guys are the best.

And to my amazing agent, Tina Dubois, who picked me up when I was very much down, thank you. I'm looking forward to all that's yet to come.

I would not have been able to do this without some of the most incredible friends a person could hope to have: Adam & Mary, Roxie & Jay, Erika & Nathan, Pam & Jon, Matt & Megan, and JJ & Cristina. I could not ask for a better posse.

And then there is family: Christopher & Pam, my awesome brother and sister-in-law, who make me smile and laugh, and who always have my back; my in-laws, Dorit & Naseem, who never once doubted I could do this; and my parents, Roger & Carol, who always bought me any book I wanted, even when they didn't think the Sweet Sixteen series had much literary merit. But those are the books that made me a reader. If you meet kids where they are, amazing things can happen. Thank you, Mom and Dad. You are the absolute best parents a kid (or adult) could hope for.

And finally, the wacky five people who live with me. My kids—Spencer, Max, Leo, and Calvin—breathe life into every character I write. They are truly my inspiration, in all ways, every day. I strive to be as good a person as each of them is. And finally, Omar. My love, my rock, and my unwavering cheerleader. It is no overstatement to say there would be no Charlie without him. Thank you, my dear, for giving me the space, time, and freedom to follow this dream. May we continue to chase—and nab!—joy for many years to come.